Thundering Mountain

THUNDERING MOUNTAIN RANCH
BOOK TWO

NICOLE NEISWANGER

Calico
publications

For questions or and comments about the quality of this book, please contact us at calicopublicationsllc@gmail.com.

Cover Design: Covers and Cupcakes, LLC
Publisher: Calico Publications, LLC
Digital ISBN: 978-1-960600-00-4
Print Edition ISBN: 978-1-960600-01-1

To my husband, Bryan, and my mother, Debbie, for being supportive of a dream I've had for years. Without either of you, I would never have had the courage to chase my dreams.

To my friends, Jamie Dodge, Hilaree Collins, Natalie Workman, Erin Torres, and Jessie Carol. You were patient and supportive as I ran my crazy ideas past you. I love all of you and couldn't have done this without you. Thank you for coming along on my wild ride.

One

August 1892

"Elizabeth, what in the name of all that's holy did you just do?"

The blood-speckled rock slid from Elizabeth's fingertips, tumbling across the dirt before it stood still mere inches from a muddy, blackened boot. The stranger lay crumpled in a heap, a worn rifle between his limp fingers. Dark blood trickled from the back of his head and seeped from the wound. She wasn't trying to kill him, but she had to stop him from harming her brother.

"I saved your hide," she grumbled.

After what it took to find her brother James, she wasn't about to lose him. If the stranger had to hide on a hill like a coward while her brother's gang robbed the stagecoach, then he deserved what he got. A real man wouldn't have hidden like a rabbit from a coyote. Of course, she was grateful he hadn't gone down the hill with guns blazing. He might have shot her brother, and she wasn't about to let that happen.

"You disobeyed me and could've been killed," James snapped,

his eyes flashing with anger. "I didn't want you anywhere near here while I did my last job. What if this man had caught you?"

Why didn't he treat her like a grown woman going on twenty-two? One with determination, grit, and a desire to be independent.

She bent to pick up the man's rifle, and her hat tumbled into the dirt, letting her braided brown hair fall over her shoulder. She snatched up the rifle and her hat before facing her brother's irritating tirade. "He didn't, and it seems to me I saved you from a hanging. You should thank me." Every man, except her poor excuse of a pa, wanted her to depend on them as though she were a helpless, dainty society lady.

"Thank you? I told you to stay at the cabin," he said, his eyes narrowing into thin slits.

"I told you I was coming. It's not my fault you didn't check to see if I'd follow."

"Elizabeth." His voice deepened. "You..."

"What did I do that was so awful?"

He sighed as he shoved his kerchief into his trouser pocket. "It's not important. Leave the rifle. We don't want to be caught with it."

She emptied the chamber of the Winchester rifle, dropped it on the ground, and pocketed the cartridges. James was right about the gun, but she'd stop the unconscious stranger from shooting it anytime soon.

She shook the dirt from her hat before slapping it on her head. "Are we going to argue or leave before he wakes?"

"You're unbelievable." He pointed his finger at her. "We need to head on out, but don't think this conversation is over."

Biting her lip to hold back her grin, she said, "I suppose nothing ever is."

She catapulted herself into her saddle and nudged her horse forward. Looking behind her, she said, "Are you coming? We've been here long enough."

A few hours later, Elizabeth, James, and his men gathered in a ramshackle cabin far off the beaten path. Considering the missing doors and windows, weather torn walls, and roof that would fall in with a stiff wind, the likelihood of anyone discovering them by happenstance was minimal.

Elizabeth stood next to her brother, watching the calculated movements of him and his men as they divided up stacks of money and bags of gold dust. She was unnerved by her own anticipation of the potential rewards from the bounty. She'd never been involved in anything of this nature and although it had been one of the most exciting days she had ever experienced, fear of consequences settled deep in her gut.

She hadn't expected her brother to be a criminal and wasn't sure her life would improve with him at her side. He'd claimed this was his last job, but how could she know that for sure? Her pa made promises as well, but he never kept them.

James had said little on the way back to the cabin and the silence was daunting. Would he send her back to her pa or would he be willing to keep her by his side as their ma had wanted?

When she had handed him the letter their ma had written, he had read it, stuffed it into his coat pocket, and then asked, "Are you sure you want to come with me? Your pa won't like it." She had looked at him hard before nodding and that had been that. James's pa had died long before their ma had married her pa, George Winslow, and while she didn't know the details of what had transpired between her pa and James, she did know her pa had likely washed his hands of James the moment he could.

A few days later, she had found herself protecting the brother who should have protected her. Her pa had raised her as if she were a boy, his rough hands a testament to his displeasure whenever she did wrong, but a helping hand when gutting a deer. She knew how to ride, to shoot, was quick on her feet, and stronger than anyone expected. She was not one to weep, wail, or fall faint. James could trust her at her word and depend on her in any situation.

"Elizabeth, gather your things and that nothing's been left behind."

Nodding, she did what he asked as he told his men to be alert. They needed to steer clear of the law or their efforts would've been for naught

"Last thing I want is to be caged like a bear or on the end of a long rope," James said.

The men chuckled as they left the cabin. They tightened the cinches on their saddles and headed out in different directions. Within minutes, only Elizabeth and James remained.

"Are you ready? We can't stay here," James said.

Elizabeth nodded and wiped the sweat from her palms onto her trousers. She then tightened the belt, securing them around her waist. They were much too big for her slight frame, and they were even baggier considering how little she'd eaten the past few weeks. The little money she'd taken had gone to feed horse and whatever she could scrounge for herself as she searched the countryside for her brother.

James's muscles strained as he loaded the money bags on the back of his packhorse. The animal shifting uncomfortably before he settled under James's steady hands. How much had James taken from the robbery? She wanted to ask, but she wasn't sure she wanted to know the answer. Best to be in the dark if the law caught up with them.

She scratched her horse's muzzle, his soft whiskers tickling her fingers as he nestled against her. Her touch was gentle before grasping the horn and catapulting herself into the saddle. Adjusting her hat so it covered her face, she tightened her hold on the reins and looked at her brother. "Where are we headed?"

"A small town where no one knows us."

"That ain't much to go on."

"I know."

"Can you tell me more?" she asked, her forehead wrinkling with irritation at his less-than-forthcoming answers.

"You'll know when we get there." His gaze stared ahead at the green and yellow hillside, his hands resting on the pommel, the brim of his brown hat tipped up to the sky.

"Why can't you tell me now?"

"Are you always this contrary?" he asked, nudging his horse forward.

"Yep, so you best get used to it." She grinned and followed. Her life and circumstances had changed, and she was going to make the best of it.

Hours after leaving the secluded cabin, Elizabeth and James arrived at the ranch James had purchased a month before. It sat a few miles west of Spring Creek, a small town south of Helena, Montana. The sun settled behind the distant mountain range, red and orange streaks of light obscuring the blue peaks. The reins rested between Elizabeth's fingertips as she slowed her horse, his head dropping to the ground to munch on the sweet grass before them. James's horse brushed against her leg as he reined to a stop next to her.

The wind rustled through the meadow. A vision of green with a smattering of pink and orange wildflowers, sweeping and rolling as far as she could see. She inhaled the fresh scent of wet barley.

During their journey, James told her he wanted to settle his roots and make an honest living. "Spring Creek is small but thriving. There's lots of opportunity here, especially since they built the rail station."

"You chose well. How'd you find it?" she asked. She could see the hidden possibilities of the ranch. It needed work, but they could make it their own.

His lips lifted into a wide smile. "I saw sales notices when I was in Helena last spring. I couldn't resist. It needs work, but I figured I'd hire a ranch hand to help with the heavy lifting. It has potential."

She grinned. "You don't need to hire a ranch hand. I can help."

"The house itself's a disaster, so I'll need a man's strength," he continued, as though he hadn't heard a word she said.

"I can do it," Elizabeth interrupted, anger boiling inside like a volcano ready to explode. It was just like a man to assume she couldn't do an honest day's work.

"You might think you can, but..."

"Dad-blame it," she said, her voice raising in volume, almost like a squeaky wheel that hadn't seen grease in months. "I worked on Pa's ranch as hard as any hired hand."

"Mayhap, but we can't draw attention to ourselves. I can't have anyone looking at me and wondering why I can't control my sister."

"Control..." she sputtered, "that's absurd. No one ever questioned Pa."

"Maybe they should've." He rested his forearms on the pommel of his horse, his hat pulled low over his brow. The silence stretched between them. "When we're on the ranch alone, you do what you please and even wear those trousers you're so fond of."

"What's wrong with them?" she said, heat radiating off her like a torch from a smithy.

"No need to get all riled up. Most women your age try to catch themselves a man and dress more..." He paused as though deliberating his next words. "More like a woman."

"Don't want a man and certainly don't need one either," she said.

"Not sure why'd you feel that way." He held up his hand at her protests. "I reckon I ain't an example to set your sights on, but one day you'll want to have a home of your own, maybe a passel of children."

She'd have to take the man to get the children, so she'd live without both. Taking a deep breath, she said each word carefully, so he'd understand. "It's not something I'll ever want." James didn't know why she was against marrying, and it wasn't his fault she couldn't imagine taking a husband, not when the man she had loved had disappeared so completely.

He shook his head in either frustration or consternation. She wasn't sure which.

"So, as to keep our lives from becoming a battleground, perhaps we strike a compromise. You wear what you want on the ranch. When in town, you act like a lady."

"Fine, but..."

"But what?" he asked.

"I... I don't own a skirt or a dress. Pa never thought I needed 'em, and since Ma passed, there'd been no one to tell him otherwise. No one brave enough to tell him, truth be told."

James said nothing, just waited. The silence stretched between them like an accordion waiting for a song's climax. She wasn't sure how much to tell him or what to tell him. She wanted to forget.

"It never bothered me." She removed her hat and swiped at the loose hairs. "Pa was a force to be reckoned with. I couldn't defy him... until I left. You know it better than most, I suspect."

He stared straight ahead, as if remembering the past. "I suppose I do. At least I can fix that. I'm gonna head to town tomorrow to pick up supplies, and I'll see if I can find you a skirt or two. You stay at the ranch and decide where we should begin." He turned in his saddle, the leather shifting across the horse's back, and faced her. "Do you think you could do that?"

"Yes." The corners of her mouth lifted. She always did what she wanted regardless, but for the sake of keeping him out of jail and for keeping the peace, she'd honor his wishes as long as he never raised a hand against her. She already had one man take a fist to her. She'd do what she could to avoid another.

James laughed, the edges of his eyes crinkling with delight. She reckoned he was in for a few surprises when it came to her.

Two

Ben's head ached. He tried to open his eyes, but they were glued shut and heavy, as if weighted down with stones. After a moment, he wrenched them open and regretted it. The intense sun burned, intensifying the throbbing inside his head.

His head rested between bags of feed on an old wagon. The tangy smell of rotten oats surrounded him. The wagon bumped and jolted, increasing the pain with every passing second. Reaching behind his head, he discovered the cause of his pain—a large, sticky, blood-covered knot. His stomach turned, and he swallowed hard to keep his morning meal where it belonged.

The wagon creaked and pulled to a stop. The world rotated in an intricate sequence of colors as he pushed his aching body to a sitting position. He closed his eyes, trying to stop the crazy spinning. When he reopened them, an old man with a toothless smile grinned at him. His eyes twinkled as though he knew what Ben's future held.

"You alright, son? Ya took a nasty hit to the head."

The man wore dingy clothes and the scent of ripe horse manure poured off him. Had he rolled in it? Ben turned his head downwind, trying not to appear rude. The stench was overpowering.

"I seem to be," replied Ben. "My head's pounding something fierce. What happened?"

"Not sure, son. You was lying dead to the world when I came upon ya." Sweat stains trailed along the sides of his ratty shirt.

Ben groaned. "Where's my horse? My rifle?"

"Horse's tied to the back of the wagon. Rifle sitting next to ya and a mighty fine one at that." Ben glanced at his fingertips and sighed. The rifle had been a gift from his pa and he treasured it.

"You remember anythin'?" the man asked.

"I..." He struggled to recall the last few hours. He'd been heading to Helena, when he heard yelling and..."Gunshots. I tied off my horse and crept up the hill to see what was happening. The stagecoach was being robbed." Shifting to ease the pain in his head, he asked, "Was anyone hurt?"

"Nope. Others are fine. Marshal's with 'em getting what information he can about them there outlaws. Since you was the only one hurt, Marshal asked me to get you to the doc."

"I don't want to put you out."

"Yer doin' nothing of the kind. I was headed back to town, so was no trouble at all, no trouble at all."

"Thank you, I'm much obliged."

Ben tried to stand, but the world swirled around him in maze of colors. He stumbled and dropped back on the hard, wooden slats. Sharp slivers stuck into his backside.

"You best lay back and enjoy the ride, 'cause I don't think you'll be able to sit a horse. Let's have the doc look at that head of yours first. Besides which, the Marshal's going to want to talk to ya in the mornin' about what ya saw and heard."

Ben eased his back against the side of the wagon. The old man was right. He couldn't ride a horse, at least not now.

"What's your name, old man?"

The man smiled. "Folks call me Digger on account of I keep

digging for gold!" He guffawed as he heaved his body onto the seat. "I keep digging but haven't struck it rich yet. One day I'll hit it." He picked up the reins and nudged the mules. "Let's get back to town, boys."

The wagon jerked and plowed forward, throwing Ben against the side of the wagon. His head and neck throbbed, but that was a sight better than being dead.

Ben headed to the Marshal's office the next morning. He found a room to let at the saloon after Digger dropped him at the doc's, declaring Ben would be right as rain in a day or two. It was time to discover what the Marshal knew and if Ben could be of help.

He pushed hard on the thick door. The Marshal sat at a large wooden desk that had seen better days. The nicks, scratches, and gunshot holes were a testament to days gone by.

"Looking better, son. How's the head?"

"Better than yesterday, I'm embarrassed to say," Ben said.

"These things happen. Have a seat."

Removing his hat, Ben sat on an old unsteady chair and extended his legs in front of him. His boots were dusty from the trail.

"What's your full name? Don't think I ever got that." The Marshal leaned over his desk, picked up a stubby pencil, and prepared to take notes.

Grimacing with the memory of his foolishness, Ben said, "Yeah, I suspect I wasn't coherent when Digger found me. Name's Benjamin Seymour."

"Nice to meet you. I wish it would've been under better circumstances."

"So do I."

"Can you tell me what you saw and heard?"

Ben scratched his chin before settling his hands on his knees, his fingers tapping out a silent tune. "I was headed to Butte when I heard a volley of gunshots. Not knowing what I'd find, I crept to the edge of the hill, staying out of sight." He sighed at the memory of his stupidity, his complacency at thinking he was alone. "I hadn't been there long when they caught me unaware, and the next thing I know, I'm in Digger's wagon with a knot the size of a boulder on the back of my head. I never heard the outlaw before he knocked me out."

The Marshal winced. "How many men were there?"

"There were four near the stagecoach, but there must've been another. I only saw the four, though."

"Did you see their faces?"

"No, I was too far away. Based on their location to the stagecoach, I'd say they were tall. My height mayhaps. They had dark hats but their faces were covered."

"Anythin' special about their horses, saddles?"

"No, not that I can recall."

"That ain't much to go on."

"What about those on the stagecoach? Did they offer anythin' useful?" Ben asked.

"No. They're as useless as a pack of hogs."

Ben chuckled at the description, although he supposed he wasn't much better. "Do you have a posse? I'd like to help."

The Marshal leaned back in his chair and scratched his head. "You seem awfully interested in helping, son. I don't know you, and to be perfectly frank, you could've been involved in that robbery and just trying to cover your tracks."

Ben stiffened. The Marshal was right. He had no reason to believe him.

Keeping his hands where the Marshal could see them, Ben said, "To set your mind at ease, you can wire the Marshal in Helena. My pa is... was close friends with him and can vouch for me. I also worked with a man named Victor Olson..."

"Now hold up." The Marshal shifted forward and the chair's

front legs hit the ground with a large thunk. "I know Olson. You worked with him?"

Ben nodded. "For going on the past five years, but I decided to head on home to my pa's ranch when... well, doesn't matter now. I'd like to help but I understand your hesitation. I'll stay in the area 'til you decide you can take me at my word."

"Alrighty then. I'll do just that."

Knowing he had given the Marshal all the information he had, Ben stood. "Well, if you change your mind about the posse, let me know. I've tracked a man or two over the years."

The Marshal tipped his head. "If you're tellin' the truth about working with Olson, I'm sure you have. I'll keep that in mind and let you know if I want your help."

"I best leave you to it then." As he opened the door to leave, Ben turned. "One more thing. Do you know of any ranches hiring?"

"Few need help this late in the season. You lookin' to be hired on somewheres?"

"If I need to stay for a bit, I might as well earn my keep." He had money saved from his years with Olson, but he'd like to keep from using it if he could.

The Marshal leaned again back in his chair again, resting on the two rickety back legs. "I heard someone bought the Triple-A ranch. It's an hour west of town. They might be searching for ranch hands. It's in shambles and needs plenty of work."

"I'll check there. If they need my help, you can find me there. If not, I'll be back in town soon enough."

Three

E lizabeth woke early the next morning feeling a mite refreshed, just as the sun peeped over the mountains. She peered out the wide window of the bunkhouse and watched it cast a soft pink glow across the valley. Birds rose from their nests as the sun roused them from their slumber, their wings flapping in the wind as they swooped and dove in the light blue sky.

She pulled on her trousers, wrapped her hair into a tight braided knot on the top of her head, and placed her hat low on her forehead, covering her hair. It was easier if it was out of the way.

Upon arriving at the ranch the night before, Elizabeth and her brother found a dry patch in the bunkhouse to drop their saddle-bags. They each had a quick bite of dried jerky before heading to bed, exhausted. Before Elizabeth's head hit her makeshift pillow of dry hay in an old flour sack, she was fast asleep. It had been a difficult few weeks, and she had been bone-tired.

Slapping cold water on her face, she washed, stepped outside, and gazed at the crumbling homestead. James thought the main house was unstable. Looking it over, she agreed. It was a collapsing monstrosity that had seen better days and would be laborious to restore to its former glory.

Eager to start but needing to stock up on supplies, James left her behind as he headed to town. The sun burned hot, and it'd be a scorcher of a day. Covered in dirt from weeks on the trail, she could stand a wash, but it'd have to wait. She might take a bath later that evening if she could find something suitable to soak in.

Wandering through the ranch house, being careful not to hurt herself, she pulled fallen wood and debris from inside and stacked it in the clearing out front. James could decide what he wanted to salvage. They'd burn what remained. After working hard for several hours, Elizabeth took a break around noon. Sweat dripped along her neck and between her breasts, and she likely stunk to high heaven. Her throat was dry from all the dirt and dust, but she remembered a working well sat behind the house. She'd head there to quench her thirst.

Taking a good long drink from the ladle, she spilled it on her shirt as horse's hooves sounded out front. Surprised James had made it back so early, she took one last drink of the cool water. She wiped her mouth with the back of her hand, likely smearing dirt across her cheeks, but it'd only mix with the rest of the dirt that covered her from head to toe. It was a good thing she didn't have anywhere special to be. She hurried out front to greet him.

Her excitement at seeing her brother was at once replaced by terror. She stopped dead in her tracks, her mouth dropped open in dismay. Elizabeth swallowed the lump of fear that had lodged itself deep in her throat. Paralyzed, her limbs refused to move. She needed to run, to disappear, but she couldn't. Twenty-four hours earlier, she'd hit the back of his head with a rock. She'd felt certain he hadn't seen her, but perhaps she'd been overconfident. How else had he found them? She would deny knowing who the outlaws were. This man would not imprison her brother, not while she had breath left in her body and fists with which to hit. She had to convince him to leave before James returned. Her heart pounded fast and furious. It'd likely pop straight out of her chest and roll to the ground in front of him if she made any sudden moves.

Taking a deep breath, she forced her stiff legs forward. She had to act calm, although her mind raced with all the implications of him finding them. Her fingers twitched, her legs quivered, but she could do this. She had to do this. She had no other choice. If she had to, she'd lead the man away from the ranch to give James a chance to escape.

The man dismounted and smiled in greeting. Stunned, she stumbled. Was this a joke? Was he deranged? She shouldn't be surprised. She was used to dealing with crazy men. What was another one?

"Mornin'," he said, his voice smooth, husky. It sent a shock-wave of tingles along her spine. His deep brown eyes were open and friendly. Was this a game to him?

What was wrong with her? Why was she noticing stupid details, like his husky voice and bedroom eyes? She shook herself from her stupor and forced words past her lips. "What can I do for you?" Her voice cracked.

"I'm looking for the owner. Is he around?" His eyes ran past her, to the barn, and back again.

Her eyes squinted. What? She wasn't good enough to own it? Of all the unmitigated gall!

"Nope," she snarled.

"Do you know if he's hiring?"

What was he up to? Did he suspect that she and her brother were a part of the band of robbers he'd encountered? She didn't understand what was happening, but she could go along. No matter what, her brother's safety was of utmost importance. She swallowed the angry response she wanted to hurl at him.

"He went to town for supplies."

"Do you mind if I wait for him, son?"

Son? He thought she was a boy. Red, fiery anger flared up her chest and into her cheeks. Her hands balled into fists.

Stop. What was she doing? Who cared what he thought? She relaxed her fingers and inched her arms behind her back. If he couldn't tell she was a girl, that was his problem, not hers. Maybe he wasn't here because she had interfered on that hill overlooking the stagecoach robbery. Was there another reason he had shown up, one she couldn't fathom?

"I suppose." Her tone was belligerent.

"Don't want to impose."

"No imposition. I just don't have time to entertain strangers. As you can see, I'm busy working."

"I'm happy to help 'til he gets back."

"Why would you do that? No guarantee he'll give you work." She glowered at him. Why wouldn't he take the hint and leave?

"I understand, but it might help my cause." He smiled, his eyes twinkled, and a dimple creased his cheek. If she were like the girls back home, she might swoon, but she wasn't. A breathtaking smile on a devastatingly handsome man wouldn't sway her. No sirree, it surely wouldn't. She had more backbone than that.

Shrugging, she said, "Mister, that's up to you, but I've got work to do. If you're determined to help, start in the barn. Plenty to do there. I'm headed back to the house. You can talk to him when he returns." The words spilled from her mouth in a rush.

Retreating to the rear of the house, she leaned against the one steady wall left and let out a swish of air. It didn't appear he had any idea who she was. She'd keep an eye on him, though. She didn't trust him as far as she could spit.

Four

The young man sauntered away, his scrawny body no match for the work needed to get the ranch up to snuff. He didn't appear to be older than fifteen years. Immature and impertinent, the boy reminded him of his brothers at that age. Ben didn't take offense to the young man's words. Trying to be a man, he had flexed his muscles and attempted to be contrary. Ben chuckled softly enough so the boy wouldn't hear him. He'd probably take offense. With any luck, the owner would be friendlier and not so petulant.

Ben looked around after the young man disappeared. The main house was standing on its last legs. The roof had caved in on one side, the windows were empty of glass, the front door hung on its side, and the porch sagged. Fence posts had fallen and overgrown weeds covered the spread. The barn was full of miscellaneous items, but the walls appeared steady and sound. It was a good thing, as you needed a sturdy enclosure to house your animals.

There was plenty of work to keep multiple men busy for weeks. He'd be surprised if the owner relied on the boy to do the heavy lifting. With fall rolling in and winter coming soon after, he'd need the help. Depending on his livestock, the fences and corrals needed to be repaired and fast. The boy might've had good intentions, but until he was older, stronger, and added meat to his bones, he'd be of little help.

Ben pushed up his shirt sleeves and headed to the barn. The sun was bright and hot, but that wouldn't stop him. He used to do back-breaking chores while toiling on his pa's ranch and his body would remember soon enough. This was the work he'd been born to do, but because of his impatience and pure stubbornness, he'd left home seeking something more than what he thought was the drudgery of the day-to-day life of living on a ranch. What he found was complicated, difficult, and lonely. He should've never left home, but he needed the time away to grow, mature, and find himself. If he hadn't, he might never have been satisfied with ranch life.

He had been headed to Butte to look for work but considering the circumstances, Spring Creek seemed a good place to begin anew. Besides, he had unfinished business here. Until the Marshal was satisfied he wasn't a part of the robbery, he needed to stick around to clear his name. With any luck, he'd be able to help the Marshal find traces of those outlaws and bring them to justice.

Over the last five years, he learned how to track and excelled at it. With the amount of money the outlaws had taken, there was bound to be a clue. Outlaws were never careful and one of them would make a mistake. He was sure of it.

Elizabeth spied on the man from the back of the house. His tanned, muscular arms bulged as he cleared the barn. He wasn't afraid of hard work. Taking a few deep breaths to calm her beating heart, she had to be on the lookout for her brother. She needed to warn him before he met the stranger.

She couldn't believe he thought she was a boy. It was annoying and bothered her, and she didn't understand why. It wasn't the first time someone called her a boy, but when he did, it was as if he'd punched her in the gut.

Realizing she was getting nothing done, she stopped her train wreck of thoughts and went back to work. She couldn't gaze at him all day. She had better things to do.

She returned to pulling out the remains of the roof from the kitchen. Being cautious, she was careful not to disturb the standing walls. She didn't want what remained to fall on her.

Before long, she had cleared the kitchen of debris, rotten animals, and the dirt and dust that had accumulated from years of neglect. Her stomach rumbled with hunger as the blistering sun baked her exposed skin. It had to be close to four in the afternoon.

James should've been back by now. She hoped he would've returned with something more than the dry bread and jerky left in her saddlebag. Although it didn't sound appetizing, she was pleased she had that much. Her food supplies had dwindled by the time she had found James. Resourceful, she had taken little when she left her pa's.

As she approached the bunkhouse, she moved around the large piles of wood, decaying straw, cow dung, and who knows what else that the man had removed from the barn. Sweat lined the back of his shirt and his dark hair curled at the nape of his long neck, just touching the tip of his collar. His muscles strained beneath the large planks of wood he carried. He dropped the load into the growing stack and then reached for a canteen on the nearest fence post, tipped his head back and took a healthy swallow. Water spilled from the canteen and dribbled across his chin and onto his exposed chest.

His head descended, and he caught her eye. A tingle curled in the pit of her stomach, and warmth flooded her chest and cheeks. She didn't know what was wrong with her. Grinning, he nodded to the pile and held his hands out as if to ask, *does this show you I'm serious*? Not acknowledging his silent question, she marched to the bunkhouse and her saddlebags.

She needed food. The lack of it had to explain how hot and faint she'd become. She found her last piece of bread and jerky wrapped in cheesecloth. Stuffing the jerky in her pocket, she took a healthy bite of the stale bread, hoping to stave off her hunger pains. She chewed as she wandered out of the bunkhouse, the bread in one hand, her canteen in the other.

Taking another bite, she slammed into a hard wall. A solid, warm, masculine wall.

"Umph," she said.

Her mouth full, she swallowed and choked. Her throat closed, and she tried to cough, but the bread stuck in her throat. The canteen and bread tumbled from her fingers, forgotten, as her chest squeezed with the lack of air. Bending over, her hat fluttered to the ground. She tried to gasp and failed, her gut seizing. She couldn't breathe and darkness blurred her vision.

He reached around her and lifted her arms to help her get air. When that didn't work, he hit her on the back. Between the force of his hands, her violent coughing attempts, and a miracle from heaven above, they dislodged the bread. With a great whoosh, it flew out of her mouth and warm, delicious air filled her. He patted her on the back as though she were a small child.

She was bent at the knees, her hands braced against them as tears ran down her cheeks. Her braid had fallen loose and dangled next to her, swinging freely. She shoved it behind her as she continued to cough, her throat aggravated and scratched.

"You alright?" he asked.

She breathed, trying to slow her pounding heart, coughs still wracking her slim frame. When she finally stopped, she wiped her face with the back of her hands. Not sure she could say much, she nodded her head in thanks.

"Here's your hat, miss," he said with a distinct touch of irony in his voice, the hat held in his hand.

She stood straight, looked into his eyes, and knew the question he didn't ask. She should explain but wasn't going to.

She snatched it out of his hands. "Thank you, Mr.?"

"I guess I never introduced myself, did I?" he said. "Ben Seymour's the name and you aren't a young man."

Avoiding his gaze, she said, "Nope. I'm not."

She slapped her hat on her head. Before he said more, she picked up her canteen and strode away as fast as her legs could carry her.

Five

James arrived back at the ranch much later than planned. Ordering lumber had been quite the adventure. Lucky for him, the owner of the mill knew the state of James's ranch and helped him decide what he needed.

Just as he was leaving town, he realized he'd forgotten to stop at the General Store for a skirt or two for Elizabeth and food staples so they wouldn't starve. He, himself, was looking forward to a hot meal—maybe a thick, juicy steak smothered in a rich, brown gravy and creamy mashed potatoes. His mouth watered at the thought. He'd ask the storekeeper to throw in some potatoes, and he'd stop at the butcher and pick up fresh steaks.

After requesting the items from the storekeeper, he found the ready-made clothing but wasn't sure what to purchase. Women's dresses, skirts, blouses, and unmentionables hung on a metal frame and were folded on a long counter against the wall. He stared in astonishment. He had no idea where to begin.

"Can I help?" A soft, lilting voice asked. A strikingly beautiful woman looked at him with an impish grin on her face. She had her hair covered in a frilly bonnet, her hands encased in white lace gloves, lips red as cherries.

He shrugged and said, "Frankly, I can use all the help I can get."

Giggling, she said, "I wouldn't expect a handsome man like yourself to be looking at women's clothing."

"Me either, but it seems I need a skirt. What do you think of this?" He pointed to one in dark green.

"Hmm, a striking color," she said. "But... I don't think the green would complement your complexion."

"What... what?" He swung his eyes from the skirt to her.

"I'm thinking red would be more your color." Her finger tapped her lips.

"Oh, no... I mean, it's not for me. I mean, I'd never..." Heat rose from his chest to his cheeks. No woman had gotten the best of him before.

Laughing, her face was full of mischief. If all the women in this town were like her, he was going to enjoy settling here.

He chuckled. "Well, I guess that's a first, young lady."

"First for what?" She cocked her head to the side, her blue eyes searching his.

"That someone as charming as you got the best of me."

"I don't understand. I was just trying to help you find a suitable skirt." Her eyes twinkled with joy.

"Well, could you help me find a skirt that'd suit my sister instead?"

Taking his arm in hers, she pulled him to her side and said, "I'd be happy to, Mr.?"

"Dodson, but please, call me James."

"And *you* can call me Suzette."

Hours later, he found himself with more packages for Elizabeth than he'd planned. Suzette had welcomed him to Spring Creek and had been gracious enough to help him buy the clothing. She insisted any young lady would love the dark green and blue skirts, as well as the white and light blue shirtwaists. Not to mention all the other accoutrements a young lady would need. If

Elizabeth didn't like any of the items, he was to bring her back to town, and they'd find her something more to her liking.

Reaching the clearing in front of the barn, he pulled on the reins to slow his horse and his mouth fell open. Was he at the right ranch? Massive piles of debris lay in front of the barn and next to the house.

How had Elizabeth done all of this? He dismounted and led his horse to the barn when a stranger walked out, holding a bucket of feed.

Startled at the intrusion, James's eyes narrowed. "Who are you?"

"Name's Benjamin Seymour, but folks call me Ben. You must be the owner?"

"Yes. Yes, I am," he said. He kept his eyes on the stranger the whole time. He didn't know what the man wanted, but he hadn't survived this long by not being cautious. The last thing he wanted was trouble considering his involvement in the stagecoach robbery, but he needed to make sure Elizabeth was unharmed.

Ben placed the bucket next to his feet, wiped his hands on his trousers, and held out his hand. James ignored it.

"Pleasure to meet you," Ben said, dropping his hand to his side and his smile losing a bit of its shine.

"Mind telling me what you're up to, Mr. Seymour?"

"I'm looking for work, Mr.?"

James paused before replying. "...Dodson,"

Ben nodded. "When I arrived earlier, I talked briefly with your sister. I told her I was looking for work. She didn't know if you were hiring, so I asked if I could help until you returned."

"Why'd you do that? No guarantee I'd hire you."

"I know, but I figure sometimes the best way to show someone you're a good hire is to show him what you can do. If you weren't hiring, then I helped a neighbor. If you are, I gave you a taste of who I am."

Removing his hat, James scratched his scalp, his mind racing.

He hadn't expected to find anyone other than Elizabeth at the ranch, but then the last few days had been full of surprises. Thinking it over for a moment longer, he held out his hand. "I guess you just found yourself a place to work."

As she returned to the rear of the house, Elizabeth tried not to run from Ben's prying eyes. After her humiliating choking episode, she had to escape. She was mortified he had seen her defenseless and then to have him put his arms around her made her uneasy. She wasn't sure how to process what she was feeling. Not that she had been trying to hide who she was, but she'd been scared when he arrived. At the time, it made sense to go along with his mistaken impression that she was a boy.

She had to warn her brother before Ben reached him. She prayed Ben wouldn't recognize her brother because if he did, then their new world could crash down on both of them. What would she do if her brother were imprisoned? She had nowhere to go. James was all she had.

After finishing what she could in the house, she moved to the corral and cleared dried weeds with a decrepit rake she found lying in the tall grass. Once finished with the corral, she leaned against the rake, her chin resting on its handle. She looked at what she had accomplished and smiled. Not bad for a day's work.

She headed to the front of the house, the rake swinging at her side, but stopped in dismay when she saw both James and Ben coming toward her. She hadn't heard James or his horse. She'd been distracted and now it was too late. They were smiling and joking. Had he not recognized Ben as the man she'd hurt during the robbery?

"Elizabeth," he called. "You've met Ben."

"Um, yes," she said as she leaned the rake up against the fence post, thrusting her hands in her pockets.

"Yeah, we had a bit of a struggle earlier," Ben said.

"What was that?" James said, looking back and forth between them.

Ben grimaced. "I caught your sister choking."

Concerned, James walked to her, but she held out her hand to stop him.

"I'm fine. I didn't need his help. Can I talk to you alone?" She pressed her lips together.

James nodded. "Ben, could you excuse us for a moment?"

"Sure. I'll head on back to the barn. We can talk more later."

Elizabeth made sure Ben was well out of sight before she spoke.

"Please tell me you didn't hire him," she said, placing her fingers lightly on his arm.

"Why not? He seems a nice enough fellow."

"He was at the robbery," she whispered, pulling him further away.

He stopped, the color draining from his face. "What? He wasn't on the stagecoach. I would've recognized him."

"He was the one I hit over the head."

"I didn't even notice," James said.

"I was afraid of that. What are you going to do?"

"What can I do? I already offered him the job. If I change my mind now, it'll look suspicious." He stalked back and forth, his hand behind his neck as he considered the situation.

"Do you think he knows who you are?"

"I hope not. He only seems interested in work. Besides, I had my face covered. How much do you think he saw?" He stopped to look at her.

"He approached the top of the hill as the shooting started. You were wrapping up by the time I got to him."

"I didn't expect this," he said. His finger stroked his ear before dropping away.

"We've got to get rid of him. He can't stay here," she hissed.

"I can't tell him to leave."

"Why not?" she asked, her hands on her hips, her face hot.

"I already explained why." A vein popped in his neck. He was clearly frustrated with her.

"We can't take the chance he'll figure out who you are. Who we are." Sweat poured down her back from both the heat and the fear that Ben was there to end their new life.

"He won't figure it out. I said little, and he was far away."

"This is a lousy idea," she mumbled.

"I'll keep an eye on him. If he makes any suspicious moves, I'll handle it." James's face wore an expression she couldn't name, but it frightened her anyway.

"What do you mean?" she asked.

"Don't worry. It's best if you don't know." He turned to walk away.

She reached out and grabbed his arm. "We can't do this. You can't do this!"

He shrugged off her grip and said, "What do you expect me to do?" His voice was low and deep with anger.

"You need to tell him to go."

"Enough. Let it go. I'll handle it my way."

Six

Thrilled he secured employment, Ben worked hard over the next few days. He needed a distraction from the events at his pa's ranch. It was still hard to come to terms with what he had found.

Working for James was pleasant, a nice enough fellow who toiled just as hard alongside him. What he didn't understand was why James let his sister help with the hard labor. Women belonged in the home, not outside working in the hot, dry weather where the blistering sun beat down on their delicate skin. Just yesterday, Elizabeth had picked up a hammer and a bag of nails and dragged fence posts and rails so she could mend the broken corral. She dragged wood that was twice as tall and almost as thick as her slim frame. Her hips filled out those tight trousers, and sweat soaked her shirt, it clung to her curves. It was quite indecent, and he struggled to keep his eyes off her.

Ben's mother would've been horrified if one of his sisters were found working in the corrals on his pa's ranch, and she would have fainted if she saw them in trousers. You could see every curve of her legs and waist, including a nicely rounded backside.

When he questioned James the day before about her doing the

work of a man, James had looked at her, shrugged and said, "She does what she wants. I can't stop her." He then turned back to Ben, one eyebrow raised. "If'n you have a problem with it, well, then you best move on." James squinted at Ben, and he squirmed under the glare.

Ben nodded. "She's your sister."

"That's right, she is, and don't you forget it." His tone was low and his jaw set. Ben knew he had crossed a line.

"My apologies, James. Ain't my place."

"No, it ain't and you best keep your mind where it belongs—right here on the work I'm paying you for."

Ben turned his attention back to working on the windows of the barn. He'd keep his thoughts of Elizabeth's behavior to himself. Lucky for him, James seemed to have forgotten their exchange from the day before as he gave him his instructions for the day.

They had woken to a harsh summer rain, but by noon, the storm had broken and the scorching sun baked their skin. Needing to refill their canteens, he and James came around the corner of the house just in time to watch Elizabeth stumble into a large muddy puddle. She held a bucket of water in each hand when her foot slipped from under her. Her arms flailed wildly as she dropped the buckets and fell backward into the mud, which sprayed across everything in its path.

"Dad-blame-it," she muttered.

James laughed, his eyes twinkling at her misfortune.

She raised her eyes and glared at her brother. "You chuckle-head, this ain't funny."

"Oh, but it surely is," James said, laughing some more. "You should have seen yourself, flapping your arms like a chicken being chased by a rabid raccoon."

"Oh, go find a hole to climb into. I don't need you gawking at me."

James shook his head, still chuckling. "Well, if you need my help, you just holler, you hear?"

She picked up a clump of mud and threw it at him, but James jumped out of the way. He turned and headed back the way they had come. Looking over his shoulder, he said, "You coming, Ben?"

"No, I'm out of water. I'll fill my canteen and be back in a minute."

James nodded and headed away, still chuckling at his sister's predicament.

Ben took a step forward, concerned. James might have thought it was funny, but she looked like a drowned rat. "Are you hurt? Can I help?" He held out his hands, but she slapped them away.

"Get away from me," she snarled.

She slipped again while trying to turn, water and mud flying everywhere. He withdrew a few steps, not wanting any of the mud to land on him. In trying to find a foothold, she put her hands on the ground, but they slid and she slammed right back into the muddy water, this time her face falling straight into the muck.

He covered his mouth to contain his laughter. She didn't need to see him laugh after her brother had done so, but instead of accepting his help, she had made it worse for herself. She pushed onto her knees and swiped at the mud in her eyes, but since it covered her hands, she only added to the problem. Clumps of mud covered her from head to toe, but she didn't quit. He had to admire her determination, if nothing else.

After a few long and painful moments of watching her fail, she crawled to drier ground and stood. She threw back her shoulders and stalked away, her boots squeaking and sludge dripping from her with each step she took.

He started to follow but stopped. She may not want him anywhere near her. Her face was flushed red beneath the thick coating of mud, and her hands were balled into fists. She was embarrassed, and his presence wasn't helping.

Humiliated, Elizabeth blinked back hot tears. She looked like a bumbling fool. To prove she didn't need Ben's help, she'd only made things worse. The mud coating her was slimy and thick.

Angry, frustrated, and mortified, she had never cared what people thought of her, yet she cared what *Ben* thought. When she looked at him, her breath caught in her throat. His rugged good looks made her heart beat too fast, but she had to remember he could ruin her life with one word to the Marshal if he figured out her involvement in the robbery, not to mention what it could cost her brother. Instead of trying to convince Ben to leave, she was mooning over him like a lovesick calf. She hated herself for that.

She headed to the lake at the far end of the property. She had discovered it the other day and thought she'd take a swim in it soon. Looks like she'd be taking that swim sooner than anticipated. She'd clean up there instead of the bunkhouse. She could jump in, clothing and all.

After an agonizingly slow walk during which she chastised herself, she reached the lake's edge. The blue water shimmered and glistened. She might have enjoyed the view if she'd been in a better frame of mind, but the mud had hardened, making her skin itch and crawl as though tiny mites and worms were slithering all over her. It was going to be difficult to remove, but she needed to get it off before she scratched her skin off instead.

She sat and pulled off her boots. Mud had collected in crevices she didn't even know existed. A cluster of trees stood a few feet from her and could protect her from prying eyes. She ran to them, her woolen socks squishing with every step. Reaching the privacy of the trees, she dropped her boots and leaned against a rough tree trunk to remove all but her camisole and drawers.

As she looked at herself, the muddy water had soaked through and coated those too. Should she remove them? *Oh why not?* She pulled the bottom of her camisole up and over her head. Shoving her drawers down her hips, she stepped out of them and picked up her mud-caked clothing.

She looked around once more before running to the water's edge. She dropped her clothes and put each foot firmly on the rocky lakebed. She could swim but she didn't know how deep the water was and didn't want to step off a ledge. She continued until she had submerged herself so only her head was above the water. Her hot skin welcomed the cool water.

She was quite wanton being in the water without a stitch of clothing on. It had been some time since she had bathed and although she didn't have soap, she could still get somewhat clean.

Dipping her head back, she ran her fingers through the thick strands of hair, trying her best to remove the guck and grime. Rubbing her hands across her body, she scrubbed as best she could until her skin tingled. Her eyes skimmed the edge of the lake. Not an animal or human dotted the landscape.

Cutting through the water until she reached the shore, she picked up her filthy clothing and soaked them in the water, scrubbing, and rinsing them. They needed a touch of soap, but at least she had gotten the dried mud removed. Once done, she placed them on large, flat boulders. With any luck, they'd dry in the scorching sun.

Not wanting to head back to the ranch just yet, she went back into the cool water, enjoying a moment alone. Fall was right around the corner, so this might be her last chance to swim. Leaning back, she floated, luxuriating in the peacefulness and the freshness in the air.

Ben located slats of wood and placed them over the muddy puddles of water surrounding the well. He didn't want Elizabeth to slip and fall again. He glanced at the sun and how far it had moved. She had been gone longer than expected. He should check on her.

He picked up a clean blanket from the bunkhouse and headed to the lake. When she left, she had headed in that direction.

He saw an enchantress as he reached a cluster of trees near the lake. Her pale slim body floated serenely in its bright blue depths. The sun's rays sparkled on the water, creating a glow around her. She stood, disturbing the serenity of the lake.

He jumped behind the nearest tree. With her back to him, all he could see was her long, brown hair hanging down to her waist. She raised her arms as she pulled her hair across her back before dropping it across one shoulder.

She was naked as the day she was born. His heart pounded in his chest like he had been chased by a mountain lion. He shouldn't be looking, but he couldn't take his eyes off her.

She finished wringing her hair and made her way to the opposite shore. She wasn't a scrawny young man or a little girl. She was a stunning young woman, the kind of woman a man would dream of having.

She reached the water's edge. He couldn't pull his eyes away and he didn't want to. Reaching a large boulder, she picked up a white cotton camisole. Slipping it over her head, it fell to her waist. Coming out of his lust-filled stupor, he was ashamed at where his thoughts had lead. She was an innocent who believed she had been alone. He shouldn't be here.

He turned and reluctantly left for the bunkhouse. The slap of the blanket against his leg reminded him of why he'd followed her, but he couldn't approach her, not now. It was of the utmost importance for him to remember she wasn't a lady. Elizabeth wasn't someone he could ever find himself with. She was everything he didn't want.

But why, oh why, couldn't he stop thinking about her?

Seven

The next day, Ben rose early. He slept poorly, tossing and turning for hours with inappropriate dreams of Elizabeth. She was tantalizing under those awful trousers, but she wasn't a woman he'd ever consider as a future wife. Not only was she unladylike, she was his employer's sister and was off-limits.

There were bound to be women in town more suitable if he were to look. Putting his best clothes on, he headed to the barn. It was Sunday, and he wanted to arrive at church on time. He also wanted to speak with the Marshal regarding the stagecoach robbery. Opening the barn doors, he headed to his horse's stall.

Running his hand down Midnight's spine, he murmured, "Going to church today. There I'll meet proper young ladies." He reached for the cinch. "I'm sure there are plenty to choose from. Some who are every inch a lady. Ones who don't cuss, wear trousers, sweat, or are covered in dirt from head to toe. Instead, there'll be ones who I'd be proud to call my wife."

"Is that how you talk to your horse? All lovey dovey?"

Startled, he pulled the cinch too tight and Midnight resisted. He peered around the corner. Elizabeth leaned against a pitchfork in the stall across from him. Dirt marks lined her cheeks and her brown hat hung low across her face. He couldn't see her eyes and once again she was wearing those trousers.

He finished before responding. "Nothing wrong with talking to my horse."

"Oh, I don't think there's anything wrong with that. It's the words you were using. No need to get riled up," she said, grinning.

"I'm not riled up," he said, his face burning with embarrassment.

"Oh, you are," she said, stepping away from her pitchfork and placing it against the wall before raising her hands to her cheeks. "Oh, Midnight, I need a clean-smelling woman." She twirled in front of him, her hands held wide and her voice high, almost like she was singing. "One who'll wash my clothes and wear pretty frilly ones. She doesn't need a brain in her head or do anything useful. No sirree, just needs to prance around the house keeping it clean for me." She spun to a stop and put her hands on her waist, her eyes flashing with mirth.

"I didn't say that," he muttered, embarrassed.

"Maybe not, but close enough." She walked up to him, her gaze sharp as she stared at him hard. "You haven't had time to get to know anyone. Why would you want someone like that? Do you want to be bored for the rest of your life?"

"That isn't any of your business."

Laughing, she said, "My, my. Aren't we testy?"

"I'm not testy."

"Aren't you? I just asked a simple question."

"I don't need to explain myself to you. You aren't a lady."

"That was awfully rude," she said, stepping closer to him, her body mere inches from his. "I'm just trying to make conversation, and you're getting upset. Saying I'm not a lady." She pushed him back, and he stumbled against the stall wall. "That isn't very nice. I am a girl." She stopped and placed her finger to her lips as if pondering something. "But then again, you thought I was a boy when we first met."

"I'm not upset, and I didn't realize you were a girl because you were wearing those trousers."

"What's wrong with my trousers?" she said, placing her hands on her hips, before she ran her palms along her sides and then turning to look behind her. "I think they're suitable for working on a ranch."

What was she trying to do?

"They aren't suitable for a lady," he muttered.

"I never claimed to be a lady, now did I?" she said, her eyes flashing.

"No, I guess you didn't, but your brother should take you to task."

"No man will *ever* do that to me."

"They should. You should be ashamed of yourself running around in them."

"I ain't a lady, but you aren't a gentleman."

"What?" he said.

"I think I was clear. But let me say it again. You ain't a gentleman. If you were, you'd be kinder."

Was she trying to antagonize him to death?

Once again, she stepped close. He tried to get away, but he had nowhere to go.

"What's wrong? Cat got your tongue?" she asked. He wasn't sure what she was thinking, but with her cheeks flushed and her full pink lips calling him, he needed to quiet her.

Before he realized what he intended, he grabbed her by the arm, pulled her close, and placed his lips on hers. *This would quiet her.* Then he lost all reasonable thoughts.

Her lips were soft, pliant under his, tasting like ripe, juicy berries. She was sweet, delicious and then it ended abruptly.

She had pulled away and slapped his face. "What are you

doing?" she yelled. Her face was red, her chest heaving as though she had run from the far-field to the barn in which they stood.

He backed away from her, his breath coming hot and fast. His palms were sweaty, and his heart raced. "Sweet heaven..." he muttered.

"Why did you do that?"

"I..."

"You're rude," she said.

His eyes flew to hers. "I'm rude," he said. "This was your fault. You're not a lady, prancing around here in those tight trousers, showing your lady parts to any man within shouting distance. What do you expect a man to do when you act like a whore?"

Her hands flew to her mouth and tears filled her eyes. She turned and ran out of the barn, her hat falling to the ground, her long brown hair trailing behind her.

He cursed. She didn't deserve his unkind words. While he may not agree with her wearing trousers, it wasn't his place to condemn. "Wait," he called, but it was too late. She was already gone.

Elizabeth ran back to the bunkhouse. She wiped her tears. She never cried or at least not that often, but he seemed to bring out the worst in her. He had just shown his true colors by calling her a word she couldn't utter. He was hateful and mean, but had she antagonized him? Had she pushed him to the point of no return?

She had lost all sense of reason when he pulled her into his arms. She hadn't expected him to kiss her, but as his warm lips had scraped against her neck, reason had intervened, and she realized what they were doing. She hadn't wanted him to stop, but she knew it was wrong, and that was when she pulled away. Instead of letting him know how much she wanted and desired him, she lashed out, and he'd responded in kind. That was her fault, and she deserved every nasty word.

Only one other man had kissed her. Timmy's kisses had been soft, hesitant. Ben's kisses burned bright and with uncontrolled passion. She didn't know what to think. Timmy's lips paled in comparison to Ben's soft lips and muscular body.

"Stop!" Her voice echoed in the bunkhouse.

This was ridiculous. She couldn't compare the two men. They were as different as night and day. She had sworn she wouldn't fall for a man again, especially for one who thought so little of her. She had no plans to marry, so she had to stop her errant thoughts.

She headed to her room in the bunkhouse and washed away the tears with the bucket of water she had filled the night before. James couldn't see her upset. He might question her, and what would she say? She had egged Ben on and deserved every hateful word he had delivered.

Closing her eyes, she held a cool cloth against her eyes, letting it soothe her soul and the puffiness from her tears. She took a few breaths to calm her beating heart. Today was Sunday and she woke up thinking it'd be a good idea to go to church. James needed to appear as a fine and upstanding member of the community and a sure way to do that would be to go to church. It would provide an air of respectability they'd need in order to keep anyone from suspecting their involvement in the stagecoach robbery.

She couldn't let the altercation with Ben to derail her plans. Convincing James to take her was of the utmost importance. She'd meant to ask James earlier but had forgotten.

She removed the trousers and shirt Ben had touched and dropped them to the floor. She'd likely scrub them clean later. She quickly washed before pulling on the new green skirt and white shirtwaist James had bought for her. She ran a quick comb through her hair, braided it, and let it swing behind her back. She looked for her hat but it was nowhere to be found. She must've left it in the barn, but there was no chance she'd return for it now. She'd look for it later.

Heading outside, she found James in the corral working with the horses. She couldn't be prouder of him and what he was trying to do. He told her that he wanted to break wild horses and sell them. Horses were necessary and it had always been his dream to have a horse ranch.

"You're in a skirt. Any reason why?" he asked, sauntering to the fence, dust billowing around his boots.

"It's Sunday, and I'd like to go to church. Will you take me?" Her hands clasped tight in front of her. What if he said no?

"I'm not a fan of church."

"Why not?"

"Haven't been in a few years and don't intend to start now. God and I don't seem to see eye to eye, I reckon, but don't let me stop you."

"I won't, but you need to come with me." Her voice pleaded with him.

"I don't know," he said, scratching behind his ear.

"Shouldn't we make a good impression? And what better place to do it than in church?" She smiled at him as though she could convince him with one look.

"I understand, but it still makes me wary." He pushed away from the fence and removed his hat, running his fingers through the hair along the base of his neck. He stopped and looked up to the sky as though he could find all of his answers looking up into its bright blue depths.

"Please."

He dropped his chin and looked at the ground for a long moment before slapping his head back on his head "Alright. We'll go."

She braced her hands against the fence railing and jumped over, the wood sturdy enough to hold her before she landed in a cloud of dust. She ran to him and threw her arms around him, kissing his scruffy cheek. His dark brown hair, almost the color of hers, was slicked back but hung low on his neck. He could use a cut and she might just have to mention that, but not now. She had just convinced him to take her to church, so she wasn't about to push her luck. "Thank you. How about a picnic after services?"

"I guess if we're going, we might as well do that, too. I just hope I don't regret this."

"You won't, I promise."

Eight

Elizabeth sat on their new wagon bench as James urged the horses to the grassy meadow in front of the church. He had purchased the wagon just the other day, and the seat bounced with each rut in the road.

Many wagons sat scattered in the tall grass. She jumped to the ground, her skirts fluttering around her. She wasn't sure if she'd ever get used to the way they hung and draped across her hips and legs, but she'd try. They impeded everything and confined her movements. Then there was the corset. It was the most restrictive device ever invented. She wasn't sure why any woman put this contraption on their body. She wasn't sure why she did. She'd never understand the things women did to be proper.

The pews were full, and the noise level was low as they headed through the wide-open doors of the church. Seeing a spot for them near the middle, she led them to the seats and settled into the pew. Sensing his discomfort, she placed her hand on James's knee and squeezed. She was excited to be there and didn't want him to be uncomfortable.

Everyone dressed in their Sunday best—women in their nicest calicos and bonnets and men in suits or their best shirts. Although she and James weren't in the fanciest of clothes, they were clean and presentable. Looking around the room, she spotted Ben up front. He sat next to a stunning woman with corn-silk hair. A sharp pang pierced her gut.

Uneasy and self-conscious, she rubbed her hands against her skirt, trying to smooth the many wrinkles. She knew she paled in comparison. The woman's dress was light blue and fitted her like a glove. Even the bonnet covering her curls caused a fiery streak of jealousy to burn through her. Elizabeth's own hair was nothing like hers and hung straight as an ironing board. She didn't know how to make it curl and didn't think she'd get a decent curl if she tried. Instead, she consistently pulled it back into a long braid.

She looked up at James and noticed that he too was staring at the woman next to Ben's side. A frown marred his lips. Did he know the woman as well?

Before she could ask James about the woman, the pastor stepped up to the front, cleared his throat, and the congregation silenced. Elizabeth turned her attention to his sermon.

"Have we become consumed by our neighbors' opinions of us, rather than being concerned with the opinion of our Lord?" The pastor seemed to gaze straight at her, his eyes piercing deep, and she shifted in her seat. "Have we let our pride overcome our ability to be humble? Have we become jealous of our neighbors and let envy eat at our souls?"

The pastor's words struck a painful chord within Elizabeth. She shifted her gazed to the woman next to Ben and was ashamed. She was grateful for what she had and would attempt to show gratitude instead of jealousy and envy. She now had a warm home, a brother who she hoped could grow to love her, and the chance to make friends in a new community who wouldn't judge her for the actions of her pa. She didn't know the woman and had no cause to judge her.

The pastor continued to discuss ways they all could overcome pride and envy and ended the service with one last thought that resonated with her—humility is freedom from pride or arrogance. She would strive to do better not only to keep James from hanging from the end of the rope but so that the two of them could become useful members of their community and perhaps with time make up for mistakes they had each made in their pasts.

She knew she wanted to return. She hoped James felt the same way. The pastor had given her plenty to ponder. They waited until their row cleared before heading to the aisle. A few ladies smiled and nodded their heads in welcome, and she grinned in return. Perhaps she could find friends here.

They joined the line to greet the pastor. When it was their turn, James shook his hand and said, "Pastor, nice to meet you. I'm James Dodson and this here is my sister, Elizabeth."

"Welcome, James, Elizabeth, I'm Pastor Williams," he said, "and my wife, Milly." He pulled an older woman to his side. She had white, grayish curly hair with laugh wrinkles in the corners of her mouth and eyes that bespoke of a woman who smiled often.

"Welcome," Milly said. Her eyes were friendly and she bounced on her feet, full of energy and enthusiasm.

"Thank you, Pastor, Mrs. Williams," Elizabeth said.

"Please call me, Milly. We don't stand on ceremony around here."

Elizabeth smiled. "Milly, it's nice to meet you. I enjoyed the service, Pastor."

"Thank you. I'm always grateful when members of my flock appreciate my long-winded sermons." They all laughed. "Will we see you next week?"

"I'm sure we'll be here every week if Elizabeth has her way," James said.

"That's what I want to hear. We just need to change your feelings so you'll be itching to come as well," Pastor Williams said, chuckling at his own words.

They talked for a few more minutes, discussing the town, the weather, and the activities available to the young people in town.

Milly even invited Elizabeth to attend their women's league, which was held every Wednesday, weather permitting. They sewed quilts, gathered food for those less fortunate, and organized special town events such as the Christmas play. It would be an opportunity for Elizabeth to get to know more of the women in town and the surrounding ranches.

∼

Families gathered their food baskets and searched for tall trees under which to sit and eat. It was a sunny day, and it appeared everyone wanted to socialize and enjoy the pleasant weather before fall and winter arrived.

"I'll grab our food. Why don't you find us a place to sit?" James said.

She nodded. "Don't forget the blanket."

"Oh, Mr. Dodson," a young woman said behind them.

James turned. "Suzette. How good to see you today."

"Thank you. Have you met Mr. Seymour?" She pulled Ben to her side as though claiming him as her own. Ben lowered his gaze and stared at Suzette with lovesick eyes.

Suzette fluttered her eyes at Ben and Elizabeth groaned inside. Then chastised herself. Hadn't she learned anything from the sermon? She would make an effort to get to know her, but did Ben have to look so enamored?

"Yes, yes, I have," James said, removing his hat in deference to her.

Elizabeth swiveled her head to look at her brother. The tone of his voice had grown low and husky. What was wrong with her brother? When had he met Suzette?

Who was this woman who had already stirred the interest of both the men?

"I'm his new ranch hand," Ben said, smiling at Suzette seemingly unaware that James eye's had suddenly grown dark. James's knuckles grew white as he clenched his hat tightly as he watched Suzette cradle Ben's arm near her chest. "He hired me on a few days past."

Raising her eyes to James, she said, "You own a ranch around here? You didn't tell me that the other day."

"What?" Ben said, interrupting. "You two know one another?"

"We met the other day," James said and then turned his gaze back to Suzette, puffing up his chest. "I'm the proud new owner of the Triple-A."

"Isn't that a delightful coincidence?" Suzette purred. "Two eligible bachelors moving into our sweet little town. The two of you'll have all the women begging for your intentions?"

Both men laughed but it was not carefree. Ben's back straightened, and he pulled Suzette a bit closer to his side while James spread his legs and placed his hands on his hips. The two locked eyes for a long moment—the tension growing only to break when children screamed and giggled next to them.

Elizabeth watched all of this was fascination and dread. James could not get into a fisticuff with his new ranch hand. It would bring unwanted attention on them.

"We were just about to eat. Care to join us?" James asked, seeming to realize that now was not the time to stake his claim.

"I'd love to," Suzette said, "but my sister, Janie, and her husband, Doc Wilson, are waiting for me." She pointed to a couple sitting near the church.

"I understand. Perhaps another time?" James said.

"I'd love that," Suzette said, her eyelashes batting at him. If Elizabeth had any food in her stomach, she would've lost it with Suzette's flirtatious behavior. She'd never understand why men fell for women like her. It was nauseating.

"I'll return Suzette to her family and then look around town," Ben said. "I'd like to speak with the Marshal again."

James stiffened next to Elizabeth. She didn't look at him

because she feared Ben would notice something amiss. It was hard enough keeping her hands from shaking.

"You having trouble with the law? Something I should know about?" James asked.

"Ah, no. Nothing like that. I stumbled upon a stagecoach robbery the day before I arrived at your ranch. I was hoping the Marshal could tell me if they had caught wind of the outlaws."

Suzette gasped.

Ben patted Suzette's arm. "Ah no, I've got a pretty thick hide. It'll take more than a few outlaws to send me to my maker."

Suzette tittered a little, but seemed to grip Ben's arm even tighter against her.

"I hadn't heard," James said. "What happened? Did you see who robbed it?"

"No, I saw little, and I hate to admit this, especially in the presence of such a lovely young lady," Ben said looking at Suzette, "but one of 'em caught me unawares and bashed me on the back of the head before I could get a good look at any of 'em."

James sighed ever so softly, but then chuckled as if to cover his relief. "Sorry, I shouldn't laugh but seems out of character for you... based on what you've told me, that is?"

Ben ran a hand through his hair. "I'm embarrassed, truth be told. I'm usually more aware. The only thing I can figure is the outlaw that came upon me must've been stealthy cause I didn't sense a thing. I was trying to be quiet and my attention was solely on the robbery. I won't make that mistake again."

Elizabeth had to smother a grin to prevent herself from laughing outright. The man had been caught unawares alright—by her. It was a good thing she had to keep quiet to protect her brother because she'd love to tell Ben it was her that had hit him over the head.

"You poor thing," Suzette said, patting Ben's hand and gazing up at him. "You could've been killed."

Elizabeth wanted to gag at her simpering tone, but neither of the men seemed to notice her annoyance.

"Lucky for me, it was just a nasty lump on the back of the head. The doc said I'd be fine and I am. Good as new."

"I'm so glad you're safe," Suzette said. "Otherwise, I might not have gotten the pleasure of sitting next to you at church today."

Ben's face grew red.

"Oh, dear me, I hope I haven't embarrassed you," Suzette said.

"No, no," Ben said. "I best get you back to your sister." He raised his head. "James, I'll see you back at the ranch."

"Would you mind if I went with you to see the Marshal?" James asked. "I'd like to know if I should be concerned. I'd hate to leave Elizabeth on the ranch if outlaws are running amok."

Ben nodded in agreement.

James put his arm around Elizabeth's shoulder and squeezed. "Suzette, thank you again for helping me in the General Store."

"You never mentioned that," Elizabeth said, turning to look at him.

"Didn't I? Suzette here was kind enough to do so. She was of great help to me."

Elizabeth looked at Suzette and said, "Thank you for helping him. I'm sure he didn't know what to buy."

"Oh, he was lost, but we got that straightened out right away once he informed me the skirt wasn't for him, but for his sister."

Both James and Suzette laughed, as though they were sharing a personal joke.

"Is everything to your liking, Elizabeth?" Suzette asked, her smile anything but kind.

"Yes. Thank you again for helping him." She could be pleasant, but the tone of Suzette's voice told Elizabeth that Suzette was only being nice because her brother and Ben were standing there. She knew if it had been just her and Suzette, the friendliness would have disappeared as fast as a snake in the grass.

"It was my pleasure. Now, I must be going," Suzette said, pulling Ben with her.

"We can head to the jail once I return, James."

Elizabeth waited until they were out of earshot before she whispered, "Why are you going with him? You don't need to go there."

"Better for me to look as though I'm a concerned citizen. Besides, it might give me an idea of what the Marshal has discovered and if I need to get rid of anything that'd tie me to the robbery."

"What could he possibly have?"

"I don't know, but I want to find out before it's too late."

"Is this a good idea?"

"Probably not, but I'll find out soon enough."

"But—"

"Ben, that was quick. Ready to go?"

Ben had come back faster than Elizabeth expected. Not wanting Ben to suspect a thing, she said, "I'll find us a shady spot. The food'll be ready when you return."

"Do you want me to fetch the blanket and basket?" James asked.

"No, I can get them. Now get."

James nodded and the two men left.

Elizabeth grabbed the blanket and basket from their wagon, found an empty spot near a cluster of pine trees and hurried to claim it. She placed the basket on the ground and shook out the blanket. Her skirt bunched as she sat, causing her ankles to show. She didn't concern herself with covering them, as she thought it was ridiculous that women couldn't show their ankles. What was so important about them, anyway? They were just attached to her legs and feet. Nothing could be more boring than that.

She leaned up against a tree and watched the families gathering on their blankets, laughing, eating, and talking amongst themselves. The children were giggling, playing, and dashing around as they chased one another or threw balls, racing up to their mothers, grabbing food and giving hugs as though it were a part of their everyday lives. She supposed it was.

Not much more than thirty minutes later, James and Ben returned.

"Are you hungry, Ben?" James asked. "I'm sure we have plenty."

"Thanks, but I'm gonna give my regards to Suzette and then head on home."

James nodded. "I'll see you back at the ranch."

Elizabeth watched as Ben walked toward Suzette. He stopped, said a few words, helped Suzette to her feet, and then they ambled to his horse.

"Elizabeth... Elizabeth?"

"What... what—"

James laughed. "What has got your attention?"

"Nothing. Sorry, just watching the children play." She reached for the basket and pulled out a few ham sandwiches. "Sit, let's eat. You must be hungry." She handed one to James and took one for herself.

James sat and with one leg bent, he took a giant bite.

She looked around, making sure no one could hear her before she whispered to James, "What did you discover?"

"Good news, at least for us," he said. "No one on the stagecoach got a good look. The passengers were so scared they didn't take notice of our horses or any identifying markings. The Marshal said they lost the trail and haven't picked up any sign of 'em."

Elizabeth sighed with relief. "That is good news."

"Yes, and as long as Ben remembers nothing, we're in the clear."

"Do you feel guilty that you... well, that you made those choices?" Elizabeth asked.

"A part of me does. I never wanted to do this, but circumstances being what they were, I felt I had no choice." He took another bite of his sandwich and chewed before continuing. "I know that sounds as if I'm excusing my behavior, and I suppose it is. I can't condone what I've done and I'm not proud of it, but I don't plan on doing it again. Now that you're with me, I plan to stay honest."

"Will you ever tell me what brought you to that?"

He paused and looked over at the church, avoiding her gaze. "One day, perhaps."

She reached over and squeezed his hand. "I'm glad I found you. We can make this our home."

"Me too," he said. "Seems like lots of friendly folk." He gestured in front of them.

"I hope so. They seem nice."

"There's lots of young men here," he said, his lips turning up in a wide grin. "You could have your pick of a husband."

"I'll not marry," she muttered, her appetite disappearing in a flash.

"Why?" he asked. Questions burned in his eyes.

"I told Pa and I'll tell you. I have no intention of ever marrying."

"That seems rash. Why do you feel that way?"

Why did he keep pushing? Couldn't he just accept that she didn't want a man? "Just don't plan to, that's all."

"That's ridiculous. Every woman needs a husband. You'll need one."

"I don't. I'll live on my own."

"That's absurd. You need a man."

"No, I don't." Frowning, Elizabeth dropped her food. "I've lost my appetite. When are we leaving?"

~

The wagon clattered on the dirt road. They had abruptly left the picnic, and she was ashamed of herself. She wanted to apologize but wasn't sure how.

When they were almost at the ranch, she gripped her skirt in both hands and shifted to look at him. "I'm sorry," she said. "I owe you an explanation."

"You don't owe me a thing." James's elbows rested on his knees, the reins held loosely in his hands. He didn't look at her but kept his gaze on the road in front of them as the horses clip clacked down the path in front of them.

"Yes, I do."

He said nothing, just waited for her to continue. Birds flew above them, startled from the rumbling of the wheels and the horses snorting and hoofs hitting the dirt.

Taking a deep breath, she thought back over the last few months. "There was this boy. His name was Timmy." She smiled at the memory of his sweet face and the love he had for her, the only love she had since her ma's passing. "We planned our wedding. Everything was perfect." She swallowed before forcing the painful words past her lips. "Then he vanished along with his family. I was devastated. I waited months for him to return, but he never came back." The painful memories of those days was hard to think about but she continued. "Months later, Pa said he wanted me to marry Mr. Wells and thought we'd make a good match. He said Timmy wouldn't have made a good husband and that Mr. Wells would. The thing is, Mr. Wells was older than Pa, and he was mean. No one in town would go anywhere near him except Pa." Twisting her hands in her lap, she continued. "I convinced Pa I needed time to think, to decide, but he grew impatient. He said I had no choice."

Before long, things had spiraled out of control. She remembered their last conversation. He had raged in front of her, a bottle of whiskey in one hand. "I told him I wouldn't marry Mr. Wells, but he said I had no choice and was to do as I was told. When I refused again, he hit me."

James pulled the wagon to a stop and placed his hand on hers, but she pulled away. She didn't want his comfort for if she accepted it, she might not finish telling him about that horrible day.

"I fell to the floor and tried to get away from him, but he... he put his boot on my back and kept me from leaving. He then grabbed the back of my neck and squeezed. It hurt so bad, but I knew I couldn't let him know how much. He told me I was to marry Mr. Wells and that he had arranged everything and if I knew what was good for me, I wouldn't give him any more trouble. I was left with two choices—marry Mr. Wells or I could leave. I chose to leave."

They sat in silence that was broken only by the rustling of the reins as he urged the horses to move again and the wind through the trees. A few long moments later, he sighed. "I should've been there."

"You couldn't have stopped him."

"But still..."

"We shouldn't dwell on the past," she said. "It's over."

Nine

September 1892

On Wednesday morning Elizabeth woke unsettled. Should she attend the women's league or should she stay at the ranch? Torn on what to do, she had woken up multiple times, her fear keeping her awake. Growing up with just her pa, she never got along with other girls. She had more in common with boys. She was always running, riding horses, going hunting, and never wearing a skirt. Her pa had forbidden her to continue her schooling once she was old enough to care for the animals on their farm. It left him more time to drink himself into a stupor. As a result, she constantly felt awkward and self-conscious, never knowing what to say or do.

James thought she should go, but it made her nauseous. What if they didn't like her? What if she made a fool of herself? As much as she wanted friends, she was petrified they would consider her unworthy of their friendship.

Throwing back her thick blankets, she swung her feet over the edge and felt the cold air seep into her toes, even through her thick wool socks. Bending, she found her slippers. The days were warm, but the nights and early mornings were chilly. Shivering, she sifted through her blankets for her wrapper and pulled it on.

She pulled back the potato sacks they had used to cover the windows and peered outside. There were dark clouds in the sky even after the rain had stopped. Thunder and lightning had rolled through for hours during the night, just as her mind had rolled with her past, her future, and her present.

No time for dawdling. No chores would get done with her looking out the window.

Crossing the room to her makeshift washstand, she found an empty pitcher. The night before, she'd fallen into bed exhausted. Knowing she'd now have to fetch clean water, she picked up the bucket and peered outside. All appeared quiet. It wasn't the best idea to go outside in her nightgown and wrapper, but she'd be quick about it. She didn't want to put on the clean clothes she'd laundered the day before until she'd washed off the dirt and grime.

Picking up the hem of her nightgown and wrapper to keep them from dragging in the dirt, she scurried across the yard. She placed the bucket under the spigot and pumped the handle, filling it with the fresh, cool water.

A warm bath sounded decadent but wasn't possible yet. She'd warm water on the nice big stove James promised her when the repairs were complete. Until then, she'd have to live with frigid water.

Once the bucket was full, she held it with both hands and hurried back to the bunkhouse as fast as she could. Her wrapper had opened and flapped behind her, but she was alone, so she didn't worry. Reaching the door, she went inside and shoved it closed with her hips.

Ben followed James back to the corral. It had rained the night before, so they'd gotten a late start and worked on the main house instead of the far pasture. The sodden ground prevented them from setting the fence posts.

With the sudden turn in temperatures, James was worried Elizabeth would become uncomfortable in the bunkhouse. It wasn't the warmest building, and although it offered shelter, it too needed work to make it sustainable during the winter months.

They stopped to discuss the remaining chores for the week when Ben saw Elizabeth in her wrapper, running to the bunkhouse with a bucket of water in her hands. James didn't see her, but Ben certainly did.

Ben tried to listen to James, but he couldn't believe his eyes. Running around outside in her nightclothes and wrapper—what was she thinking? This was another example of unladylike behavior. Every day, it was something new. He couldn't list how many things she'd done that were just plain wrong. If he had been her brother... well, thank heavens he wasn't because he would've locked her in the bunkhouse for her deeds a long time ago.

As he watched her, a wind gust picked up her wrapper and blew it behind her. Her nightgown wasn't gauzy, but the light hit it just right and he saw every inch of her. He struggled to forget what she'd felt like in his arms. It wasn't proper for him to see her dressed this way, but as before, he couldn't keep his eyes off her.

"Ben, you listening?"

"What? Oh, um, sorry. What did you say?" He pulled his coat tight around his waist. If James realized what he'd been thinking, he'd be furious, and Ben would likely find himself thrown off the ranch.

Shaking his head, James continued explaining what he wanted done. Ben tried to turn his thoughts back to the tasks at hand. Unfortunately, the image of her from the lake, kept returning. Between having his arms full of her and the memory of her body, he couldn't stop imagining her in inappropriate ways. It was just fantasies, and ones he didn't truly want. He wanted a lady for a wife and Elizabeth was far from that.

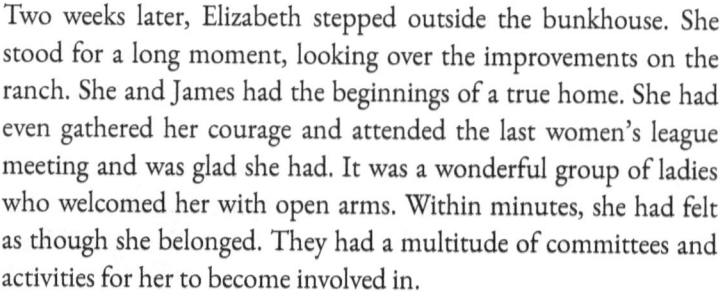

Two weeks later, Elizabeth stepped outside the bunkhouse. She stood for a long moment, looking over the improvements on the ranch. She and James had the beginnings of a true home. She had even gathered her courage and attended the last women's league meeting and was glad she had. It was a wonderful group of ladies who welcomed her with open arms. Within minutes, she had felt as though she belonged. They had a multitude of committees and activities for her to become involved in.

Milly, the pastor's wife, had introduced her to several young women, including Suzette, whom both her brother and Ben were panting after. Milly appeared to think highly of Suzette. At first Elizabeth wondered if she had misjudged her, but as soon as Milly disappeared, Elizabeth's first impression held true.

Suzette was deferential to the older women, but she and her friend Nancy were quick to gossip and hurl rude, unflattering, and condescending words about the women from the outlying ranches when they thought no one was listening. Elizabeth felt her disapproval from the moment she entered the church that first night. Lucky for her, there were plenty of other women who were nothing like Suzette. She felt certain she'd make lifelong friends.

Loud banging resonated from the roof of the house and it pulled her from her musings. She was excited to see their home come together. They had shored up the kitchen walls and roof the week before, giving her a cozy place to prepare meals. The fireplaces were next. With any luck, she'd be out of the bunkhouse and away from Ben in the next few days. He had been living in the same room as James but it was too close for comfort.

With a jauntiness to her step, she headed into the kitchen to start their morning meal of oatmeal and fried ham. Her cooking skills needed help but showed improvement. James had stopped hiding his uneaten food.. He never said an unkind word and was always encouraging, even if she herself couldn't force the food she'd prepared between her lips.

Elizabeth put the hot meal on the table and went outside to find James. She was headed to the barn when she heard a yelp and a loud thump. Startled, she turned around.

A body lay crumpled in the dirt. "Help," she screamed.

Her body quaked with fear. Was it James or Ben?

She ran to the man's side and fell next to him. With gentle hands, she turned him over. It was Ben.

Fear pierced her. Were his injuries serious? Looking him over, she ran her hands over his limbs, feeling for any breaks.

James came running around the corner. "You alright?" he asked, crouching next to her.

"I'm fine. It's Ben. He fell off the roof." Her breath hitched. "He isn't moving."

Just as she uttered those words, Ben stirred and opened his eyes. He had the most exquisite dark brown eyes with long, black lashes. He stared at her like he was looking deep into her soul. Goosebumps prickled her skin. The hair on the back of her neck raised. Then the moment faded away. He tried to sit but she put her hand on his shoulder and stopped him.

"Don't move. We don't know if you're hurt."

"I'm alright," he said. Ignoring her, he brushed her hand away, rolled, and stood.

"What if you broke a bone?" Her eyes scanned him from head to toe, trying to see if anything was wrong.

"I'm not hurt, just had the wind knocked out of me." Shaking his arms and flexing his neck, he said, "Everything's in working order."

"What happened?" James asked as he held out his hand. She didn't need the help but wouldn't embarrass her brother by making a scene, so she took his hand and stood.

"I was hammering the shingles, turned to grab more, and my foot slipped. I tried to stop but wasn't quick enough."

"Are you sure you're alright?" James asked. "I can go for the doc."

"No need for that. Let me catch my breath." He chuckled. "At this rate, I alone may keep the doc in business. I'll be fit as a fiddle in just a moment."

He walked back and forth, sinewy and graceful. Her body was very much aware of him. *What is wrong with me?*

"I've had worse happen. This is nothin'."

"Alrighty then. If you're sure, I'll let you get back to work." James headed back to the barn.

"I don't know if you should go back up there," Elizabeth said as Ben put his foot on the ladder.

He turned. "I appreciate your concern, but I'm fine. That roof won't get done with me standing here."

Grinning at her, he climbed up the ladder as though nothing had happened.

Disgusted, Elizabeth returned to the house. What a stupid, stubborn man. He'd get himself killed at this rate. She turned to look at him one last time and opened her mouth tell him to be careful but stopped herself. He wouldn't want her to mother him, and she didn't want him to know she was worried. Instead it was better to leave him be.

Ten

October 1893

One Saturday morning, Elizabeth stirred under her warm, thick blankets as she considered everything that had happened since she had found James. The weeks flew by working at the ranch and attending church and women's league meetings. She had even met a young woman named Susan, and the two of them became friends. Susan was brimming with happiness. Her smile was the first thing Elizabeth noticed when she met her. Taking her arm in hers, Susan had immediately led her to a group of women sitting in front of a quilting frame, introduced her, and then proceeded to regale her with stories of the young men in town.

She stretched one last time before she climbed out of bed. She couldn't lay there all day. There was a barn-raising at a nearby homestead followed by a town dance. She had never gone to a dance before and couldn't wait. She didn't own a fancy dress, but she convinced herself it didn't matter. She still had the green skirt and white shirtwaist James had bought when they'd arrived in town. The skirt was big around the waist, but she'd cinch it with a belt and be presentable. She felt more comfortable in her trousers, but she promised James she'd wear a skirt whenever they were off the ranch. He had given her so much, and she'd make him proud.

"Elizabeth, you ready?" James hollered from the front porch.

Elizabeth grabbed her hat and ran outside. "I'm not too late, am I?" she asked, breathless.

"Nope, we've got plenty of time." He gazed at her closely. "Are you wearing that for the dance?"

What a strange question to ask. He knew what she owned. He was the one who had purchased her skirts. "Yes, is something wrong with it?" She dropped her eyes to see whether she'd put it on backwards. Perhaps her shirt was buttoned wrong?

"No, but I thought you might prefer this," he said, handing her a package wrapped in brown paper.

Her eyes widened. "What's this?"

"Go ahead, open it." He smiled.

Elizabeth untied the string and pulled the paper back. Inside was an elegant lavender dress. Startled, Elizabeth was at a loss for words. She shook the dress from the packaging, the brown paper floating to the ground, forgotten. Holding it against her, she blinked back the tears. It was gorgeous. She never imagined owning a dress as nice as this.

"Go try it. I wasn't sure if I got the right size," he said.

With the dress in one hand, Elizabeth ran to him and threw her arms around his neck. She loved him so much and was grateful he was in her life.

"Go on now. I want to see you in it," he said, his voice thick with emotion.

She stepped back and wiped away the tears. "Thank you." She went inside to her room and changed within minutes. It was as though the dress had been made for her. It had big, puffy sleeves that tightened just under her elbows and extended all the way to her wrists. The waist was slimming and the skirt had ruffles galore. She was surely a princess, if this was what it felt like.

She returned to the porch to see James's reaction. The wide grin said it all. "You look lovely," he said. "You'll be the prettiest girl at the dance."

She blushed and caressed the fullness of the skirt. It amazed her how grand it was. "Let me change. I don't want to soil it before the dance." She ran back inside and twirled one last time. The skirt flared around her, and she knew she'd be a princess tonight, even if she were only the princess of the Triple A Ranch.

The women at the barn raising called the men to eat. They'd worked hard on the barn most of the morning and early afternoon, and were famished. The walls and rafters were in place. Only the roof remained, and once that was complete, the dance could begin. All the young women and men were brimming with anticipation, while the older, more seasoned adults grinned at their enthusiasm.

Elizabeth was having a fabulous time. She stood behind the table in the wide meadow in front of the ranch house and served potato salad. Plenty of young men nodded their thanks and smiled. If she'd been interested, she might've found herself a beau. Her heart was still broken from Timmy's disappearance, and she wasn't willing to put herself through that pain again. She had to stop dwelling on the past, though. Her future was bright, and she wanted to dance the night away.

She gave generous helpings to everyone, including her own brother, who had just stopped in front of her, holding out his metal plate brimming with tender roast beef, crisp corn on the cob, and baked beans. A thick piece of buttered bread was held in his other hand.

"How's the building going?" Elizabeth asked.

"Quite well, I think. The barn's going up mighty fast. We should be done in plenty of time."

"That's good to hear," she said, putting a large serving of potato salad on his plate.

"Thank you." He pulled the dish back and took a piece of potato and stuffed it in his mouth. "Are you having a good time?"

"I am."

"Have any young men caught your eye?" he asked, his eyes twinkling with mirth.

She wanted to strangle him. He was always teasing her, but she wouldn't let it bother her today. "No."

"And why not?"

"I don't need a husband when I've got you," she said, smiling.

"You say that now, but you might feel different later."

She pushed a thick lock of hair behind her ear. "I don't think so. I have no intention of ever marrying anyone."

"Well, that's a sad sight," a young man said. He stood behind James. "Why would a charming young lady like yourself not want to marry?"

"Excuse me?" James asked, his eyebrow raised at the intrusion.

Taking off his hat, the young man said, "I apologize, sir. I just couldn't help but overhear your conversation and seems unfortunate this delightful young lady wouldn't want a home of her own. Didn't mean to overstep."

James smiled and his shoulders relaxed. "I agree with you," he said. "I don't believe we've met."

"Name's Michael Seymour, and that's my brother, Luke." He pointed to the man behind him with bright green eyes. He was just as handsome as the man in front of her.

"Any relation to Ben Seymour?" James asked.

"Yes. He's our older brother. We were hoping we'd find him here."

Elizabeth looked at the two men and could now see the resemblance. Michael had the same dark brown eyes as Ben, but a much more pleasing grin. Their builds were similar, although Ben was inches taller than the both of them.

"This just might be your lucky day. Your brother works on my ranch."

"That's great news. We've been looking for him for weeks. Is he here?" Michael asked as he turned his head, his eyes searching the crowd of men clamoring for food.

"Not yet. He's planning on coming by later. He's repairing a broken fence in my far pasture."

"We knew he was working at a ranch near here but didn't know which one," Michael said.

Luke interrupted. "We better get moving. We're holding up the line."

"Do you mind if we join you?" Michael asked.

"I'd like that," James said.

Holding their plates, the men continued through the line, and as Michael held his plate for Elizabeth to fill it with potato salad, he said, "I meant it. You're quite fetching, and any man'd be lucky to win your hand."

Flustered, Elizabeth almost dropped the spoon.

Michael caught it before it fell and removed it from her fingertips. "Let me help you with that." He piled potato salad onto his plate and handed it back. "Better be careful with that. Wouldn't want you to lose your spoon."

She blushed.

"Hope you'll save me a dance later, Miss?" he asked, his head cocked to one side.

She stuttered, "Elizabeth."

"Elizabeth. What a beautiful name. Hope to see you soon."

"Michael, get moving," Luke said. He shook his head and nudged Michael forward. "You're holding up the line."

"Probably right, but I can't help myself when all these pretty young women are stealing my attention."

She laughed. He certainly differed from his brother, Ben.

After the men made it through the line, the women followed. Holding two plates piled high with steaming hot food, Elizabeth found her friend Susan and handed her one of them. "I hope you don't mind. I filled one for you before everything was gone."

"Thank you. I got distracted and hadn't made it back." Her blue eyes shined with excitement, her smile just as pleasing as always.

"Do you want to sit with your family?" Elizabeth asked as they stepped piles of lumber and the families sitting on the ground to eat.

"With those handsome men sitting with your brother, we need to sit there," Susan said, nodding in James's direction.

Grinning, Elizabeth said, "Isn't there someone who might interest you more?"

"There is, but it might be time for him to realize he isn't the only one vying for my attention," Susan said. "Besides, you need a beau." She held up her hand in defense. "I know, I know, but I heard what he said to you," she said, her head nodding toward Michael.

"I'm sure he was just being nice," Elizabeth said. "But they are handsome, aren't they?"

Giggling, they sauntered toward James. As they approached, James stood and spread a second blanket on the ground for them. Holding out a hand, he took Susan's plate and helped her sit.

Jumping up, Michael hurried to her. "Elizabeth, may I?" he asked, holding out his hand.

She nodded and with his help, settled on the ground before balancing the food in her lap. "Would you care for a drink?"

"That'd be nice, thank you," she replied.

Michael asked Susan the same. "Be right back." There was a happy jaunt in his step as he grabbed two tin metal cups filled to the brim with lemonade. He handed a cup to each of them.

"Can I join you, Elizabeth? With your brother's permission, of course?"

"It's alright with me if it's alright with Elizabeth," James said.

He reclined against a pine tree, his knee bent, his hat pushed high on his forehead.

"It'd be my pleasure, Mr. Seymour," Elizabeth said.

"Please call me, Michael. Mr. Seymour sounds too stiff for a gent like me," he said, the twinkle in his eyes a far improvement from the censure she received from his brother, Ben.

"It sure is a gorgeous day, isn't it?" he said, sitting next to her.

"It certainly is, Mr... Michael," she replied. "Remind me again how long you've been searching for your brother?"

"A few weeks. He'd sent a telegram but didn't say which ranch. It's nice to know we've found him."

"I'm sure he'll be happy to see you."

"Not too sure about that," Michael said, his grin losing a touch of its sparkle.

"May I ask why?" she asked as she put a spoonful of spicy beans into her mouth. The zesty flavor came in stark contrast to the smooth texture of the beans.

He hesitated a moment before replying, "Our brother, Stanley, made him leave. We aren't too sure if Ben blames us."

"I hope he doesn't," Elizabeth said. "Did you know he'd be here?"

"We stopped at the General Store yesterday. They said we'd likely find him here or someone might know of him. We thought we'd give it a shot. I'm glad we did. But enough about that, I'd sooner hear about you."

Heat flooded her neck and up to her cheeks. It had been some time since a man other than James had asked her about herself.

"I... well... um."

"Beggin' your pardon. Did I make you uncomfortable? I didn't mean to."

His smile fell, and he looked so serious. She worried she had offended him. "No." She took a quick sip of the lemonade. She could handle this. He was just a man, and she'd been around them her whole life. "I'm sorry, I..."

"No need to apologize." He patted her hand and then changed the subject. "Has Spring Creek always been your home?"

Elizabeth answered his questions and before long, it was as though they were old friends. Michael made her laugh at his silly comments and jokes. Before she realized it, the meal ended. As the men began leaving their blankets to go back to the barn, Michael stood. He took her empty plate and placed it atop his. "Let me carry these back for you," he said. Holding out his hand, he helped her stand.

"Thank you, but I'll take them," she said, reaching for the plates, but he playfully held them out of reach.

"On one condition?"

"And what might that be?" she asked, her hands on her hips as she tried to give him a stern look, but failed miserably when she saw the twinkle in his eyes.

"You let me have a dance tonight?"

She blushed once again, heat filling her cheeks. She hadn't been this discomfited around a man in some time. "I don't know..." As much as she enjoyed his company, she wasn't looking for more than friendship.

"Please, I'd like to be your friend."

She paused for a long moment and looked at him to see how sincere he was being. "Alright," she said. "As long as we're just friends."

"Swell," Michael replied. "I'm looking forward to it. Guess I better get back to work."

Michael turned, still holding the dirty dishes.

"Um, Michael?"

"Yes," he said, looking over his shoulder.

"You might want to hand me those dishes. I don't think you can use a hammer if you're holding them."

Chuckling, he looked at his hands.

"I guess you're right. My mind's been overrun with thoughts

of a charming young lady." He winked at her before handing her the plates. Her skin warmed all over as she watched him trot back to the worksite.

Hours later, Elizabeth and many of the younger women strolled to the rancher's house to change into their party dresses. Gossiping and giggling, they were eager and brimming with enthusiasm. After dressing in their finest, they gathered on the large front porch, watching as the older women went ahead of them to the barn.

Then the young men walked by, laughing and ribbing each other as they passed the porch. Throwing knowing glances at the young ladies, they jostled each other in anticipation. They were just as excited as the young women.

Soon Elizabeth heard the strings of a violin.

"What are we waiting for? Let's go." Susan pulled Elizabeth's hand, and they followed the others.

Entering the barn, the freshly cut wood sparkled by the light of many lanterns hanging from the beams. Chairs of various sizes and shapes lined the walls. The tables were laden with cakes, cookies, pies, and sweet breads the women had brought with them. Another table held a large punchbowl, and the older women were filling cups for anyone who became thirsty. The air was festive and full of anticipation. Young women gathered on one wall while young men hovered on the other.

Musicians began tuning violins, banjos, and an accordion, but no one ventured onto the dance floor. Soon, the older married couples took pity on the young folks and took to the floor. As they danced, young men gathered their courage and started asking young ladies to join them. Within minutes, Michael made his way to Elizabeth.

"Elizabeth, would you do me the honor?"

Elizabeth nodded and placed her hand in his. Taking her in his arms, Michael swung her around in time to the music. Her eyes wide, she laughed as they swung to the lively tunes.

Eleven

B en arrived late but in time for the dancing and socializing. He wasn't overly fond of dancing, but he knew the women-folk enjoyed it.

Standing at the barn door, Ben looked for Suzette. It had been a few weeks since he last saw her, and he was eager to continue their budding relationship. He especially didn't want James to garner her attentions any more than he had.

Suzette would make the perfect wife, and he was determined to make her his. She was the epitome of everything he had ever wanted—beautiful, charming, a lady through and through. His ma would've been proud to call Suzette her daughter-in-law. He needed to make his intentions known, but there never seemed to be a good moment. Perhaps tonight he'd let her know he wanted to make it more official. She had many suitors, and he didn't want someone else to sweep her off her feet.

He saw James standing against the far wall, so he walked toward him. On the way, he saw Suzette in the arms of another. Her pale pink dress sparkled, enhancing the gleam in her eyes. A surge of jealousy roared through him. He didn't want her to be with anyone else besides him on the dance floor.

"Ben, glad you could make it," James said. They shook hands. "I was wondering what was keeping you."

"It took longer than I'd expected. Quite the crowd, isn't it?" He removed his hat and smoothed back his hair before placing it on the table next to them.

"Yes. I think most folks from town and the surrounding ranches are here tonight."

Ben couldn't stop staring at Suzette. He wanted, no, he needed to make sure he staked his claim, and fast.

"Ben... Ben, you with us?"

Pulling his eyes from the dance floor and Suzette, Ben said, "Sorry, I missed that."

Chuckling, James said, "Your attention is on the dance floor and all the lovely young ladies."

Smiling, Ben replied, "What can I say? There are many beauties here tonight, but only one has caught my attention."

"Must be something in the air. I'm feeling the same way." James stared hard at Ben and then glanced toward the dance floor, where he too directed his eyes on Suzette. Ben pulled at the string tie around his neck. It suddenly felt constrictive. The last thing he wanted to do was to compete with James for Suzette's attention, but he'd stop at nothing to have the woman of his dreams.

"Got a surprise for you," James said.

"What's that?" he said, his eyes still on the dance floor.

"Two men showed up looking for you."

"Oh?" Ben swallowed and his back stiffened. He had left Olson's employ months before and not on pleasant terms. He hadn't shared that information with the marshal as he wanted to move on with his life. He had done nothing against the law but had made enemies over the years. Was there someone from his past looking to exact revenge?

"Don't need to look like you swallowed a cup or curdled milk. I believe you'll be pleasantly surprised."

The music stopped and couples drifted off the dance floor.

James's eyes focused on something beyond his shoulder. Ben followed James's gaze and saw Elizabeth. She looked fetching in a lavender dress. Her brown hair flowed behind her and shimmered under the lights. It was striking and made him want for things he couldn't have. He'd only seen her with her hair down once, and that was at the lake, wet, dripping, and cascading along her bare back. She still didn't compare to Suzette, but he was amazed to see her dressed as a proper young lady for once.

Elizabeth giggled and turned to the gentleman behind her. The man raised his head. Wait, was that his brother Michael? It couldn't be. He squinted, trying to bring him into focus. He must be more tired than he realized. It *was* Michael. But why was Elizabeth with him? Michael grinned and whispered something in Elizabeth's ear. She glanced up and grabbed Michael's hand. Ben and James headed toward the couple, closing the distance between them.

"Michael?" Ben said. "What are you doing here? How do you know Elizabeth?" He reached toward his brother, and the two of them hugged.

Stepping back, Michael said, "Looking for you, and I just met this charming young lady today."

Red bloomed on her cheeks. She turned her gaze downward, but Ben hardly noticed. His focus was on his brother.

"How'd you find me?" Ben asked.

"Dumb luck. Yesterday, we stopped at the General Store. They told us about the barn raising and dance, so we thought we'd stop in and help and see if anyone knew of you. We got lucky running into Elizabeth and James."

"I'm glad you found me. Are you here by yourself?" Ben looked around for more of his siblings.

"No, Luke's with me."

"Where is he?" He was thrilled his brothers had found him. He missed his family.

"Somewhere sulking in a corner, knowing him," Michael said, waving his arms.

The owner of the ranch stood on a wooden chair and waived his arms. The conversations silenced.

"All, thank you for comin' today and givin' up your time to help with the raisin' of our new barn. You've been kind and taken a worry from me and my sons. We couldn't have made it through the upcoming winter without your helpin' hands. My family's blessed to have such good friends and neighbors. Because of your generosity, there's plenty of refreshments. For those of you looking for a stronger drink, join us out back." Men in the crowd laughed. "Thank you. We'll return the favor anytime."

The room burst into applause. Then Luke appeared and pounded Michael on the back. "I see you had your first dance."

"I did, but look at what I've found," he said, pointing to Ben.

Ben and Luke shook hands, their grins as wide as could be. "Luke, it's good to see you."

The musicians warmed up their instruments for the next set. James turned to Elizabeth, holding out his arm. "Dance with your brother?"

"Yes, I'd love that." She placed her hand on James's arm and they disappeared into the crowd.

As soon as James and Elizabeth were out of earshot, Ben asked, "What happened? Why'd you two leave Thundering Mountain Ranch?" He stared hard at his brothers. As glad as he was to see them, he was surprised they had come to Spring Creek.

"Stanley wanted us gone," Luke said. "He made it clear we had to go, just like you."

"That makes little sense. I understand why he wanted me to leave, but you two weren't a threat."

"I became a threat," Luke said, "especially to Connie. Something isn't right about how Pa died, and I was asking lots of questions I don't think she wanted me to ask."

"I thought Pa died of the influenza."

"Ma did, but Pa was recovering."

"Didn't he take a turn for the worse? Why are you so suspicious?"

"Not sure, but something ain't right," Luke said, his voice becoming deep, hoarse.

"Are you looking for something that isn't there?" Ben asked, concerned that Luke was making something out of nothing.

"No. Stanley claims he just died of a broken heart once he knew Ma was gone. But I don't believe it. You know Pa loved the ranch above many things. I suspect you know that better than anyone else."

"Unfortunately, I do." Ben's history with his father was complicated. He loved his pa, but they had butted heads one too many times over the years. The last time had sent him away for years. He had never gotten the chance to apologize and now it was too late. In his heart he knew his pa had likely forgiven him but his head told him otherwise especially once he was told of the details of his pa's will. Being cut out completely was a hard thing to accept, but he had no choice when Stanley presented it and told him to go.

"Sorry, didn't mean to bring up poor memories. This ain't the time or the place," Luke said as he ran a hand across the back of his neck.

"It's alright, Luke. We can talk more later. Where are you two staying?"

"The closest open field, I reckon. We've been sleeping on the road."

"Let me talk to James. I'm sure he wouldn't mind you bunkin' down on his spread."

Dancers filled the floor. "Boys, let's catch up after the dance. There's something I need to do." Ben needed to ask Suzette quick if he wanted to dance with her.

"Go ahead," Michael said. "We can talk later. Besides, these pretty ladies are just waiting for me to ask them to dance." He cracked his knuckles and sauntered into the crowd of eligible young ladies.

"He's quite the character, isn't he?" Luke said, shaking his head.

"Yep, although his infatuation with the ladies is different." Glancing around the room, Ben found Suzette next to her sister Janie and Doc Wilson. "We'll talk later, right?" Ben asked before he walked in Suzette's direction.

"Yeah, go ahead." Luke's words faded as Ben looked at the woman he was going to marry.

Right before he reached her side, another gent asked her to dance. Smiling at the man, she walked to the dance floor, not sparing Ben a glance.

Another surge of jealousy filled Ben. He'd never have time to stake his claim at this rate. He headed to her sister, Janie and the doc. Maybe if he got their blessing, he'd stand a better chance. If nothing else, he'd be right there waiting when she finished so he could ask her next.

"Hello, Doc Wilson, ma'am," he said, nodding cordially to them. "Nice evening for a dance."

"Good evening, Ben," Doc Wilson said. "Why aren't you out there dancing with everyone else?"

"Just got here, but everyone appears to be having a good time."

"Yes, everyone is enjoying themselves. Are you looking for Suzette?"

Ben smiled. "Is it that obvious?"

"Only because you haven't taken your eyes off her since you came over here," Doc Wilson said, his eyes crinkling with suppressed laughter.

"May I ask her to dance?"

"Isn't up to me, but you have my blessing all the same."

"Thanks, Doc."

A few minutes later, the song ended, and Suzette joined them.

"Mr. Seymour, I was afraid you weren't coming tonight," she said, her voice curt. She avoided looking at him and instead gazed around the room as though she didn't have time for him.

"I couldn't miss seeing you. Would you grant me the next dance?"

"I'm parched," she said, fanning her face. "I'm going to sit this next one out. Perhaps later?"

Startled at her less than enthusiastic response, Ben was taken aback. It wasn't the same reaction he had received from her before. Had he done something wrong? He hadn't been in town of late, but she knew he was busy. Maybe she was only thirsty, and he'd misunderstood.

"May I get you something to drink?"

"Yes, thank you."

She turned, leaving him without saying another word. He left to get her punch and brought it to her side.

"Suzette, your drink."

Taking the cup from his hand, Suzette's eyes skimmed past him and, with a distracted tone in her voice, said, "Thank you, Mr. Seymour."

She then turned her back to him and ignored him.

Surprised at her dismissive behavior, Ben didn't know what to think. Not wanting to appear overeager, he headed back to Luke. He'd try again later.

Throughout the evening, Elizabeth danced and danced. She had never learned the proper steps, but the men were so enthusiastic it didn't matter. She didn't know what she'd been missing. Michael asked her a second time and even Luke swung her around the floor. Luke was serious compared to his brothers, but more of a gentleman than Ben. She wondered why their brother couldn't be as charming.

Elizabeth took a break and walked to the sweets to get a bite to nibble on. Seeing Susan, Elizabeth dropped a few treats on a plate and scurried through the groups of people. Soon James, Luke, Michael, and even Ben had joined them. Before long, they were laughing, talking, and sharing stories.

Luke told them about the time Michael had decided he needed to fly like a bird from the barn loft. "He'd gathered a bunch of chicken and goose feathers and tied them together with a heavy string he found in the barn. He then waited 'til a day where the wind was blowing something fierce—"

"I thought for sure the wind would help," Michael said laughing.

Luke shoved Michael's arm playfully. "He hung them from his arms and stood at the end of the barn loft, his arms held wide. Before Pa could stop him, he took a running start and leapt. What he didn't anticipate was the fact that those feathers wouldn't help. Lucky for him, Pa had just brought in a load of hay and it sat on the wagon just outside the barn doors. Michael fell straight into the bales of hay." Luke chuckled. "Hay flew everywhere, flying out like the bird he wanted to be."

They all laughed hard at the vision Luke described. Michael and Luke told a few stories before Luke asked Susan to dance and led her to the floor. Then, Michael left to find another dance partner, and James and Ben talked ranch business. Elizabeth sat watching all the many couples twirling and stomping their feet when Milly and the pastor joined them.

"Elizabeth, what are you doing sitting here?" she asked, her white, grayish curls bouncing on her head as always.

"I'm taking a break. It's fun to watch everyone."

"Have you danced tonight?" It was as though she had made it her mission to make sure every lady had a dance partner.

"Yes, I have. A few times."

"There's no reason to be sitting out again. There are plenty of young men to dance with. Let's see who we can find."

"No, no. It's alright. I can sit out the next one."

"Nonsense." Her voice told Elizabeth she shouldn't argue. "What about Ben?"

"Oh, no. He's busy. I don't want to bother him."

"I'm sure he won't mind." Milly patted Elizabeth's arm before touching Ben's shoulder in a subtle interruption. "Ben, why don't you take Elizabeth onto the dance floor for the next set?"

Ben stopped mid-sentence. He looked sick to his stomach but said, "Yes, ma'am. I'd be happy to."

Elizabeth wanted to sink to the floor with embarrassment. It was obvious he was *not* happy to do so. She didn't want to force anyone to dance with her.

"You're busy discussing business with my brother. I don't want to be an imposition," she said.

"Don't fret. I haven't danced with anyone, so it might as well be you."

Disgusted by his indifferent reaction, Elizabeth wanted to refuse, but she didn't want to make a scene. It'd only reinforce his negative feelings toward her. She swallowed her ire and held back a rude retort.

The music stopped and the couples on the floor returned to their seats or to seek new partners.

Ben stood and held out his hand. "Elizabeth?"

Elizabeth took his hand, hers clammy in his. He led her to the floor as the music began for a waltz. She groaned. Waltzes were intimate, and she'd never danced one. She prayed she could follow without making a fool of herself.

Taking her into his arms, he pulled her in close.

"Let's get this over with, shall we?" he said. His eyes focused beyond her.

Shocked, she held back her tears. Why did she always feel the need to cry around him? He was a brute, an insensitive cad. She couldn't wait to be done. If she wasn't worried about drawing attention to herself, she would've slapped his arrogant face and left him standing alone on the dance floor.

Ben only had thoughts of Suzette as he led Elizabeth in the waltz. Why couldn't Suzette be in his arms? Instead, he was stuck with a woman he didn't want. No matter how hard he tried, he couldn't even pretend that the woman in his arms was anyone other than Elizabeth. She was taller by a foot than the dainty Suzette, and she kept stepping on his toes. It was a good thing he had sturdy boots, or he'd be wincing in pain every time she stomped in the wrong direction.

He glanced at her. She was aloof, her head turned away, unhappiness written across her face. Why wasn't she having a good time? He was dancing with her, wasn't he?

Then he thought back to how he acted when Milly asked him to take Elizabeth on the floor. She hadn't asked him to dance. In fact, she had tried to give him an excuse not to. She wasn't enjoying herself, and it was because of him.

A pang pierced his gut. It wasn't her fault he wanted to dance with Suzette. He shouldn't treat any woman this poorly, regardless of his personal feelings. His ma would've been horrified and likely yanked him by the ear to remind him she had raised him as a gentleman.

Clearing his throat, he said, "Elizabeth, pardon my behavior. I was rude."

Startled, Elizabeth looked at him, her long lashes framing her dark brown eyes.

She hesitated a moment before replying. "You were busy and Milly forced your hand. She put you in an uncomfortable position. No harm done."

"Thank you for being kind, but I was raised better than that. I shouldn't have treated you so terribly. My ma would've slapped me silly if she'd heard what I said."

She frowned, her eyes dark with confusion and anger. She didn't trust him, and he couldn't blame her. Their relationship had been tumultuous.

After a moment, her expression softened and she smiled tentatively. Her eyes sparkled, and her cheeks brightened with color.

"Shall we start over and enjoy the rest of the dance?" he asked.

She nodded and with a jaunt in his step, he twirled her around the floor. Dancing with her might not be as dreadful as he thought. He could have fun, even if it wasn't with the woman of his dreams.

Once Ben apologized, Elizabeth relaxed and enjoyed the rest of the waltz as they laughed and conversed. It was a side of Ben she hadn't seen. He was captivating when he tried. By the time the dance ended, she wished it hadn't.

"Ben," Suzette called, her voice as sweet as a baby bird chirping in the wind.

Ben dropped Elizabeth's hand and turned, leaving her standing alone as though she were an awkward little girl who'd been dumped in the dirt, alone and forgotten. Dismayed, Elizabeth stood alone, not sure what to do.

Watching Ben head to Suzette's side, she heard Suzette ask, "Where have you been? I've been looking for you for ages."

"My apologies. I didn't mean to ignore you," Ben said.

"Who were you dancing with?" her voice was full of scorn and derision.

"No one special. Forgive me?" he said.

"You're forgiven as long as you ask me to dance next." She batted her eyelashes at him, her head cocked to the side as though

Ben was the only man in her life. Heavy curls cascaded down her back. She was wearing an exquisite pink dress, all frothy and elegant. It put Elizabeth's new dress to shame.

Elizabeth's heart constricted. No one special. That was what he thought of her. *No one special.* She shouldn't have been surprised, and it shouldn't have bothered her, but it did. She observed Suzette's coy behavior. He couldn't get to her side fast enough.

"I'd be delighted to dance with you. Would you do me the honor?" Ben asked, holding out his arm.

"Yes," Suzette said, placing her hand on his. She glanced at Elizabeth, her eyes full of hatred and disgust. Suzette despised her, and Elizabeth didn't know what she had done to deserve it. They'd had little interaction in the time Elizabeth had been in Spring Creek, but Suzette was angry with her as though Elizabeth had stolen her man. Elizabeth didn't want Ben and never had. Suzette could have him.

New music filled the air and Ben pulled Suzette to the floor. Elizabeth hadn't expected Ben to fawn over her, but that he could dismiss her so easily was painful. She stumbled back, her palm hiding her mouth to hide the cry of dismay before she regained her composure. She wouldn't let Ben see her cry.

"Elizabeth, what are you doing standing here alone?" James asked. She looked over her shoulder and saw her brother. "Did you just finish dancing?"

She blinked a few times to hide the tears and shoved back her displeasure at the abrupt way Ben had dismissed her, she forced a smile to her lips and said, "I did."

"Dance with me again?" he asked. "Unless, of course some other gent has caught your eye."

"The only gent I'd love to dance with is you." This time there was no hiding her feelings. She enjoyed dancing with her brother. She took his hand. Unfortunately, James led her right next to Ben and Suzette.

"Alright folks, this'll be the last dance," the owner of the barn said, "but I thought we'd try something new. Throughout the dance, I'll call out *change partners*. You'll change with the couple that's closest to you. We'll continue to do this, giving you a chance to meet your neighbors and making it right enjoyable." Everyone cheered and clapped with enthusiasm. Giggles and jitters rippled through the crowd, but everyone was up for the challenge.

The music started. Couples two-stepped to the music and twirled their partners around the room.

"Change partners," the man called.

Looking to their right, James let go of Elizabeth and exchanged her with Suzette. James's grin widened when he realized he was getting a chance with Suzette, but Ben's was filled with anything but pleasure. It matched her own. She didn't want to be with him any more than he wanted to be with her. Luckily, they didn't take but a few steps before they changed partners again. On and on it went, switching from partner to partner.

Laughter rang out as dancers stepped on each other's toes and fingers lingered. Confusion reigned when everyone changed partners, but overall, they enjoyed the dance. In the last exchange, Elizabeth ended up in Ben's arms once again, which was just her bad luck.

Instead of smiling at him, she held herself stiff in his arms, trying to make sure she didn't touch him anymore than she needed to and didn't utter a word. He tried to engage her in conversation, but she had nothing to say to him. What was there to say? He wanted nothing to do with her, so there was no reason for idle chit-chat.

The dance ended, and they twirled to a stop. Everyone clapped. When the noise dimmed, Ben asked, "Did I offend you?"

Avoiding his eyes, she focused her attention over his shoulder and said, "No, what a strange question to ask."

"You sound angry."

"What could I possibly be angry about?"

"I don't know. Why don't you tell me?"

"It's not worth the effort. Why don't you go find the woman you want and don't bother me again?"

With that, she left him standing alone. Let him see what it was like to be discarded. Maybe then he'd think twice before doing it to someone else.

Twelve

Late November 1892

Fall turned to winter and life fell into a routine. Church on Sundays and chores, repairs, and improvements on the ranch continued during the week. Ben convinced James to let his brothers stay and help on the ranch. James agreed and with the extra help, the repairs went quick. With all the Seymour brothers on the ranch, she limited her trouser wearing to when she was alone or riding her horse. As much as it pained her to put the skirt on daily, it seemed the prudent thing to do. She was getting used to them, although she definitely preferred wearing her trousers when she was alone.

Elizabeth wasn't aware of James's long-term plans, but he was determined to get the ranch in full working order as fast as possible. She wondered if he had an ulterior motive that had something to do with Suzette. Both he and Ben made frequent trips to visit her but kept it civil, though they both stated their intentions. Elizabeth was worried James might try to marry Suzette, and she couldn't imagine being her sister-in-law.

The men continued to be oblivious to Suzette's real personal-

ity, as she appeared to have a sweet disposition with them, but not
with anyone else. Suzette would cast scathing looks in Elizabeth's
direction anytime the men's attention was diverted and would
whisper hateful words in Elizabeth's ears every chance she had. It
was as though she believed Elizabeth was competing for Ben's
affections. Elizabeth had no designs on Ben. She would've
preferred it if he'd left town, but for whatever reason, James and
Ben worked well together despite their mutual attraction to
Suzette.

Before they knew it, November flew by like a faint whisper,
and Christmas was right around the corner. The women of Spring
Creek were organizing Christmas festivities, and Elizabeth was
volunteering for a few committees.

Michael showed more than a passing interest in Elizabeth and
took her on many wagon rides and picnics. She enjoyed the attention but knew her interest in Michael was brotherly. He was jovial
and made her laugh, but he was nothing more than a friend. She
was happy with her new life of spinsterhood and saw no reason to
search for a husband.

Early one Wednesday afternoon, James asked Ben to escort
Elizabeth into town for her women's league meeting. Ben agreed.
He hadn't seen Suzette in some time and it gave him an excuse to
call on her. He thought he'd stop and pick up a gift for her, a small
token of his appreciation.

As Ben readied the horses and wagon, he looked at the sky
and hoped the weather wouldn't turn. The sky was dark and
ominous, but he thought they'd make it back before it turned
unpleasant.

By the time they reached town, the winds had increased. Trees
bent under the strength of them. The horses pulled hard, turning
their heads side to side. They had picked up their pace despite

Ben's hold on the reins. Once they reached the church, Ben pulled the horses to a stop.

"I'm unsure about the weather. What time do you think you'll be done?" he asked.

Elizabeth lifted her skirt, revealing her shapely calves as she climbed out of the wagon. "Around four," she said. She grabbed her basket from the back.

"I'll be back to pick you up, then. We don't want to dally. I don't like the looks of the sky." He tugged on the collar of his coat to protect his neck.

She glared at him. "I won't dally, but it may go late. We have much to get done."

"Just be ready to leave at four. We don't want to get caught in a snowstorm."

"I'll be out when we're done. You worry too much." She sauntered to the church, her slim hips swinging in cadence with her steps.

He shook his head, disgusted at her cavalierness, yet also entranced by her. He couldn't pinpoint why he was so infatuated. She wasn't for him. She was always contrary, and over the last few months, it'd only gotten worse. Just the other day, he caught her trying to move a bull from the far corral away from the heifers. She had been wearing her skirts more frequently, but that day she was wearing her hip-slimming trousers. Once again, his eyes were drawn to her. She could have been attacked if the bull had a mind to it. They were unpredictable on the best of days and if they had caught the scent of any heifer, then there would've been pandemonium. He'd yelled at her to get out of the corral, but she had bucked his suggestion and continued as though he was a fly she had to swat away.

Looking back at her, he watched her walk inside the church and then shivered as another fierce breeze blew through the trees around him. The weather was turning and her disregard for his opinion and knowledge was irritating on the best of days. She could find herself in a heap of trouble if she wasn't careful. Just one more reason he needed to remember who he really wanted in his life, and it wasn't Elizabeth. He released the brake, shook the reins, and headed for the General Store.

Ben left the store after spending a great deal of time looking at the various options while considering what Suzette might enjoy. He purchased a decorated comb wrapped in pretty blue paper. It wasn't much, but Mr. Crockitt, the storekeeper, said all the young ladies enjoyed the little trinkets.

He rapped his knuckles on Doc Wilson's door.

"Ben, what a surprise. Everything alright at the ranch?"

"Yes. James asked me to bring Elizabeth into town, so I thought I'd stop in and see Suzette. Is she available?"

"She isn't here. She went to dinner with Mr. Breckenridge."

"Who's Mr. Breckenridge?" Ben asked.

The doc leaned against the door frame, crossing his arms. "He's a dandy from back East. He knows my father-in-law, or at least claims to. He arrived in town a few weeks past. They've been seeing one another quite frequently."

"Does Suzette..." He stopped. He didn't have the right to ask the doc about Suzette. She wasn't his to question, no matter how much he wished to claim her as his.

The doc smiled; his eyes filled with sympathy. "Did the two of you have plans?"

"No, I just... I thought. Well, not sure what I thought," he said. He hoped it wasn't serious between Suzette and Mr. Breckenridge. He believed he only had James as competition, but it appeared he had more than one man to fight for her affections. He'd just have to make his intentions clearer.

"Come in and have a drink?" Doc Wilson asked, holding the door open wide.

"No, thank you. Can you let her know I stopped by?"

"Certainly. I'd be happy to."

He turned to walk away but remembered the gift in his hands. He turned back to the doc and held out the blue package. "Can you see that she gets this?"

The doc took the gift, looked at Ben and nodded. "I sure will. Have a good night, Ben."

Leaving the doc's, he headed to a saloon. It'd be another hour before he needed to return to the church, so he might as well drown his sorrows in a glass of whiskey. He had to beat this Mr. Breckenridge in the courtship game. He just needed a chance to prove that to her.

Thirteen

Noting the late hour, Ben left the saloon to pick up Elizabeth. He'd likely had one too many drinks, but he needed to calm his nerves after discovering Suzette had a new suitor.

The fierce wind raised the hair on the back of his neck. The dark clouds had moved in sooner than he'd expected and were hovering above them. If they didn't hurry, it could make for a long ride home.

The wind ripped his jacket open, and he shivered. Yanking it closed, he fastened the buttons and pulled up the collar to protect his neck from the biting cold. The weather had worsened, and snow was in the air. He could smell it.

Arriving at the church, it appeared he'd come just in time. Women came outside and ran to their wagons and horses, holding their bonnets from flying from their heads. Snowflakes drifted to the ground. If they didn't head out soon, it might be too late to make it back to the ranch in one piece.

Sitting in the wagon, he waited and waited. Ten minutes passed, then twenty, and she still hadn't appeared. In the time he sat waiting, an inch of snow had fallen. Uneasiness, then anger filled him. She should've been waiting for him. No one had stepped outside in the last thirty minutes. What was she doing?

Frustrated, he climbed from the wagon seat and tied off the horses when the door opened and she appeared. Eager to leave as soon as possible, he stalked toward her, grabbed her basket, and threw it into the back. "Climb in. We need to hurry." His voice was curt, tinged with barely concealed anger.

Sighing, she said, "No reason to be rude. I'm sorry it took so long, but they needed my help."

She climbed into the wagon as though she had no care in the world, which infuriated him further.

He sat in the seat next to her and shook the reins. He could sense the horses' uneasiness. They didn't want to be out here anymore than he did.

Twenty minutes later, Ben knew they were in serious trouble. He could no longer see the road in front of them. The only thing guiding him were fenceposts from the ranches, and before long, they would disappear under the thick snowdrifts and a darkening sky.

The snow was falling in thick sheets, covering everything in front of them. It had turned into a blizzard. They would not make it back to the ranch. He'd have to find them shelter soon, but he didn't know where.

He glanced at Elizabeth, trembling under her thin cloak. Her teeth were chattering together like a woodpecker against a tree. He knew she was cold, but he was too angry and frustrated to care. If she had left the church when they'd discussed, they wouldn't be in this mess.

Moments later, while considering huddling under the wagon for shelter, he saw what he thought was a structure. It appeared to be standing and had a roof. No lights blazed, but a dilapidated structure was better protection than being outside in the snow and wind.

He shook the reins and turned the horses toward what he

hoped was a road, but it didn't matter—the horses were having a hard time pulling the wagon through the snowdrifts even on what he thought was a road. Their steps were slow and sluggish, but they were giving it all they had. Stopping in front of the cabin, he grimaced. It was in deplorable shape, but they were out of options. They needed to escape the weather, and fast. There also appeared to be a small barn off to the rear, which would house the horses and keep them relatively safe from the piercing wind and growing snowdrifts.

He helped Elizabeth from the wagon. She shook from the biting temperatures, and her unease matched his own. He banged on the door but no one answered.

They were desperate, so begging the owner's forgiveness, he shoved open the door. A musty, empty smell greeted them. This place hadn't seen human contact for some time, which worried him further. He hadn't made a mistake like this since he was young man. He must have taken a wrong turn because there wasn't an empty homestead between the town and the ranch.

"I need to get the horses to the barn. Will you be alright?"

"Yes, go. I'll see what I can find to start a fire."

Ben left her inside and returned to the horses. He unhitched the wagon as quick as he could with numb fingers. Releasing the horses from their hooks, he grabbed their bridles and led them to the barn. They sensed safety because they picked up their pace and didn't fight him.

It wasn't pretty, but the barn was still standing. Settling them each into a stall, he brushed them with an old brush he'd found to get the wet snow off their backs and legs. A small well stood outside the barn and he rushed toward it, dumped the bucket inside, and prayed it still contained water. He sighed with relief when he heard a splash. They'd have water for the horses and for them to drink.

He filled the troughs for the horses and found dry hay for them. He stepped outside and looked around. At least one inch of snow had fallen in the few minutes he'd been with the horses. It just added to the foot of snow that had already accumulated before they had reached the ramshackle spread and there were no signs of it stopping.

The severe wind blew ugly around him and it took all his strength to close the barn door. Straining, he secured it and looked toward the cabin was. Snow was coming down so thick he couldn't see more than a foot in front of him. He couldn't make out the cabin, but he needed to trust his judgment. If he was wrong, he might freeze to death. Holding onto the bucket of water, he trudged through the snow toward what he hoped was the cabin.

He returned to the porch with pure determination. Throwing a small prayer up to God for helping him, he fumbled for the door latch and pushed it open. Snow billowed in behind him and he struggled to close it. Elizabeth rushed to his side and helped him. He sank to the floor, exhausted, the bucket of water sloshing.

"Are you hurt? Is there anything I can do?" Her words came at him in a rush.

His hands hurt from the freezing air and his hair dripped wet with snow, but he was thankful they were safe from harm, at least for the moment.

"Ben," Elizabeth said again. She touched his shoulder. "Say something, please."

Lifting his head, Ben peered at her. "I'm alright. Just need to catch my breath and warm up a bit."

"Oh," she said, her voice hesitant, as though she was afraid he'd lash out. "There's... there's a fireplace, but I can't see well enough to tell if there are any matches or wood to start a fire." The sun had disappeared behind dark clouds and the cabin was empty—morose as though it too wanted to hunker down.

He pulled off a sodden glove, reached into his vest pocket, and pulled out a set of matches. His fingers shook, and it took him a moment before he got one to strike. It gave him enough light to see an old lantern hanging on a hook.

He scrambled to his feet and grabbed it, shaking to see if it held any kerosene. They were in luck; it was full. Striking another match, he lit the wick and held it up so he could see around the small cabin. He saw nothing that would keep them warm. The remains of a rope-strung bed with a straw mattress were all that remained. There wasn't even a chair to sit on.

No wood, no food, and the temperatures were dropping fast. He needed to start a fire or Elizabeth would freeze and her brother would kill him. He shook his head, her brother was going to kill him just because he hadn't gotten her home safely.

One problem at a time. There was nothing he could do about the state of the cabin, but he could try to warm them. First up was wood. Looking out the small window, he saw a pile on the porch. He thanked the heavens above. Whatever had guided them to this cabin had been looking out for them, for if they hadn't found this place, they would've been out on the road with no shelter. When he pulled open the door, the wind yanked it from his hands, slamming it back against the outside wall. Snow flurries roared inside like a small tornado.

"Elizabeth," he yelled over the howling wind. "I need your help. I'm going to grab the wood I saw outside. Can you take what I hand you?"

She nodded and hurried to his side. Within seconds, snow covered them both as she waited for the handfuls of wood. He picked up one last armful and shoved the door closed.

Her eyes were enormous with fright, and she clasped her hands in front of her. "Are we going to have enough?"

"I hope so," he said.

He didn't want to frighten her, but they were in a rough spot. He didn't know how long they'd be there, and if they didn't have enough wood, well, he'd have to think on that later.

"We'll make it through the night. I promise," he said.

He knelt in front of the well-used fireplace and started a small fire. It took a moment, but with a bit of encouragement and a lot of luck, the fire blazed to life. It took the chill off his bones.

"I'm not sure if the fire alone is going to keep us warm," he said.

He walked around the room, looking for anything to keep them from freezing to death but finding little.

"Let's put the bed near the fire. You can at least sleep off the floor and maybe that'll help," he said, his tone softening at her obvious fright.

He knew she needed comfort, but he wasn't the person to give it to her. His mission was to get her home to her brother unscathed. He shoved the bed as close to the fireplace as he dared. It scraped across the floor, yet didn't collapse. It was ricketier than it appeared at first glance.

Once the bed was moved, the dim light from the fire illuminated a thick lump against the wall. He hoped it wasn't a dead animal. He walked over and kicked at it. It didn't move. He smiled and sighed with relief. It was a few old woolen blankets. He picked them up and dust and dirt fell from them. Shaking them to remove what dirt he could, he carried the blankets to the bed.

She sat on the edge, her cloaked wrapped around her, shivering. Her hair hung in clumps and the misery in her eyes made him uncomfortable. He was doing the best he could, and he hoped it would it be enough?

Elizabeth shuddered with disgust as Ben draped one of the smelly woolen blankets across her shoulders. He huddled under the other.

"I know it stinks, but it's all we've got," he said, his tone suggesting he was in a foul mood.

She didn't have to say a word for him to read her thoughts. She knew she should be thankful that he found them, but they reeked of dead skunks and rotten onions. Seeing the look in Ben's eyes, she didn't complain. He was trying his best to make the awful conditions bearable.

Her feet were at least thawing. The rest of her should warm, she hoped. It'd be a long, miserable night if she couldn't get warm.

As her body tingled from the fire's heat, she became restless. She needed to use the privy but didn't want to go outside. Who knew how close it was, if there even was one? Not sure how to broach the subject, she clasped her hands to her belly and started wringing her fingers.

She fidgeted for a moment before Ben snapped at her. "Is something wrong?"

"Um, well, um."

"Yeah, spit it out," he said.

Swallowing hard, her throat croaked when she spoke. "I need to use the privy."

"Oh." His face grew red.

"I don't want to go out there, but I can't make it through the night." It was embarrassing enough just asking, so she avoided looking at him.

"Let me see if I can find an alternate solution." He searched the room before pointing to a second old bucket, one that was covered in a layer of dust and cobwebs. "That's the best we've got."

Mortified, she cringed. "You can't be serious." Her horror was likely written all over her face.

"No skin off my back what you do, but I'd use it unless you want your..." he paused, "Well, I'd just use it is all."

Resigned, she stalked over to it. "You can't watch me. Are you going outside while I—"

"Nope. It's cold and windy. I'll turn away until you're done."

"I can't do"--she waved her arms in frustration--"this with you here. It isn't proper."

"We are way past the point of propriety. Just use the bucket and be done with it." His tone was curt.

Disheartened and out of options, she went to pick it up and

screeched when large, black, hairy spiders tumbled out. She scooted back, trying to hide her horror but not succeeding.

"What's wrong?" Ben yelled. "Are you hurt?"

She pointed to the spiders as shivers ran up and down her skin at the thought that she could have sat on those spiders.

Ben laughed. "It's just a few spiders."

"A few spiders! You... You—" She stomped her foot in a fit of frustration.

He took a look at her and swallowed his laughter, but she could tell it took quite the effort. He then pounded his boots on the ground killing the creepy, crawly spiders before bending down and picking up the tainted bucket. Pulling out a handkerchief from his pocket, he removed the cobwebs and checked it near the lantern before handing it to her.

She shuddered but took it from his hands and went to the far corner of the room. Ben turned as promised.

Elizabeth put the bucket on the floor and pulled up her skirts. Awkwardly squatting above the bucket, she relieved herself.

"What do you want me to do with it?" She picked it up and held it in front of her, annoyed she even had to ask.

"Give it here," he said. He took it from her and threw the contents out into the snow. The wind blew through the cold room, causing the flames to flicker, but miraculously they hung on until he closed the door. "I'll leave it here in case you need to use it later." He placed the dirty bucket next to the door.

She hoped it wouldn't come to that, but depending on how long they were stuck in this dreadful cabin, it might come in handy again. She nodded and then glanced at the only piece of furniture in the room. She dreaded the thought of sleeping there. The rough cotton had yellow and brown stains scattered all over it. It was probably full of all kinds of nasty diseases.

Her eyes were heavy with fatigue, her limbs sluggish. It'd been a long day, but her mind continued to race. Trying to hide her yawn from him, she sat on the bed, pulled her scarf from around her neck, and wrapped it atop her head and across her ears. She then yanked her cloak tight around her, and dragged the stinky blanket on top. She was sure she looked a fright, but she might stay somewhat warm if she prayed hard enough.

Ben watched Elizabeth unsuccessfully try to hide her emotions. Her hands trembled, and she wrung them in fear.

The wind whistled through the open cracks and unmaintained crevices, but the fire held and kept the room a touch warmer than when they found it. He'd have to keep an eye on the flames all night to make sure it didn't burn down low. It was their only source of heat.

"You should get some sleep," he said.

"I'm fine," she muttered, her head buried beneath the scarf she had wrapped around her ears.

"I doubt that, but it's a sight better than being outside in the snow." He threw another log on the flames.

"Could we talk instead?"

Talk. Now that wasn't something he'd expect her to ask of him, but why not, especially if it kept her from thinking about how frigid it was. "What would you like to talk about?"

"I don't know. Why don't you tell me about yourself?"

He chuckled. The animosity between them sizzled, and this was what she wanted to talk about. "I'm not that interesting."

"Why did you come to Spring Creek?"

Boy, she was persistent. "I hadn't planned on settling here, actually." He leaned against the edge of the mantle, the heat from the fire warming his legs.

"Where were you headed?" Her big brown eyes searched his as though what he had to say was of utmost importance.

"I was making my way to Butte when I... well, when I decided to stay."

"Why did you?"

"Stay?"

She nodded.

He paused a long moment before answering. "A lot of reasons, I suppose, one of which was the stagecoach robbery. I still wish I could've been of more help to the Marshal."

"I'm sure you did all you could." She shifted on the bed, pulling the blanket more firmly across her shoulders.

He shrugged. He didn't agree with her on that, but he'd tried. With any luck, more information would come to light, and he'd be able to bring the men to justice.

"Where are you from?" she asked.

The fire snapped and popped as the logs shifted. Ben knelt and pushed another log onto the fire. Staring into the embers, he took a minute to respond.

Without turning, he said, "From up North. My pa owned a ranch outside of Helena."

"Why aren't you working there?"

"I..."

He stood, his knees cracking from the bent position. Holding his hands near the flames, he felt a chill run through him. He didn't want to remember, but it came rushing back: the pain, the betrayal, the loss.

"Did I say something wrong?"

"No," he said, before turning to look at her. For whatever reason, he felt as though he could trust her and before he stopped himself, he began telling her about those few days about five months earlier, right before he had arrived in Spring Creek.

Fourteen

Five Months Earlier

Urging his horse to the gates of Thundering Mountain Ranch, Ben pulled Midnight to a stop and gazed at the wide pine arches. The sun had risen high in the sky and it reminded him of the warm spring day when they'd installed them.

His pa had called the ranch Thundering Mountain due in part to the large mountain peaks that sat behind the end of the property. Ma liked the name, and that was the end of that.

Pa had taken him and Stanley into the forest that flocked the west side of the ranch where they chopped two of the biggest pine trees they could find and even a few smaller ones. He and Stanley had stripped off the branches and dragged them to where their pa stood. They'd placed the stripped logs on either side of the path, creating an archway as their pa looked on. They'd both felt like men that day.

Pa had wanted it to be a grand entrance for the grand woman he had married years before. The ranch was for her, he'd said, after she had lost what she had worked so hard to build. He had never told them what their ma had lost, but he was determined to make her proud that day.

Over the years, they planted lots of pine trees along the drive, and it looked like the tradition had continued while Ben was gone. Smaller trees were sprinkled in with the ones he himself had planted. The trees had grown taller and broader, and they beckoned him home.

Urging Midnight into a gentle canter, he approached the ranch house. An eerie quiet and unease filled the air. Black wreaths on the front doors of the house caused his heart to stop for just a moment, giving it a painful tug. The wide front doors opened and somber faces spilled from inside. No happiness, no excitement, only despair and heartache. What happened? Who was gone?

He dismounted and went up the wide stairs to a plank-covered porch. A strapping young man stopped him as he approached the front door. He looked strangely familiar. It was as though he were looking at a younger version of himself.

"Ben? Is that you?" The young man embraced him and held his shoulders in welcome. "It is you. You're home. I can't believe it. Stanley's gonna be so surprised."

It was his younger brother, Michael. Gone was the lanky youth he remembered, replaced now by a man, broad-shouldered and tall.

"Who's gone?" Ben asked, dreading the answer.

"You don't know?"

"I haven't heard from anyone in months. I've been on the trail for weeks. Who is it?"

"It's Ma and Pa," Michael whispered, his eyes red-rimmed from crying.

Gazing at him in shock, Ben couldn't believe it. "No, it isn't possible." He pushed past Michael and continued inside the house he had once called home.

Nearing the front parlor, he saw his brother Stanley leaning stiffly against the windows. The sun glared through the room, casting a bright glow on a striking young lady by his side. Her silvery blonde hair was piled high on her head in an elaborate updo that highlighted her heart-shaped face. She was petite and barely reached the middle of Stanley's chest. Her crystal blue eyes gazed at him with sympathy. If he'd been in a better frame of mind, he might've stopped and introduced himself. As it was, his head and heart were fighting reality.

"Stanley, what's going on?"

Startled, Stanley looked at Ben. His eyes swam with tears at the sight of him. Ben had forgotten how much Stanley looked like their pa. He had light brown hair, a square jaw, and a nose that was slightly crooked because of a tussle the two of them had when they were younger.

"You're alive. You were rumored to be dead," Stanley said once he gained control of his emotions. The woman next to him wrapped her arm around his waist and leaned into him.

"I've had some close calls but nothing serious. Tell me it isn't true."

Stanley grimaced. "I'm sorry. They're gone. Within days of each other. Influenza took 'em both." He choked back a sob.

"No!" Ben shouted. The ground rippled out from beneath him. He fell into a chair. Tears burned. He bent his head forward, the thrill of coming home replaced with a despair so deep and personal. It was a nightmare he'd never wake up from. He'd never have the chance to talk to them again.

The next morning, Ben headed through the hall, looking for his brothers and sisters. Loud angry voices boomed from his pa's study. Concerned, he headed there to find out what was causing the ruckus. Standing before the closed door, he hesitated a moment. He'd been gone so long. Did he have the right to interrupt? He wouldn't have when his pa was alive, but he was now the head of the family. He stepped inside the fracas.

A firestorm brewed in front of him. Stanley and Luke were nose to nose, faces red and hands clenched into fists at their sides. Luke looked more like their ma with his ash brown hair and wide green eyes, but he still had the same broad build all the men in the family had.

"Stanley, Luke. What's going on?"

They stepped back from one another but continued to glare, neither giving an inch.

Luke spoke first. "This isn't over, Stanley. Not even close to being over." He pushed past Ben, the door crashing into the wood frame.

Running his hands through his hair, Stanley tried to smile, but it was more of a scowl. "He's furious. Pa appeared to be improving, and then he was gone. It surprised us all. We expected him to survive."

Stanley strode to the sofa where the woman from the night before sat. Eyes soulful, he looked at Ben as if expecting him to understand.

"Ma went quick, didn't suffer, but Pa he... he held on. He wasn't willing to give up, but it was just too much."

Putting his head in his hands, Stanley sat there for a moment in silence.

The woman put her arm around his shoulders and squeezed. "It's alright, Stanley. Luke'll come around." With a grim smile, she looked at Ben. "I'm sorry you had to see that. I'm Connie, Stanley's wife." She stood, held out her hands, and walked toward him. "I'm sorry we had to meet this way."

Taking her hands in his, Ben replied, "Me, too. It's nice to meet you."

She smiled before letting go and returning to Stanley, settling close to his side.

"I wish I'd gotten here sooner," Ben said.

"Your pa hoped you'd come. He talked about you all the time," she said.

Ben thought he saw something in her eyes. Something he couldn't quite name, but she blinked, and the moment passed. Ben shook it off. Must be grief.

"Why's Luke so angry?" Ben asked.

Stanley shook his head. "He's been sullen from the moment Pa passed," he said. "Luke blames me, thinks I should've known something was wrong and sent for the doc sooner."

Connie put her hand on Stanley's. "It isn't your fault. We all thought Pa was improving."

"Doesn't change the fact that Luke blames me," Stanley uttered.

"He's angry. Give him time," Ben replied.

"I hope you're right. I do."

"Where are Anne and Katie?" Ben asked.

"I believe they're still upstairs. The funeral was rough on them," Connie responded. She settled back into the sofa, her yellow dress rustling.

"Thank you. I'll leave you two alone."

Connie's voice followed him out the door. "Stanley, what are we going to do?"

"Not now, Connie. We'll deal with it later."

Fifteen

Elizabeth had fallen asleep. He wasn't sure why he confided in her, but a weight had lifted from his shoulders. She had listened and was sympathetic to his pain. He had seen another side of her he hadn't expected. She hadn't interrupted and let him tell her of his past.

He hadn't told her everything, for he didn't want to admit that his own brother hadn't wanted him back home. Stanley had kicked him off the ranch two days after he had arrived and told him to never come back. He was no longer welcome. Stanley told him that when he had left five years past, their pa had been furious and threatened to write him out of the will. That didn't sound like his pa, but Ben hadn't been home since that horrible night. All he had was Stanley's word and the document Stanley waived in his face. The will was clear. Ben was left nothing.

He shook off the pain from that day and shoved his hands into his pockets. The cabin continued to be frigid, and he was powerless to stop it. As the wind blew outside, it seeped through the cracks of the walls, and the flames flickered as they fought to stay alive.

Elizabeth whimpered, her body twitching from the chilly air seeping under the thin woolen blankets. He had put the second one on her over an hour ago, but it wasn't doing much to help. He stifled a yawn, blinking his eyes a few times to clear his head. The day had been long, and he wasn't any warmer than Elizabeth.

Putting another couple of logs onto the fire, he considered his options. He could continue to sit, watch the fire, and let both of them freeze or he could climb in the bed next to her and share their body heat. It wasn't proper by any stretch of the imagination, and if anyone were to discover, it could ruin their future.

Another wintry breeze seeped through the cracks and chilled him to his core. His decision was made. He climbed into the bed next to her. Trying to unwrap her from the blankets, she woke with a start.

"What are you doing?" she cried. She grabbed one blanket as if it were a shield of armor. "Get out of this bed at once."

"You're freezing and the cabin isn't staying warm. The only way you're going to stay warm is if we share our body heat."

"No. You shouldn't be here. Get out." Her hands trembled.

"I know this isn't proper, and I certainly don't want to compromise you, but we're both going to freeze. This is the only way I know of to make sure we live to see the morning."

"I don't believe you," she snapped.

"Do you have any other ideas?" His patience with her was wearing thin.

"The fire..."

"The fire is not keeping the wind out. You're shivering."

"No, I'm not," she said, her chattering teeth betraying her words.

He sighed and held out his hands in surrender. "Please, your brother will kill me if anything were to happen to you. Your virtue will stay intact. I promise."

He could see the struggle within her, but she seemed to

consider his words. After a long moment, she nodded and settled into the bed. He threw the blanket over them and pulled her tight against him. She kept trying to adjust as if keeping an inch of space between them would keep it proper. Eventually, his body heat seeped through to her chilled limbs. She snuggled against him and fell asleep.

Ben warmed as well, but he wasn't sure if it was because of their shared body heat or the fact that Elizabeth's curves were tight against him. The last thing he expected was the rush of desire exploding inside, but at the same time he should have considered what would happen, as he hadn't stopped thinking of her in months. It was as if she were made for him.

He couldn't help but remember the kiss they shared, but to have further encounters would not happen. He might've shared the pain he had endured, but that didn't mean he had any genuine feelings for Elizabeth.

Suzette was to be his wife, not this unruly woman. It was just lust. That was all. He hadn't been with a woman in some time. The last time had been a month before he had headed home and to the pain of his parent's passing. He rarely stopped at brothels, but the men he once worked with were invited to a high-end brothel in Helena one evening after a long and intense job. They had wanted to let off steam after a job well done, and a brothel had been their first choice.

He had indulged his physical urges, but there had been something missing, something emotionally unsatisfying about the encounter that made him swear he'd never visit a brothel again. No matter how fancy it appeared, it was still full of women who appeared to want to please them. In rare, unguarded moments, he could see the pain and desolation in their eyes. He didn't want to be party to their pain and was ashamed he had taken part, even if he had paid them for their services.

Having Elizabeth near him was difficult, but his pa taught him to respect women, all women. A hint of rose petals filled his nose. It reminded him of his ma. She had always smelled of roses. Whether she had worn rose-scented perfume or filled their home full of freshly cut flowers, it was a scent he'd never forget.

Elizabeth shifted and snuggled even closer to him. Her hands tucked between them and her head nestled into the crook of his shoulder. He breathed in deeply as her hot breath tickled the skin below his chin. She was hard to resist, but he was a gentleman and he'd never take advantage, especially of someone in his care.

As she fell into a deep sleep, he couldn't help but look at her long lashes as they lay against her smooth rosy cheeks. Her hair was a tangled mess but was still thick and luxurious. She had removed her boots and had slipped her small feet next to his legs. Why he ached for the woman in his arms and not for Suzette, he didn't know. He grew hotter by the minute, and it wasn't because of the fire blazing in the fireplace. It was the fire burning within him, but he would contain it and keep it where it belonged.

Late in the evening, he climbed out of the bed and away from the woman lying in it. He put another log on and stoked the flames. His feelings were in a turmoil. He couldn't sleep as he thought through the last few months and what had happened this evening. Elizabeth had shown compassion while listening to him tell her of his parents' passing. He had been surprised at the kindness in her eyes, in the words she whispered while he spoke of the worst days of his life. Seeing her now made him want things he shouldn't.

She could barely cook, wore trousers, used words that only men should utter, rode her horse like a man, and even handled a rifle and revolver like an expert. All of this was quite unladylike. Not to mention she was James's sister. He wouldn't live to see another day if James had any inkling of what was going on in his head.

The wind howled outside, and he shivered. He was unsure if he should return to the bed. His body burned with a heat that intensified with every subtle movement she made. She needed his warmth as much as he needed hers. Forcing his passion back, he threw another log on the fire.

He pulled her into his arms and lifted the blankets back over them. Elizabeth turned and murmured something unintelligible. He smoothed back her hair and pulled her close. He would keep her warm, even if it killed him.

It took every bit of strength he possessed not to brush her pink cheeks with his lips. He wanted to touch her so he could memorize every inch of her. It might be the only chance he'd ever have to be close to this woman who had somehow crawled under his skin.

His eyes closed and he willed himself to sleep, but his mind raced. There was no way he was sleeping with her in his arms. She fit perfectly next to him and it was a reminder of things he swore he'd never do.

As the flames climbed high in the fireplace, sleep came. It was fitful, full of dreams of a woman with long, brown, silky hair, lips as ripe as berries, who was meant to be his.

At some point, hours later, Ben shifted and found her warm body still in his arms. He buried his face in Elizabeth's neck and kissed her delicate skin. His hands skimmed over her sides and pulled her closer to him.

Murmuring something unintelligible, she wrapped her arms around his neck. He placed sweet kisses along her neck until he drew her plump lips to his. She moaned, and he deepened the kiss. Any reasonable thought he might have had disappeared with the passionate woman in his arms.

His breath grew heavy as his heart knocked hard in his chest when her eyes flew open and she squealed. She yanked her arms from around his neck and pushed at his shoulders. He didn't want to stop. She was delicious, like a ripe peach begging to be sucked and devoured.

"Stop. What are you doing?" She scrambled to get away from him.

As he looked at the terror in his eyes, his desire was squashed like a spider under his boot, dead and forgotten. He backed away. "Damnit! I don't know what came over me."

Elizabeth swung her legs over the edge of the bed and bolted away. Wrapping her arms around herself, she cowered in fear and disgust on the other side of the room.

He had forgotten where he was.

He had gone too far.

Elizabeth was horrified. She'd been as shameless as a woman with loose morals. How could she have responded as though she'd enjoyed his touch? In her sleepy state, his lips had ignited a primal awareness and her insides had quivered with excitement. Now fully awake, she knew better. She wasn't his wife. She hadn't acted like a lady. No one could ever know.

What was Ben thinking? What would her brother think? Would James throw her out? Demand they marry? She didn't want to marry this man. He didn't care for her, didn't like her, and certainly didn't love her. Her head spun with all of the implications of what had just happened and tears welled in her eyes.

She couldn't let Ben see her cry. She scurried to the window and looked out through the dirty panes to a winter wonderland. There was sparkling white snow as far as she could see. Needing a moment alone, she opened the door and stepped outside to compose herself.

Standing on the shaky porch, she took a few deep breaths, letting the clean, icy air fill her. A few drops of cold, wet snow fell on her head from the low overhang, melting and trickling down her scalp. She ran her fingers through the tangled strands, braided it, and tied it off with a string. Feeling a mite better and in better control of her emotions, she considered her behavior and what she would say to Ben.

Reacting to him, she had given him another reason to disrespect her. She shouldn't care, but she did. Her pa always said it was up to the woman to control a man's needs. She should have stopped Ben as soon as he ran his hands across her sides and nuzzled her neck, but she had been half asleep, believing it was a dream—a delectable, intensely satisfying dream. His face had been blurred, and the sensations he stoked had awakened a desire she had long forgotten. It wasn't until his fingers brushed across her skin that she had realized it wasn't a dream. It was entirely her fault, and she'd have to live with the consequences unless she could convince Ben to keep quiet and forget it happened.

She buttoned her blouse and took a deep breath, then went back inside to face him. She couldn't avoid him forever. He knelt before the fireplace, adding another log to the flames. As the door closed, he stood and faced her.

"Elizabeth—"

"Say nothing."

"I'm so sorry. I made a mistake, I shouldn't have—"

"Please, stop. There's nothing to apologize for. We need to forget this ever happened."

"I can't do that. I've compromised you." He stalked back and forth in front of her, his movements agitated, angry.

"No one needs to know," she argued.

"I went too far. It's unforgivable. I'll talk to your brother, explain, and ask him for your hand in marriage."

What a lackluster and unemotional proposal. If a man asked her to marry him, she wanted to be filled with joy. Instead, she was filled with dread. She had already run from a potentially disastrous and dangerous marriage. She wasn't about to marry a man who disliked her. Her emotions were scattered from wanting to cry, to wanting to belt him over the head with a frying pan.

"I will not marry you. You love someone else," she said with clenched teeth.

"Love has nothing to do with it. We have no choice."

"It has everything to do with it. I won't tell anyone. You won't either. As far as anyone is concerned, we rode out the storm in this cabin. Nothing happened!"

"I've ruined you."

"Stop it," she yelled, holding out her hand as he took a step toward her. "Don't come near me. I don't want to marry you, and I won't. If you tell James, I'll deny it. I had no intention of getting married before, and I have no intention of getting married now."

"Please be sensible. This is the only way." He held out his hands.

"I am being sensible. There's no reason both of us need to be unhappy because of a lapse in judgment. I will not marry you out of a sense of obligation."

"This is about honor and dignity. I can't, in good conscience, walk away from this." He ran a hand through his hair. "You're beautiful and while I can't condone some of your behavior, we'd likely make a good match."

"A good match." Her eyes widened. He thought she was beautiful, but then she realized what else he said and her hands tightened into fists. "You can't condone my behavior. You insufferable brute. I won't let you do this to me," she cried. "I'm not gonna let another man dictate my future."

His eyes softened as he looked at her. He lifted his hand as though he wanted to touch her, but then let it drop woodenly to his side.

"If you have any shred of decency left, you'll forget everything that happened." She couldn't look at him anymore, so she turned away, wrapping her cloak tight around her. She had to convince him to keep quiet. She so desperately wanted to hide from him and the despair that filled her.

A long silence filled the room. He sighed. "If this is the way you want it, I'll never mention it again."

She nodded, relief coursing through her. "Can you take me home?"

"As soon as the snow melts."

"Why do we need to wait?"

"There's no way the horses are going to be able to pull the wagon through this mess. The sun is bright, and the temperatures seem to be rising. Hopefully, it'll melt enough for us to leave in a couple of hours. If not, we'll just have to wait until it's safe to leave."

He turned away from her, staring into the flames. What more could she say? He was right as much as she hated to admit it.

Two days later, they were finally able to leave the dilapidated cabin. They were both starving but at least had had water to drink. They had barely spoken to one another, both lost in their own thoughts, but they slept wrapped together on the bed every night in an effort to stay warm. She hadn't wanted to, but he'd convinced her it was the wise thing to do. However, he kept his hands and lips to himself no matter how much he wanted to explore her.

Ben pulled on the reins and set the brake with his foot. It took longer than he expected for the horses to get through the thick snowbanks, but he got her home. When they pulled up to the ranch, the front door crashed open and James rushed out.

"Where have you been? I've been worried sick," he said as he yanked Elizabeth from her seat. "Are you alright?" His hands rested on her shoulders.

She mumbled, "I'm fine. Hungry, but fine. We got caught in the blizzard because of me. Ben found shelter for us." She gave him a hug. "It was bitterly cold, but we managed with a fire. As soon as it melted enough to leave, we made our way home."

Ben jumped to the ground and looked at James warily, preparing for a scolding. Might as well get it over with, he thought. "I'm sorry. I should've been prepared and gotten her home before the snow started."

"It wasn't his fault," Elizabeth said. "I got caught up in my meeting and wasn't watching the weather."

"Wasn't her fault, was all mine. I could've gone inside the church and gotten her when I realized we might have a problem," Ben said.

"No," Elizabeth said. "It was my fault."

"No," Ben said, "It was mine."

"The two of you sound like an old married couple. If I didn't know better, I'd think you'd plan to be stranded and all alone in that shelter you'd found." James laughed.

Ben's back straightened and his head swiveled to look at Elizabeth. Her face was stricken with horror, but James didn't appear to notice a thing. Instead, James wrapped an arm around her shoulders and pulled her close to his side.

"I'm grateful you kept her safe." He looked down at Elizabeth. "Let's get you inside where it's warm. You're shivering. I've got a stew simmering on the stove. Won't be the best you've ever tasted but at least it'll fill your belly."

James led her up the stairs. After he ushered her inside, James turned to look at him. "Ben, you coming?"

"No, go ahead. I'll care for the horses. They need to be fed." Ben unhitched the horses from the wagon and led them into the barn, his steps slow and steady. His heart was heavy, and he wondered if he was making a monumental mistake.

He couldn't turn back time, but he could have done the right thing and he hadn't. He'd abided by Elizabeth's wishes, wishes that gave him the future he always wanted, but a decision that might ruin hers if anyone were to discover what had happened. A part of him couldn't help but wonder though what a life with Elizabeth would have been like. Her stubbornness, determination, and lack of decorum might be interesting to watch from afar but it wouldn't be appropriate for him. She wasn't anything like what he had ever imagined, but she was a strong woman who would likely make the right man very happy.

What he had a hard time with was that no matter her denials, he had compromised her. Luckily, it hadn't gone too far, but it had gone far enough. He was ashamed of himself, but what more could he do? She didn't want to marry him, and he didn't want to marry her, but as he had watched her go inside the house with James, his heart felt like a piece of him was suddenly missing.

Sixteen

February 1893

Winter continued with a fierce vengeance in Spring Creek. Christmas had come and gone. The snow fell heavy, blustering around them, coming without end. The temperatures dropped drastically, which made it difficult to go outside, even for water from the well.

Elizabeth had been stuck in the ranch house for weeks with no one to talk to except James. She hardly saw the Seymour brothers. They stayed in the bunkhouse in the evenings and worked in the barn or in the fields during the day. It was as though they were avoiding her, and although she didn't want to see Ben, she missed the banter she had with Michael.

Elizabeth was worried someone would discover what had occurred between her and Ben. She was ashamed of her actions, but there were moments, especially in her dreams, where she remembered the comfort and strength of his arms and the sweetness of his kisses. Her feelings were developing in a direction she was unprepared for.

She had decided on her future and it hadn't included a man. She had to remind herself she didn't admire Ben. He was rude and inconsiderate, but in those rare unguarded moments she could remember his fingers on her hot skin, and heaven help her, she wanted to experience it again.

On occasion she would catch a glimpse of him, but that was it. A part of her longed for his love. She thought she had put those feelings behind her when she'd lost Timmy, but Ben had awakened a hope deep inside her. He had only offered to marry her because he felt guilty, but there had been a brief moment when she wondered what it would have been like to be his wife. Then she was reminded that Ben had powerful feelings for Suzette and none for her.

Shaking her maudlin thoughts away, she looked out the window and stared at the never-ending sight of snow. It would be at least two more months before they saw anything green. It would be a blessing if the snow stopped for a few days. Blue sky and a hot sun would be a welcome sight from the thick, dark clouds that hovered over them almost daily.

Days later, as though she had willed it to happen, the snow stopped and melted enough that James considered taking her to town, but it'd have to wait. Doing the wash came before any jaunts away from the ranch.

Soon she was wiping sweat off her brow from the heat and the exertion of lifting the heavy sheets and blankets in and out of the water. She had rolled up her sleeves to keep them from getting wet, but it was useless. The front of her was soaked clean through.

Between the heat from the fire and the warm sun, it didn't take long for Elizabeth to wish she had worn her trousers, but she was trying to wear the skirts whenever possible as much as she disliked them. Humming under her breath, she washed the dirty linens and hung everything to dry.

As she moved along the clothesline, Ben stepped out of the

barn. He wasn't wearing his hat, and the wind ruffled his dark brown hair. He hadn't shaved and had a thick beard covering his cheeks. Although she preferred him clean shaven, she had to admit the beard gave him a rakish look that was exceedingly attractive.

Catching herself gawking at him, she was glad he didn't see her. He didn't need to see the look of longing, which was likely written all over her face. He wasn't for her.

Ben spied Elizabeth. She was washing their clothes and sheets, a chore his own mother hadn't enjoyed, and doing it in the best of weather was difficult but had to be done. Her hair was askew and her cheeks tinged with pink.

He'd been overrun with thoughts of her during the most inopportune moments. She was a hard worker, never complaining and there were times like today where she was even more alluring. He couldn't help but remember their interlude at the cabin, the way her lips felt under his, the softness of her body, and how she had fit perfectly against him.

He should dream of Suzette and of winning her heart. Instead, his thoughts were centered on Elizabeth. Between his desire and the guilt he felt over his actions, he struggled with the decision he had made. No one had discovered what they had done. She had kept quiet and hadn't uttered a word of his deplorable behavior, and he had also not mentioned his part. He knew he should ask for Elizabeth's hand in marriage. That was the honorable thing to do, what he had been raised to do, but he had agreed to Elizabeth's demands because he hadn't wanted to give up his own dreams of marrying Suzette.

Suzette was reluctant to commit, but he believed she needed time to get to know him. The weather was not cooperating, however, and he hadn't been in town since before Christmas. The last time he had seen her, she had given him the cold shoulder. His courtship of Suzette would fizzle like a flame snuffed between two fingers if he couldn't spend time with her. He was convinced that once Suzette accepted his marriage proposal, then his errant thoughts of the enticing Elizabeth—her long, glossy hair tangled in his fingers and her soft curves nestled against his chest—would stop. He was sure of it.

Seventeen

April 1893

Before long, spring was upon them, and the snow melted allowing the first green buds of spring to push through the hard ground. Leaves were beginning to appear and even a few early wildflowers sprouting their yellow, pink, and pale red petals. There were days when Elizabeth woke to the mist of her breath but removed her jacket by mid-afternoon.

During church service on the last Sunday in April, Pastor Williams announced their annual trek through mountain trails for the young adults and encouraged them to attend. They would leave Friday morning, walk a few trails that afternoon, stay overnight in tents, and then return on Saturday. The pastor and his wife, Milly, along with two other married couples, would act as chaperones. There was loud clapping and even a few yippees in the back of the congregation when the pastor told them of the details.

Elizabeth was excited. It sounded like a fun adventure after the drudgery of the snowy winter. After services, Elizabeth whispered to James and asked if she could attend.

"I don't see why not. I think you'll have a good time."

"I love sleeping under the stars. Pa used to take me when I was younger, especially when he'd go hunting."

"Then I see no reason why you should miss it," he said, grinning at her.

"Do you want to come too?"

"No, I'm sure Ben and his brothers will go, so someone needs to stay at the ranch. But you go. Have fun."

"I don't want to leave you alone," she said, her forehead crinkling with concern.

He chuckled and lifted her chin with his forefinger. "I've been alone before, you know."

Smiling, she said, "I know, but..."

"No buts. Go, have fun. Besides, you'll only be gone for two days. I'll survive."

May 1893

Friday morning arrived and Elizabeth was bursting with enthusiasm. She packed what she needed the night before, and her bag was waiting by the door. She wanted to wear her trousers but feared the gossip, so instead, she put on a thick pair of woolen stockings sewn together like tight trousers. She had fashioned them to keep her warm and paired them with a woolen undershirt. Together, they were similar to a man's union suit but fitted to her needs. They added bulk to her waist and made her skirt a tad tight, but she'd rather be warm than thin any day of the week. They'd be easy enough to remove if need be.

Just as she put the morning meal on the table, James appeared. Rubbing his hands over his eyes, he smothered a yawn.

"Morning," he said. "Isn't it a bit early?"

Elizabeth knew it was, but she'd been too excited to sleep. "Perhaps, but I wanted to give you a decent meal before I left. You'll be on your own today and tomorrow."

"I'll make it through, I'm sure," he said, laughing.

"Stop laughing," she said with a wide grin. "Sit and eat before it gets cold."

"What do you think I did for food before you came along?" he asked as he pulled out a chair.

"That's a good question," she said. "Probably ate better, that's for sure."

"I won't argue with you 'bout that." His lips lifted into a teasing grin.

"Oh, you," she said, swatting him with a towel. "Eat, before my hard work goes to waste."

After eating and insisting that she sit and eat with him, James loaded the wagon with her bag and tent. Although spring was in the air, it was still chilly at night, and she packed a few thick woolen blankets as a precaution. She didn't want a repeat of the night she had spent with Ben when her body had shivered uncontrollably for hours. Better to be over prepared than not be prepared at all.

Ben, Michael, and Luke had left just moments before, and she watched as they and their horses disappeared around the bend.

"Hurry. I think we're late." She was jumping out of her skin with anticipation.

"We have plenty of time. Don't you worry, they won't leave without you."

An hour later, they arrived at the church. Laughing young adults had gathered and energy resonated amongst them. Three wagons sat waiting for their occupants. One wagon would hold the gear and the others would carry the young women. All the men were riding their horses.

Elizabeth jumped from the wagon seat and went to gather her belongings. Michael stood joking with the men, but when he saw her, he excused himself and hurried to her side.

"Let me help you with that." He took her bag and tent, and left her with her blankets.

"Thank you." She grinned at him. He was always eager to help her, unlike his older brother.

"Is this everything?" he asked, his eyebrow raised.

"Yes," she said, looking to make sure she had forgotten nothing.

"There isn't much here. Others had much more than this."

She grinned at him impishly. "I've camped plenty of times. Besides, it's only one night. How much do I need?"

"I certainly don't disagree with you. It's just surprising considering what I've seen this morning. I assumed you'd be like the others."

Leaning over to him, she whispered in his ear, "If I had my way, I would've shown up in a pair of trousers, but I thought better of it."

Laughing out loud, his eyes twinkled. "You amaze me."

Whistling, Pastor Williams stood at the top of the stairs and gestured for everyone to quiet their voices. "Now that everyone's here, we need to get goin'. We'll want to arrive at the campsite as soon as possible."

The group cheered and clapped before heading to the horses and wagons. Elizabeth found her friend Susan and the two of them scrambled inside the same wagon. Realizing too late they had climbed into the one containing Suzette and her friend Nancy, Elizabeth groaned inwardly. She didn't want to be near them. They were both so judgmental, and were always whispering and giving her dirty looks. She shook her head. She wouldn't let her spirits be dampened by Suzette.

Before long, the wagons headed up the mountain road. They sang songs and laughed, the mood merry and carefree. Soon, they were in the foothills and arriving at the campsite. Sunlight broke through the trees, shimmering on the tiny, green leaves. The tall pines created a canopy over them that kept the sun from burning their skin, and a pleasant breeze swirled around, lifting the leaves from the ground. It was cool enough for a jacket, but she knew once they started their journey on foot, it wouldn't be needed.

The pastor gathered the group and explained the sleeping arrangements. "I don't believe any of you will give us any cause for concern. We trust each of you, but to be cautious—"

The young adults laughed, their eyes dancing nervously and feet shifting with embarrassment. There were relationships budding amongst some of them, but no one wanted to break the rules, so they would be on their best behavior.

The pastor gave out work assignments and everyone scurried to do their part. Elizabeth watched as Suzette and Nancy perched themselves on a fallen log and settled in. They wouldn't be helping. This didn't surprise her but was irritating nonetheless. They'd expected the men to wait on them.

Before long, Mr. Breckenridge headed toward them, his hat in his hands. He was quite the dandy gentleman who had arrived in town last fall. Always wearing pinstripe suits and a bowler hat on his head. He strutted around like a peacock, and was condescending to anyone who didn't live in town. He had set his eyes on Suzette, just like her brother and Ben. She collected men like queen bees gathered their workers. "Miss Suzette, is everything alright?"

Beaming at him, Suzette said, "Of course. I wanted to sit here for a moment out of the sun. I was a little dizzy and didn't want to fall. I'll get my things from the wagon here soon."

"No need for that. I'll be happy to get your things. I don't want you feeling faint. Can I get you something to wet your lips?"

"Mr. Breckenridge, that's so kind of you. I can't let you do that. Everyone needs to do their part." She stood and then stumbled toward him as if she had lost her balance. "Oh, my. I'm sorry. I must be woozier than I thought."

"My dear, please sit." He helped her back to the log. "You don't need to do anything except rest. I'll get you a cool drink and take care of everything else." He patted her hand and left to do her bidding. A moment later, he returned with a canteen of water. "Here you go. Drink this. It should help."

Smiling at him, she took a small sip before dotting her lips with a white handkerchief she held in her hands.

Elizabeth watched this unfold as she set up her tent. Disgusted at the fawning, she grumbled to herself. She'd just ignore Suzette and stay as far away from her as she could get. However, she couldn't resist watching the way Suzette manipulated Mr. Breckenridge. It was something to behold.

Suzette handed the canteen to Nancy. "Would you like a drink?"

"Thank you." Nancy took the canteen and swallowed some water.

"Now you two ladies relax and save your strength for our walk. I'll let you know when your tent's erected." He walked off, a skip to his step.

Elizabeth strode to the wagon to get more supplies when she heard Nancy say, "How do you do that?"

"Do what?" Suzette said.

"Get men to do your bidding?"

"Very carefully," Suzette said as she giggled. "Men think we're helpless and are happy to do everything. I just encourage them."

They laughed and tucked their heads together, whispering conspiratorially, and Elizabeth heard nothing more. It was a good thing, as she wasn't sure she could contain the scathing retort threatening to pass her lips.

Her stomach turned when she heard Suzette. Elizabeth didn't understand why she did it. Why did they even come on the trip if they didn't want to take part? As she came around a thicket of trees, her mind elsewhere, she tripped over a fallen log. Before hitting the ground, muscular hands grabbed her and kept her from falling flat on her face.

Raising her head and seeing that it was Ben, she muttered, "Watch where you're going, you, you, oaf." Mortified at being caught unaware, she didn't want his hands on her as it brought forth feelings she'd rather keep tucked away.

Pushing his hands aside, she stepped back. Anger roared through her. He was likely headed to Suzette's side right now, presumably to sweep her off her feet so she wouldn't have to walk.

Startled, Ben retreated. "I'm sorry. I was only trying to help."

"I don't need your help."

Ben's eyes darkened in fury. "Maybe you should watch where you're going and watch your language as well."

"Don't lecture me. I can say whatever I want."

"A lady should never utter such language, especially on a church sponsored trip. Why can't you act like the others?"

"Like who? Someone like your precious Suzette?" She sneered, growing angrier with every second. But was she angry at him or herself? He was right. Her language was inappropriate on a church trip, but she'd never admit it to him. Besides, what right did he have to lecture her?

"She's a perfect example of a lady. You might find it wise to follow her behavior."

"I don't want to be like her, let alone follow anything she does. She isn't as perfect as you men think."

"I think you're jealous, and it doesn't become you."

Furious, she pushed around him to go to where she was going to set up her tent. She was not jealous of her and had nothing more to say. As far as she was concerned, he could rot with her. They'd be perfect for each other.

Taking a deep breath, she shook off what had just happened. Her trip wouldn't be ruined because of him. She could ignore them both.

Eighteen

Within the hour, everyone had gathered for their trip through the woods. They had erected the tents. The firewood was stacked and ready to use, and the food supplies were stored for later. One of the chaperoning couples was staying behind to prepare supper.

"Everyone, I've divided you into two groups," Pastor Williams said. Reading from a piece of paper, he continued. "Those going with Milly and I are Suzette, Nancy, Tami, Susan, Elizabeth, and the Seymour brothers. Those going with Doc Wilson and his missus are Sarah, Emma, Louise, Mary, the Erickson brothers, Mr. Edwards, and Mr. Breckenridge."

They talked animatedly to each other, excited and eager to leave.

"Your leaders have the maps. Make sure you've dressed warmly with a light jacket you can remove. It's chilly now, but you might not want it later. Don't forget your canteens. Have a good time, and we'll meet back here in a few hours."

Ben couldn't believe his good luck. Mr. Breckenridge was in the other group, and he'd have Suzette to himself. The pastor and Ben led their group, with Luke and Michael in the rear. The ladies were clustered together in the middle. The men each carried a rifle as a precaution. It was early spring, and animals looking for their next meal filled the mountains. They couldn't be too cautious. Suzette was near the back with Elizabeth, so Ben couldn't converse with her, but he was sure he'd have ample opportunities.

As they walked, they broke through the shelter of trees. The sun warmed their skin and cast a glaring glow to the budding greenery. Delicate wildflowers bloomed, creating a cascade of rainbow colors after the spring rain. Those who'd brought jackets were removing them.

They stopped at a wide clearing where boulders sat jumbled in a disorganized fashion, as if in a game of marbles. They took a moment to rest and drink water before continuing up the trail. Suzette ambled near Ben's side.

"It's so hot, I'm feeling faint," she murmured

"You should remove your jacket. That should help." He could see the sweat glistening off her forehead, and her face was flushed. "I don't want you to overheat."

"Will you carry it for me?" she asked, gazing at him, her eyes wide and innocent, a look he found so alluring. He didn't want to carry the extra weight, but he wanted her to be pleased with him. He agreed and put it in his knapsack.

"Thank you. You're such a gentleman. I don't know what I'd do without you." She ran her fingers across his forearm.

"It's my pleasure. Are you enjoying the walk?"

"We're moving faster than I'd prefer, but the scenery is breathtaking. Are you?"

"I am. I love walking through the forest. The view is supposed to be amazing at the top."

"How much further?" Her forehead crinkled with concern.

"It'll be a while yet. We'll walk alongside the river for maybe a mile and then go up a slight incline to the top. Or at least that's what the pastor said. He said we need to watch our step as we get farther up."

"I hope it isn't dangerous," she murmured.

"Don't you fret. I'll be up front with the pastor. I'll make sure it's safe for you."

Her bright blue eyes brimmed with adoration. He could get lost in those depths if she'd let him. His heart swelled with emotion.

She stepped close to his side, her lavender scent overpowering his senses. "You're so strong and courageous. You won't let any harm come to us, I'm sure."

He blushed at her flowery words and felt like an awkward youth, unprepared for the rush of love he felt for this young woman.

"You're so good to me. I'm glad we're here together."

Ben swallowed hard. When she looked at him like that, he lost his words. It took him a moment before replying, "I'm glad, too."

The pastor clapped his hands and said they should continue. Ben made his way up to the front while watching Suzette move to be near her friend Nancy. Her petite form moved gracefully over the dirt and rocks as though dancing a waltz in a brightly lit ballroom.

Elizabeth viewed the exchange between Suzette and Ben. Jealousy pierced through her like a hot poker in a flaming fire when she saw how enamored Ben was. She was disgusted with herself. She shouldn't be jealous of their relationship. While she had never meant for Ben to mean something to her, it was clear he did.

As she watched Ben put Suzette's jacket into his knapsack, she wondered how Suzette got what she wanted every time. It was a mystery to her. If Elizabeth complained and didn't want to carry her jacket, Ben would have no sympathy for her. She couldn't let it bother her and soon forgot about their exchange as they continued up the trail.

Looking down to her left, Elizabeth saw the raging river below them, swirling, overflowing the banks as it rushed against large boulders. White surf smashed, twirled in circles and then extended out in wavy lines. It had a mind of its own and was something magical to behold. All that strength and power. The river was wide, curling around the bend and likely went for miles. There was no telling how deep it was, but it wasn't meant for a quick dip.

Elizabeth looked ahead and saw that the trail narrowed halfway up the incline. There also appeared to be a rocky cliff. They needed to be extra cautious as they crossed that part of the trail. It'd be treacherous if any of them fell.

As they climbed and arrived at the narrow path, the pastor stopped. "This part of the trail is smaller than I remember," he said. "Please be careful and watch your footing as you cross. We should be fine, but please, no sudden movements. We'll cross it one person at a time. Let either myself or Ben know if you need our help."

He stepped slowly, testing for safety. Each person followed with deliberate, measured steps, taking care to tread lightly. When it was Suzette's turn, a scream burst through the air, but it wasn't human. Elizabeth recognized it at once. It was a mountain lion. Suzette reached for Elizabeth's arm, frightened, and asked, "Whaaaat is that?"

Elizabeth whispered, "Be quiet, that's a mountain lion."

"A... a... what?" Suzette's fingernails dug into her arm, gripping it so tight she was bound to leave marks.

Trying to peel Suzette's fingers from her, Elizabeth gritted her teeth. "I said, a mountain lion. Now be quiet. Don't move."

Ahead, Elizabeth could see Ben and the pastor cock their rifles. Not letting go, Suzette squeezed Elizabeth's arm even more painfully, her nails breaking through tender skin.

Ben lifted and pointed his rifle. Suzette screamed and then wrenched Elizabeth, shoving her out of her way. Elizabeth tried to keep her balance, but Suzette forced her toward the edge. Elizabeth fought her footing as the rocks and dirt skidded behind her, falling into the rushing water.

"Stop. We're going to fall," Elizabeth yelled, fighting in desperation to keep her balance.

Suzette screamed again and shoved Elizabeth hard as she ran. Arms flailing, heart pounding, Elizabeth tried to stop her fall but within seconds, she lost her balance. As she tumbled toward the edge, Elizabeth saw Suzette slip and fall. In the moment before Elizabeth slid down the hillside, she prevented Suzette's descent by pushing her atop a massive boulder jutting out the side of the ridge before Elizabeth plummeted straight into the water.

Hitting with a splash, the intense, roaring water sucked her into its depths. Her skin burned, sharp pinpricks on every each of her like she was being poked with thousands of needles. She had never felt anything like it. Her lungs closed and she couldn't breathe. The weight of her skirts pulled her further into the darkness, into the deep crevices of the frigid water. Trying not to panic, she ripped at the ties holding her skirts and they fell from her hips and it was swept away.

She struggled with every bit of strength she had and propelled upward until her head broke through the surface. Forcing herself to suck in a deep breath, she wanted to cry out with agony. It burned, a scorching, stinging sensation that was worse than burning her hand on an open flame. She kicked her legs and arms, but it was as though she was being torn apart. If she wanted to survive, she had to force her way through it.

She tried to breathe, while fighting to stay afloat. Water splashed into her face, up her nose, and into her mouth. Trying to move her arms, they didn't cooperate and she feared she didn't have the strength to swim to the shore. The water moved too quick and pulled her along so fast it was impossible. She only hoped the current would move her toward dry ground.

The freezing, fast-moving water sucked and pulled. If she stayed in it much longer, she didn't know if she'd survive. She knew the consequences of exposure to bitter temperatures, and she would not let this be the end of her.

Praying hard, her eyes scanned the banks of the river. Ahead of her, she saw an enormous tree trunk that had fallen across the water. If she could grab one branch, she might pull herself out. She had to swim to it. The chill was zapping her energy quicker than expected. Her chance of survival was disappearing, and she prayed the current would help her, not hurt her.

Just as she thought she wouldn't be able to grab the tree, the current shifted just enough to move her toward the fallen tree. Reaching her arm as far as she could, her frozen, numb, stiff fingers screamed with protest, but she wasn't going to die, not if she could help it. She grasped the branch. Relief swept through her, and she wrapped her arms around it, holding on tight. She shook violently, and she was weak. The water roared past her, trying to pull her from her precarious perch.

Her eyelids were heavy with fatigue. She wanted to close them and sleep, but the advice her pa had given her at a young age surfaced. If she fell asleep in the water, she would never wake. She needed to fight.

She anchored herself as best as she could, reaching high on the branch. Kicking with all her might, Elizabeth pulled her body up, inch by inch, until she reached the steadiness of the immense trunk. Taking another deep and painful breath, she wrestled her legs out of the water. She said a quick prayer of thanks that her boots were still on her feet. They helped her gain traction on the slippery wood. She rested her head, her arms wrapped tight around the wood, the bark damp across her cheek as she watched the water churn and spin past her. She had survived.

Her energy had drained, and she shook with such force it was a wonder she didn't slip right off the wood. She had to get to dry, steady ground. She also couldn't take the chance the tree would shift and push her back into the frigid water. On her hands and knees, she crawled with purpose, testing her weight and steadiness until she reached solid ground. Trembling but grateful she was alive, she tried to gain her bearings.

She wasn't sure how far downriver she'd traveled, but as she looked at the sky, it became clear she had another, more dangerous problem. The sky had darkened with ominous clouds, and the wind was picking up sending additional chills up and down her skin. Her priorities shifted. She needed to find shelter and find it fast. She couldn't waste time trying to find her way back to everyone. She removed her clothing, standing as naked as the day she was born, and wrung the water out of them as fast as she could.

Shivering, her teeth chattered as the cold wind whipped around her, but she took a moment to take stock of her injuries. Scratches and bruises covered her arms, legs, and chest but none appeared life threatening. Her right palm had a ragged gash and bright red blood trickled from it. Ripping a ruffle off the bottom of her shift, she quickly wrapped her hand to stop the bleeding, grimacing from the sting but it was the least of her problems.

Goose bumps prickled on her skin. She put her damp drawers, shift, and shirt back on and carried the thick woolen undershirt and pants. She was grateful she had worn them. As soon as they dried, they'd help keep her warm, but for now they were a sodden mess. She walked briskly along the riverbank, stumbling over the rocks, looking for a cave or shelter that could protect her from the thunderstorm that brewed above.

Nineteen

Ben pulled the trigger, and the shot reverberated through his shoulder. He missed. The pastor was ready with his rifle for a second shot when the mountain lion raced away. They had startled the animal as they came around the bend, none too happy to be interrupted while feasting on a dead deer on the side of the trail. Blood pooled around the carcass; the lion's meal was left to rot.

Ben thanked God the shots scared it away. He shuddered to think what would have happened if they hadn't succeeded. Hearing the frightened screams of the women behind him, he didn't turn until he was positive the mountain lion was gone. The women were terrified, and their safety was his priority.

When he finally turned, commotion and unrest lay before him. Suzette had fallen over the cliff. She hung on, her fingers grasping what she could, whimpering in fear. He was too far away to help.

A giant boulder appeared to have halted her fall, but if she shifted one inch, she could plummet to her death. Luke hung over the edge while Michael held fast to his feet. Luke grasped Suzette's hands. Her body scraped against the rocks that ripped her clothing when Michael pulled them both up to safety.

The other women huddled together, frightened and crying.

Milly was doing her best to calm them as Ben ran to them. Reaching his brothers as they pulled Suzette to the trail's edge, Ben knelt and gathered her into his arms. She cried great sobbing tears as he tried to reassure her.

"Everything's alright. You're safe," he whispered.

Tears poured across her cheeks. Her hair had fallen from its braided coiffure, her blouse was ripped, and dirt covered her face and arms, but she was still a delicate flower he needed to safeguard. She clung to him, and a surge of protectiveness filled him. She was fragile, precious. He could have lost her. He hugged her close, rocking, and murmuring calming words to her.

"Ben," Luke said, interrupting.

"What?"

"It's Elizabeth."

"I'm busy. She can take care of herself," he said without taking his eyes off Suzette.

"She fell over the side and into the river. We couldn't save her. Suzette pushed—"

"What?" The roar of the river below muffled Luke's words. Ben head twisted fast to look at Luke. "I don't understand."

"Elizabeth fell. I'm not sure what happened to her after she hit the water. We need to find her and fast," Luke said. "The water's moving readily, not to mention frigid from the snowmelt.

"I didn't keep her safe," he said. Suzette stiffened at his words, but if he hurt her feelings, he'd have to deal with it some other time. He helped her to her feet and put her in Milly's capable hands.

"No, don't leave me," Suzette cried. "Elizabeth deserved what she got." Ben was shocked and gave her a stern glare that quieted her at once. He softened his expression when tears filled her eyes. She was just frightened and likely didn't mean her harsh words regarding Elizabeth's safety.

The men gathered and conferred. The pastor would lead the

women back to camp. Michael, Luke, and Ben would follow the riverbank to search for Elizabeth.

Fear etched the women's faces. There was no guarantee Elizabeth had survived the fall or the roaring water. Once it was determined Suzette had suffered no actual damage and could travel, the pastor and Milly left with the others.

Michael, Luke, and Ben moved carefully but quickly along the path until they could safely climb down the steep ravine to the river's edge. Scanning the riverbed and the rushing water, Michael looked up into the sky and pointed out the dark, thundering clouds building above them. Wind gusts had developed and were rushing through the trees.

"The weather's turning. We need to find shelter or head back," Michael shouted over the roar of the wind.

"We can't leave her out here," Ben yelled, fighting to be heard.

"I know, but a storm's rolling in. If we get caught in it, we won't be able to help. We need to find shelter. That lightning's gonna be dangerous." A bright flash exploded in front of them and thunder echoed through the valley moments later. "See?" Michael yelled. "Once it's passed, we can continue our search."

They agreed and looked for a haven to ride out the storm. As they walked along the edge of the river, Ben scanned the edge and his eyes focused in on a cluster of rocks. Running to it, he pulled the thick fabric out of the water. It was a green woman's skirt, torn to pieces, a ragged mess. His heart sank. It had to be hers. This wasn't a good sign. She could be anywhere.

He turned to his brothers, the skirt in his hands. Sorrow filled him and his chest ached. She had snuck into his heart and he'd let harm come to her. He had to fix this and bring her home safely.

Michael pointed to a cave covered in foliage, and they followed him as the roaring wind and crashing thunder made it difficult to hear. Pulling back tangled vines, Michael peered inside the cave. It was big enough to hold the three of them, and they went inside the dark cavern just in time. The sky opened and torrential rain poured.

Elizabeth woke the next morning, curled under a massive fallen tree trunk. She had hiked for about a mile before finding the tree. The roots had created a shelter with hanging roots protecting her from the worst of the wind and rain.

She had shouted with joy when she discovered the tin box containing her matches still in the pocket of her woolen pants. She had shoved them in there that morning at the last minute, never thinking she'd fall into a raging river and would need them. Once the rain had subsided, she had started a small fire with sticks and broken logs she found. She hung her woolen clothing on the roots, letting the heat from the fire dry them. Once they were dry, she pulled them on. The warmth from the fire still in the woolen fibers.

She had stacked an enormous pile of leaves and pine needles to keep herself off the hard ground and then pulled what she could on top of her. Wasn't the most comfortable night's sleep, but it worked. She made the best of her plight and didn't freeze.

Rising out of the semi-warmth of her makeshift den, she wiped the sleep from her eyes. Her head ached and was painful to the touch, and her hand still smarted from the nasty cut. She must have hit her head during her fall, but she didn't remember when and there was nothing she could do to fix it. She pushed the thought aside. Finding her way back was her priority. Her head could be tended to later.

She looked at the sky. The sun's brightness cut sharply across her field of vision. It made her head hurt even worse. She closed her eyes for a long moment before opening them again to gain her bearings.

If she kept the sun to her left, she could make her way back to camp. She assumed they were looking for her, but considering how fast and dangerous the water had been flowing, she feared they might have given her up for dead. She hoped she was wrong because she didn't want to spend another night alone.

Trudging forward, she ignored the sharp hunger pains and loud stomach growls. She kept repeating, "I can live without food." As long as she found water, she'd do just fine. It was just a matter of finding it again.

As she marched through the thick foliage, she kept an ear out for the river. When she left the swirling, raging water the day before, her focus had been on finding shelter. She hadn't noticed where she was going. She regretted not being more cognizant of her path.

She was thirsty. Considering how much she had swallowed yesterday, she hadn't wanted more, but today her dry throat craved the moisture. Her mouth and lips cracked from the lack of water.

After climbing through thick brush, over rocks, and up and over hilly inclines, Elizabeth heard the welcome sound of water rushing in the distance. Her body ached, her head hurt, and she just wanted to fall back asleep. Keeping the sun to her left until it reached high in the sky, she walked over another small hillside and wept with relief.

Clambering to the embankment, rocks and dirt skidding as she tried to find footholds, she made her way to the river's edge. She knelt and scooped up handfuls, bringing it to her parched lips. She tried to drink deliberately, knowing if she drank it too quickly, she might get sick, but nothing had ever tasted so good.

Once she had her fill, she sat back on her rear, pulled her knees to her chest, and said a small prayer of thanks. With a renewed sense of hope, she washed her hands and face. She pulled apart her ragged braid and winced as her fingers brushed against the tender bump on the back of her head. Ignoring the ache, she combed through it with her fingers and fashioned a new tight braid.

Considering how sharp her headache was, the tender and

swollen lump likely explained the pounding between her eyes and along the back of her neck. She'd likely need a doc, but it wasn't as though she could conjure one up in the middle of the forest, so she'd have to make do. She was alive, and that was a reason to celebrate. A brief swim in a raging river would not stop her from finding her way home.

She stood, looked at the position of the sun to get her bearings, and tried her best to continue heading north with the sun settling on her right. As the hours passed, however, frustration threatened to overwhelm her. She saw and heard no one and was afraid they had given her up for lost.

Taking a quick rest, she sat on a broken tree stump. Her heart heavy, she put her head in her hands and the tears she had kept at bay fell unheeded. Would she ever see James or Susan, or even Ben? Or was it her destiny to die out here alone, cold, and afraid?

"No!" she screamed. "I'm going to make it."

Stomping her feet and wincing as the pain in her head reverberated from her furious actions, she swiped at the tears and refused to let anymore fall. With fists at her side, she stood and kept going.

"I'm going to get out of here," she muttered. "I'll find my way back if it takes a day, a month, or a year. I will survive this."

A horse neighed, breaking through her rambling rampage. Then she heard it again.

"Help," she hollered, her voice cracking. "Is anyone out here?"

She ran and hollered as loud as she could, holding one hand at the back of her head to keep it as still as she could. She burst through a cluster of trees and saw men on horses galloping away.

"Stop!" she yelled, dying inside when they didn't halt. They didn't look behind them. It was as though she was hollering to an empty forest. She was too far away and was doomed to be left here to survive on her own?

Twenty

Frustration lined the men's faces. There hadn't been a sign of Elizabeth since they found her shredded skirt. Michael, Luke, and Ben had continued to search once the rain stopped. They kept going until it was too dark to see their hands in front of their faces, and they'd risen early the following morning. They made their way back to camp, deciding they needed their horses to make better ground. All the men except for the pastor had headed out to look for Elizabeth. No one wanted to say it, but they all thought it: she hadn't survived. Their search was now just a chance to recover her body.

Stopping for a quick rest, they watered their horses and ate a small meal. The doc warned them that if they found her alive, they should be mindful of her injuries. A fall that steep would likely cause serious injury if not death. After finding no evidence of her in the river, they wondered if she made her way inland and searched for hours before heading back to paths along the river-bank. Clustered together in pairs, Ben and Luke brought up the rear.

Ben's horse, Midnight, began behaving erratically—pulling on the reins and not wanting to move forward. He dismounted to check his shoes. The last thing he wanted was for Midnight to go lame from a pebble. It was best to remove them if he could. Running his hand along Midnight's flank, he picked up a foot and bent to look at it when he heard something in the wind. Turning, he saw someone waving their arms and yelling. It had to be Elizabeth. His heart raced with anticipation. Who else would be out here, far from the nearest town or ranch?

"Stop," he yelled. "It's her."

Dropping Midnight's foot, he jumped into his saddle and galloped toward her. She stumbled and fell to the ground before he could reach her. He came to within a few feet, leaped off, and ran to her.

"Elizabeth?" He crashed to the ground and knelt in front of her. He placed his hands gently on her shoulders. Was she injured? Tears framed her lashes, dirt covered her face, she was wearing a strange getup of a woolen shirt and pants, and her hand was wrapped in dirty, white cotton, but looked otherwise unharmed.

She shivered. "I didn't think you heard me."

He shrugged out of his coat and draped it across her shoulders. She grasped it and hugged it tight.

"I almost didn't," he said. "If it hadn't been for Midnight acting skittish, we might've missed you. Are you hurt?"

"No, I don't think so." His eyes scanned her body as his hands gingerly touched her arms, checking for breaks, and then pulled her into his arms holding her tight. She buried her face in his neck for a long moment before she pushed him away. "Don't touch me."

He abruptly removed his hands. "I'm sorry, I didn't mean..."

She struggled to her feet. "I'm fine. I don't need you to act as if you're concerned for my well-being." Her eyes blazed with fury.

He stared at her in shock. Where was this anger coming from? "I'm just trying to help."

She glared at him. "I don't need your help. Why don't you—" Her words faded, her eyes rolled back into her head, and she started to fall. Grabbing her around the waist, he swept her up into his arms and held her close. Her body was limp from fatigue.

Doc Wilson approached. His medical bag in one hand, his hair standing on end, and his eyes crinkling with concern. "Is she hurt?"

"I'm not sure. She was talking and then collapsed."

"Let me look at her. You can put her down."

Ben shook his head. He couldn't let her go. He needed to hold her, to protect her. There was no way he was letting her go this time.

"Ben, please. I need to make sure she's alright. Why don't you sit over here?" He gestured toward a fallen log. "It'll let me get a good look at her."

Ben strode to the log and by the time he reached it, she had woken. She looked around, confused. "What are you doing? Let me go."

"We're just trying to help, Elizabeth," Doc Wilson said as Ben set her on the log, being careful not to jostle her. "You fainted and Ben here kept you from falling." She shrugged out of Ben's grasp, but he didn't go far. He didn't want to leave her side. She was his responsibility. James would expect nothing else but there was far more to it than that. His emotions were boiling over and he wanted to hold her, protect her, comfort her from all harm.

The doc knelt in front of her. "Are you hurt?"

Raising her head, she said. "I'm alright, I think." She raised her hand to her head. Ben's coat fell off her shoulder. "My head hurts, I cut my hand, and I have a few bruises, but I think everything else is fine."

He unwrapped the dirty cloth from her hand and probed it gently before pulling clean gauze from his medical bag and wrapping it again. "I'll clean that better back in my office. Let me look at your head."

"I think I hit it when I fell in the river," she said, shivering.

The doc stood and moved behind her. Ben watched as the doc

undid her braid, revealing thick, dried blood. He put his fingers on the wound, probing it. She grimaced with pain.

"Doc, be careful," Ben said.

"I'm sorry. I know it hurts," Doc Wilson said. He separated the strands of her hair. A large, jagged gash covered the back of her head, but no fresh blood appeared. Coming back to face her, he knelt again. "Are you dizzy or nauseous?"

"No. Just tired and cold." She shook her head and then reached out as if to catch herself. The doc steadied her.

"I think you might be dizzier than you realize. You have a nasty gash and bled profusely. Frankly, I'm surprised you're up and walking." He chuckled. "Most grown men wouldn't be as strong as you. You're something, young lady." He patted her knee and gestured to Ben. "Once we get you back to town, we can get it cleaned and bandaged. You'll be fine for now, but let's get you home."

Ben couldn't believe how stoic she was being, how brave. His stomach churned from uneasiness and dread. He wished he had been able to guard her from harm. As she rose, he stopped her and picked her up in his arms.

She protested, but took one look at his tender gaze, and quieted at once. He was surprised she didn't continue to argue. It wasn't in her nature. At the same time, he was glad. He wanted to avoid saying something regretful. He was angry, happy, frustrated, and something else he couldn't put a name to. *What is going on with me?*

Luke held Ben's horse steady while he carefully placed her in the saddle.

"Is she going to be alright?" Luke asked, his eyes full of more questions, but he was astute enough to know that now wasn't the time to ask. They'd likely talk later when they were alone.

"I believe so, but the doc wants to look her over at his office. We'll know more then." He untied his bedroll and draped it across her legs. He didn't want her to be uncomfortable or cold.

She whispered, "Thank you."

He nodded and mounted behind her. Midnight shifted with the extra weight but settled with Ben's stern commands. Elizabeth squirmed, trying to keep herself far up in the saddle. After letting her fidget for a brief moment, he wrapped one arm around her waist and pulled her back, so she was firmly tucked against his chest. Her soft curves felt so right. He didn't want to ever let her go.

Leaning, he murmured in her ear, "You're safe, sweetheart. I'll protect you."

Why did I just say that? His neck burned with heat.

She slumped back against him, and a wave of tenderness swept through him. She'd been through hell in the past twenty-four hours. He didn't know what had happened, but she'd survived.

Amazed and in awe of her strength, he thought of his sisters. They were strong women, and they wouldn't have done such a remarkable job if they found themselves where she had been. He wasn't sure Suzette could have survived the same ordeal. If they had both fallen in the river, they might have found something entirely different.

A few hours later, the tired but jubilant group reached town. Ben stopped Midnight in front of the doc's office and dismounted, being careful of Elizabeth's injured head. Reaching up, he lifted her from the saddle and held her close with one hand under her legs and the other around her waist.

She pushed at him. "I can walk. Put me down."

"Please let me," he implored. "I think you've done enough walking in the last twenty-four hours, don't you?"

She looked at him with hundreds of questions in her eyes, but complied. He was recognizing her behavior and actions and he wanted to be the one who was there for her. *What does this mean for my future?*

He carried her into the office and placed her on the examination table. She sat, gripping the blanket and his coat as if they were the only thing holding her steady.

Janie, the doc's wife, rushed into the room and gave Elizabeth a big hug filled with love and concern. He backed away and closed the door with a soft click. His heart hurt, and he didn't understand why.

Twenty-One

A sizable crowd cooled their heals outside the doc's office waiting to hear if Elizabeth would be alright. James had been sent for and had arrived moments before. Mr. Crockitt ran out of the General Store. Breathing heavily, he stopped and handed Ben an envelope.

"Urgent telegram, Mr. Seymour," he said, bracing his hands against his knees as he tried to catch his breath.

Ben ripped it open.

COME HOME STOP

STANLEY HURT STOP

CONNIE GONE STOP

ANNE

"What's in the telegram?" Luke asked.

Ben's lips fell into a frown. "We need to return to Thundering Mountain."

"What's wrong?" Michael asked.

"It doesn't say. Just says Stanley's hurt and Connie's gone."

They strode to their horses as James walked out of the doc's office. Pastor Williams had sent someone to collect James when he had returned to town with the women the day before. He had been waiting when they had arrived with Elizabeth, and Ben was lucky James had been too distracted to worry about strangling him for not watching out for his sister.

James asked, "Is something wrong?"

"I don't know for certain," Ben said as he mounted his horse. He hated to leave Elizabeth but his family needed him. "Just got a telegram from my sister, Anne. We need to head home. I'm sorry to put you in this position..."

"Go... I understand."

"Will you be alright without us?" Ben asked.

James raised a hand behind his neck. "After everything that has happened to Elizabeth, I'm the last person to stop anyone from taking care of their family."

"How is she?" Ben asked.

"She's gonna be fine. She just needs rest."

"Tell her..." Ben said and then stopped. What could he say? His emotions were in turmoil. He didn't know how he felt anymore. He had planned on proposing to Suzette, but it was Elizabeth who frequented his dreams.

"Tell her we hope she recovers soon," Luke said.

A few days later, Ben, Michael, and Luke rode their horses onto the Thundering Mountain Ranch. No sounds filled the corral and no ranch hands bustled around. It was too still, too quiet, and eerily similar to the last time he was here. There wasn't a black wreath hanging on the door.

The wide wooden doors opened, and his sisters rushed out to greet them. Giving them each a hug, Ben asked "How's Stanley?"

"Stanley's in terrible shape, but the doc says he'll recover," Anne said.

Ben squeezed her shoulder. "Where is he?"

"He's upstairs resting." She took his hand, keeping him in place. "He feels awful and hates himself for making you leave—making all of you leave." Anne looked at each of her brothers.

"I won't hurt him, Anne."

"I know that. I just—"

Ben gave her a quick hug. "All will be well, I promise."

He left his siblings and walked slowly up the stairs to Stanley's room. He had to control his anger. Whatever had passed between them was in the past, and he'd do good to remember that. Standing in front of Stanley's bedroom door, Ben hesitated, took a deep breath, and then knocked.

"Come in," Stanley said, his voice weak.

Ben pushed open the door and closed it behind him. He wanted to let Stanley have his say and felt it best they keep it between them until they cleared the air.

Stanley rested against the pine headboard, the knots in the wood clear as the day the two of them had sanded it smooth. Stanley's shoulder was bandaged. He looked small and gaunt in the enormous fourposter bed. "Ben..." Stanley coughed. "I'm glad you came."

"Kind of surprised you'd want me back, to be honest."

"About that. There aren't words to express..." Stanley swallowed as he fought for control, his eyes avoiding Ben's eyes. "I let my feelings for Connie interfere. She convinced me that the best thing was to have you and the boys gone. That y'all needed to have your own lives. She insisted we couldn't have a future with you here and I... I shouldn't have kicked you out." He raised his good hand to his face and scratched his beard. "I should've examined Pa's will myself and not listened to her."

"I'm not sure I understand."

"The will..." Stanley paused, hanging his head in defeat. "It was a forgery. It wasn't what Pa wanted."

Shock rippled through Ben.

"What?" Ben's voice ripped through the room like a tornado, hard, strong with enough force it could have blown all of them away, but Stanley withstood the anger as though knowing he had no other choice.

"Connie planned it. Somehow, she got ahold of Pa's original will and made a forgery." Stanley sighed and shifted on the bed. "Since we hadn't heard from you in years, no one questioned it. After your fight with Pa that night you left all those years ago, I believed he was still angry with you. He didn't say your name and only talked about you when he had too much to drink. I mistakenly believed he left everything to me. I was wrong. I should've listened to Luke. He thought something was amiss, but I guess even he couldn't imagine what she'd done."

Standing at the foot of the bed, Ben waited. He was at a loss for words especially now.

Taking a deep breath, Stanley said, "Pa's will, the real one, left the ranch to you. Pa wanted you to have it. The rest of us were left with plots of land he'd bought over the years, land I didn't even know he owned. Pa invested his gold money well. I found the original in Connie's things."

"Anne didn't mention the will," Ben said. He had forced his voice to be even keeled. His anger was near to a boiling point. All the time wasted, all the hurt that had occurred over the last few months—all gone because of the woman Stanley had married.

"The girls know nothing. I didn't have the energy to explain. After everything settled, I didn't want them to hate me as much as I hated myself. I realize that's selfish, and I'll let them know how complicit I was. I just wanted you to be here, so they'd realize I wasn't hiding anything, that I'm trying to make things right." The words were expelled in a rush, as though he had practiced the speech for when Ben arrived.

Not believing his ears, Ben sank into a chair and stared hard at his younger brother. His Pa hadn't forsaken him like he had believed.

"I should've known the will wasn't right." Stanley's eyes were downcast, his voice hoarse. "I was selfish, and I hate myself for it. I guess what's happened is penance for my mistakes."

Gulping, Ben focused his eyes on Stanley. He had returned to the ranch after five long years wanting to mend the rift between him and his pa. Because of Stanley's wife and her evil plan, he had missed out on apologizing to his pa and letting him know how much he had loved him.

"I'm so sorry, Ben. I hope you can forgive me one day, but I likely don't deserve it." Stanley covered his face with his good hand, his shoulders shaking with grief. His world had collapsed, and it appeared he could no longer handle the pressure.

"You didn't know what she was doing or what she planned?" Ben asked.

"No, but it gets worse."

"What could be worse than that?"

"Pa didn't die from the influenza."

Ben sat up straight, his hands grasping the hard edges of the chair. The wood dug into his palms.

"He was recovering and Connie had the ranch hand—the one I fought and killed—smother him. It was part of her plan to inherit the ranch."

"How do you know this?" Ben asked, his voice thick with anger.

"She told me the night she escaped."

"She told you!" Ben banged his fist into the wood of the chair causing it to rock under him.

Stanley avoided Ben's gaze. "Yes, she was positive gleeful when she told me how she'd planned on having that ranch hand kill both Ma and Pa."

"But I thought Ma—"

"Connie claimed she didn't kill Ma, that Ma died from the influenza. I don't know whether or not to believe her, but Ma hadn't been left alone, unlike Pa, so there's likely a ring of truth to that," Stanley said, his lip quivering with the evil thought that Connie had planned on killing their beloved mother.

"Heaven help me," Ben muttered, rubbing his hand across his eyes. Emotions swirled around him, causing his eyes to glaze over from anger and pain, mixing together and creating a volatile mixture that he had to control otherwise he'd explode.

"Why didn't you lock her up when you found out?"

"I did, but..." Stanley hesitated. "She... She threatened to kill our sisters, and I couldn't let that happen. I would've rather died than let her harm them. But then, her lover, the ranch hand interrupted us. The look in his eyes..." He shivered. "I knew he'd hurt them so I... He was able to get a shot off before I wrestled the gun away and killed him. We locked her in the study, but..."

Horrified, Ben swallowed hard.

"How...did...she...get...away?" Ben asked, the words coming out harsh and unfeeling.

"I don't know. In all the confusion, she slipped away."

Ben held his tongue. His body rigid, his throat swallowing hard, murderous heat climbing up his chest.

"I feel horrible. If I hadn't married Connie, none of this would've happened." Stanley's voice broke.

Ben wanted to yell and tell him he should have known; he should have done more. He took a deep breath and was deliberate with his next words. "You couldn't have known what she was planning."

"I should've known," Stanley yelled.

Ben sat silent.

"I'm to blame for this, and I don't know how to fix it." Stanley's fist hit the blankets, his face red with anger. His body was rigid, as though he was prepared to fight Ben if need be.

His Pa would not have wanted them to fight. There had already been too much damage done to his family. He was now the head of the family, and he had to find the strength to act like it. "There's nothing you can do now. You've got to heal. In a few days, we can discuss what to do next." He pushed out of the chair and started toward the door, but Stanley's words stopped him.

"I'll bring her to justice, Ben. I swear I will. She'll pay for this. I promise!"

Ben turned and looked at his brother. "Why don't you rest? We can discuss this more later."

Stanley's shoulders sagged with anguish. Tears filled his eyes, but he blinked them back. "Will you ever forgive me?"

"There's nothing to forgive." He forced the words past his lips. He wasn't sure he believed them, but it was clear Stanley needed to hear them.

Stanley slumped against the bed frame. "The girls don't know what Connie did to Pa." He took a deep breath. "I'm not sure if you'll agree, but I don't think they need to know."

"I agree. They've had a shocking week. I won't tell them Pa was murdered, at least not yet. We'll talk more later." Ben left and stood outside the door, astonished. Stanley's wife had killed their pa. He hadn't died of influenza as everyone believed.

He had to tell Michael and Luke but not today. Too much turmoil, hurt, and anger had torn their family apart. He had been gone far too long. If he had come home sooner, he might have stopped Connie. Instead, she had infiltrated their family, killed their pa, and almost killed Stanley.

Hot anger burned inside of him. They would find Connie. She would pay for this, but something told him it wouldn't be as easy as he'd like. She had been crafty in arranging the forgery, in manip-ulating a ranch hand to do her dirty deeds, and then to escape after she had been caught. This was a woman who knew exactly what she was doing and wouldn't be easy to catch, but they would find her and bring her to justice, of that he was certain.

～

Their evening meal was a somber but happy affair. The six of them were together again. It had been way too long. Warmth and laughter filled the room. Under an unspoken agreement, no one mentioned the last few weeks. Instead, the conversations revolved around the good things in their lives. Ben told them he planned on proposing to Suzette. Michael mentioned the young ladies he had met in Spring Creek and even Luke interjected with a few humorous stories from over the last few months.

As the evening wound to a close, Stanley turned quiet. When Ben rose and said he wanted to check on the horses, Stanley stood as well, made his excuses, and headed up to his room.

Ben left for the barn to find their foreman, Sam. A mentor to him growing up, Ben trusted his opinion. Sam had been a second father, and Ben knew he'd be honest with him.

Opening the barn door, Ben walked into the warmth. The horses were content in their stalls, munching on hay. A few stuck their heads out, nudging his hand for a treat. Sam came out of his room in the rear, a soiled rag in his hands, his limp more prominent tonight than normal. He was still the lanky, tall cowboy with ears that were too big for his head, and bushy eyebrows and mustache that had both grown white. Wrinkles lined his cheeks and in the corners of his eyes, but he still had a strong presence that Ben had always found comforting. Sam had been with their pa for years and had been hurt while trying to save their ma from a man from her past. No one knew the real details except Sam and his pa, and Sam would likely never share.

"I'm glad you're back home," Sam said.

"So am I."

"Come on back. Have a glass of whiskey with me." He shuffled across the dirt floor, his leg dragging behind him.

Ben followed.

Sam brushed off a cluttered chair for him. "I just finished eatin'. Would you like a bite?"

"Thanks, but no. We just finished up at the house."

Picking up a bottle of whiskey and two glasses, Sam placed them on the small, worn table that had seen better days and poured them each a healthy glass. Sitting, Sam pulled a cigar out of his vest pocket and offered it to Ben, which he declined. Sam shrugged, lit it, and took a deep breath, letting the smoke lazily flow out of his mouth and circle up to the ceiling before dissipating.

"It's been unsettled around here," Sam said.

"That's what I've been told. How much do you know?"

Taking another puff, Sam inhaled the smoke, held it in his mouth for a moment, and then released it. "Enough to know your brother made an error with his choice of a wife."

"Humphh, you could say that."

"Yep. Not the best decision he's ever made. No one really knew her."

"It's worse than that. Turns out she had something to do with Pa's death."

"I hope you ain't serious?" He leaned forward in his chair, his posture changing from one of relaxation to one of fight.

"I wish. Connie had that ranch hand kill Pa. He smothered him to death."

He stood and pounded a fist loudly on the table behind him. "Luke thought something was wrong with the way your pa died, but no one thought he'd been murdered. It looked as though he died in his sleep. When are we going after that lying piece of..." Sam took a deep breath, shuddering with anger.

"Soon, but Stanley needs to heal before we try and find her."

"I ain't sure I want to wait, Ben. Your pa..."

"I know how you feel but not just yet."

Sam glared at Ben but settled back in his chair.

"I'm angry with Stanley, and I know that ain't fair. I should be sympathetic, but I don't know how to be."

"Hmm," Sam said, scratching his chin. "You've got much to consider."

"He told me more. Pa's will. It was a forgery. The ranch is mine, not his."

"Well, that makes a sight more sense than Stanley gettin' all of it. I didn't understand, but no one was questioning it, so wasn't my place to say nothin'." He took a quick whiff of his cigar and leaned back; his long legs relaxed in front of him. "You've a couple of options. You can be angry and let it fester and tear your family further apart, or you can forgive. Work on fixing what's broke. Ask yourself, what would your pa have done? Then you'll have the answers you're looking for. And when you're done with that, we go after that woman."

His pa had forgiven Ben for his actions if he had left the ranch to him, as he'd always promised. He just wished he could have told his pa how sorry he was for the way he had acted. He had been young, stupid, rash, and impulsive—all the things his pa had shouted at him as he had left the ranch that June morning.

He could still remember his pa standing there tall and true, his face red with anger at what he perceived as Ben's stupidity. His ma had stood behind him, her eyes filled with tears. She, too, believed he had been making a mistake.

Ben had been convinced that joining Olson's vigilante gang was the right thing to do. There had been a rash of robberies and rustlers that had plagued the region, and he thought he was doing right by joining them. His pa had lost several heads of cattle to the rustlers, and Ben had been determined to bring them back. He never did.

Olson had started out with true intentions, but as the years passed Olson started to believe that no one deserved a second chance. He became jaded and harsh. The last job had been the last straw for Ben. He had left knowing he could never join anything like that again. He had headed home with every intention of begging his pa's forgiveness, but he had been too late to stop the actions of a devious woman.

Enough was enough. It was time to let go of the past.

$\mathcal{Twenty\text{-}Two}$

A few days after her ordeal in the river, Elizabeth headed to town to visit with Susan. Being cooped up in the house with James fussing over her was driving her insane. James tried to convince her to stay, but she told him she'd walk to town if he didn't hitch up the wagon. Reluctantly, he agreed, but asked her to be cautious.

Before heading to Susan's, she stopped at the General Store. She climbed from the wagon, using the wheel to help her get to the ground. Her head was still sore, and abrupt movements could make it pound something fierce. She tied the horses to the hitching posts. Pushing her hat so she could see better, she climbed up the stairs. Suddenly, the door opened, and her worst nightmare stepped in front of her.

"Elizabeth," he drawled, his evil eyes raking over her. "What a pleasant surprise. I wasn't sure I'd find you, but here you are." His large, meaty body loomed in front of her like an enormous bear. Mr. Wells, her pa's friend, was here to bring her to submission.

Terror ran through her, but her legs refused to move. He stepped closer until his hot, foul breath fanned her cheeks. Jerking, she tried to move, but it was too late. He gripped her upper arm, his fingers digging into her soft flesh.

"Now, my dear, no need to leave. We've much to catch up on."

"Leave me alone," she cried. She tried to pull her arm away, but he held fast.

He bent his head and muttered, "If you know what's good for you, you'll come with me."

"I'll do no such thing! No! Let me go!"

She wrenched her arm away and ran down the wooden steps to her wagon.

"No point in running from me," he cackled with sickening glee. "Your pa's with me. He means to see us hitched."

He ran down the steps and trapped her against the wagon, her back to his front. She couldn't climb inside, and his beefy arms had her pinned. She twisted and turned, trying to escape, but she couldn't. He blocked her every turn.

"You'll be my wife." His body was pressed into hers, smothering her with his revolting scent. He smelled like dead skunk and horse dung. He never bathed and her stomach rolled from the pungent odors. "It's unfortunate you ran away, making me find you, but don't ya know, distance makes the heart grow fonder as well as other things?" His steamy, liver onion breath sent chills down her spine as he whispered threats in her ear. "Your pa's given his blessing, and I see no reason to wait. You'll make a fine wife, and I can't wait to make you mine." His hand reached around and gripped her breast painfully, squeezing it until she emitted a small screech. Tears leaked from her eyes. He chuckled menacingly and released it. "My, my. Yes, I like 'em feisty. You'll learn your place soon enough. I ain't afraid to give you a few wallops to show you who's boss."

He flipped her around and placed one of his enormous, dirt soiled hands on her face. He grabbed her chin and turned it to him. "Don't you think it's time to give your future husband a kiss?" he asked with a sneer. He bent and covered her lips with his own. Trying to push him away, she only got her hands caught between them. He ground his mouth on hers, his legs keeping her trapped with nowhere to go.

She struggled and fought, but he had her pressed tight against him, and she didn't have the strength to break away. His tongue pushed through her tense lips. In disbelief, she bit down–hard.

Outraged, he bellowed with fury, and his fist slammed into her face, snapping her head back. She fell, her head hitting the wheel of the wagon. A loud ringing reverberated in her ears. Pain radiated along the side of her head, her neck, and into the small of her back. He kicked her hard in the side, one, two, three times. She groaned with each hit, her body lifting from the force and fury of his kicks.

"You bitch," he spat. "You'll learn your place. Never do that again." He kicked her again, his boot hitting her side, her ribs caving with the impact. She tried to crawl, but it was too much. The boot slammed into her side, her legs, her arms again and again.

"Hey, you there. Stop!"

"Stop!"

"What are you doing?"

"Stop!"

Screeches of horror and the sounds of fists pounding flesh reached her ears, but the agony behind her eyes and through her mid-section was too severe for her to crawl away. Her vision grew black and hazy. Giving up the fight, she closed her eyes and let the darkness overtake her.

Elizabeth shifted, her ears hearing far away sounds—feet shifting on the wooden floorboards, doors closing, voices whispering, but her eyes refused to open.

"Elizabeth. Elizabeth. You're safe. Please open your eyes."

With every bit of effort she possessed, she forced them open. Blurry shapes appeared that swam disjointedly in front of her. She couldn't focus. She rubbed her eyes. Her arms ached. She tried to sit, but the pain was unbearable. The room spun, dizziness threatening to overwhelm her.

Gentle hands pushed at her shoulders. "Don't try to sit. You're bruised all over."

Everything rushed back when a man's wide shoulders came into view. Fear choked her, and she whimpered. Pushing, she fought to get away. She had to run, she had to hide.

"Elizabeth, it's alright. We're only trying to help." A woman's voice pierced through the fear. Janie, the doc's wife, appeared before her eyes.

"What... what happened?" Elizabeth asked.

"You were attacked. No one knows what happened, but Mr. Crockitt's son saw a man strike you. Before he could get to you, you'd hit the wagon wheel and collapsed."

"Where is he?"

"Who?"

"Him." She couldn't utter his name.

"The man who hurt you?" Janie frowned but smoothed back Elizabeth's hair. "The Marshal ran him out of town. No man like that is welcome here in Spring Creek."

Relief surged through Elizabeth. She had time to get away. But where could she go? Her pa was here. If he found her, there was no telling what he'd do.

Elizabeth tried again to push to a sitting position and Janie tried to stop her. Slapping her hands away, Elizabeth sat, but the room swirled, and her head exploded with pain. She had to get to the ranch, grab her belongings, and leave. Go somewhere far away. Putting her feet on the ground, she tried to stand and promptly collapsed.

Janie knelt next to her. "Please, let us help. You need to stay here."

Struggling against Janie, she fought. She had to leave. She wasn't safe here. She wasn't safe anywhere.

Doc Wilson promptly knelt next to her and placed a wet rag over her nose and mouth. It smelled sweet, almost like a ripe pear. Elizabeth tried to fight him. She wasn't sure it was from the pain in her head, the fear in her heart, or from what she just inhaled; but regardless, blackness won. She lost the battle as the medicine entered her lungs, and she slid straight into oblivion.

Elizabeth stirred on the unfamiliar bed. Opening her eyes, she looked around the room. Her head no longer throbbed and the room no longer spun. Sitting, her mid-section hurt like the devil. Looking down, her ribs were wrapped in a stark white cloth and a look in the mirror showed that her face was bruised and swollen.

It appeared she was in the same room she had been in after her fall into the river. Why was she at the doc's office? She was in a nightgown, but it wasn't hers. Wondering what happened, she tried to stand, but her legs shook from fatigue. She sank back onto the bed, thinking hard.

As she tried to remember what happened, it rushed back. He had grabbed her, forced his lips on hers, and then hit her when she bit him. Where was he? Where was her pa? She couldn't stay here. What was she going to do? Could her pa still force her to marry Mr. Wells? She didn't think so but she didn't know for sure. She could take her horse, leave, and run until she was safe. But where would that be? She had nowhere to go, no money, and no way to support herself. Despair rippled through her. Her life was over. Her pa would beat her again if she didn't marry Mr. Wells, of that she was certain.

Maybe she could try to change his mind, but she knew her pa had other plans. He wanted the money Mr. Wells had offered him and he was determined to get it. She couldn't convince him months ago. Why would now be any different? If they'd been searching for her, there was no way he would let her walk away from this marriage. If only they hadn't found her.

A knock sounded at the door. She took a deep breath and said, "Come in."

The door opened and Janie peered inside, her face filled with concern. "How are you feeling?"

"Alright, I guess."

"How's your head? Does it still hurt? Are your sides hurting?" Though the questions came fast, Elizabeth could see the worried look in Janie's eyes. She didn't want to frighten Janie any further.

"My head doesn't hurt much, but it hurts to move. I got dizzy when I tried to stand."

Janie peered at her more closely. "Can I help?"

"No... I, um, I just—"

"Are you worried about something?" Janie knelt and took Elizabeth's hands.

Tears filled Elizabeth's eyes and spilled down her cheeks.

"My dear, you've nothing to fear. The man who attacked you hasn't been seen. You're safe here."

Forcing a smile, Elizabeth knew Janie was trying to comfort her, but if her pa had his say, she'd marry the man of his choosing. Mr. Wells would return. Men like him always did.

Her future was over. She had everything to fear.

Twenty-Three

James slowed the horses in front of Doc Wilson's office. With any luck, he'd bring Elizabeth home today, but the joy in bringing her home would be shadowed by the bad news he dreaded sharing.

Elizabeth's pa had guessed at his involvement in the stagecoach robbery and James couldn't hide it. He had come to James's ranch and was threatening to tell the Marshal if Elizabeth didn't marry the man who had beaten her. Mr. Wells was a friend of her pa's, and the two of them had an arrangement. Nothing James said changed his mind.

Her pa's menacing grin sent chills down James's spine as he described the plans he had for his daughter. It was a stark reminder of why James left when Elizabeth had been nigh on a few years of age.

In the beginning, when his ma had married Elizabeth's pa, he had been hard but not cruel. As time passed, his struggle with liquor became all-consuming. He hadn't wanted to raise another man's child and tried to beat James whenever he had the chance. His ma tried to stop him, but he would raise his fist to her, and James knew he had to go.

Leaving his ma's side had been the last thing he wanted to do, but both of them were safer when he did. Unfortunately, their ma passed six months later. Elizabeth had been left with a pa who hadn't wanted a daughter, and James had gone down a path he never would have if his own pa had lived.

His steps heavy, he walked inside the doc's office and took a deep breath. Once he got her home, he'd find a way to tell Elizabeth what her pa's threats entailed.

James convinced the old man she'd be more amiable once she healed. It was the only way he could get the man to give him some time. The old man had agreed with a full bottle of liquor in his hands, and James prayed he could come up with a solution soon. He didn't want his sister forced into a cruel marriage. He'd rather serve time for his crimes than allow that to happen. The problem was, he didn't think that would stop her pa.

"James, it's good to see you," Doc Wilson said. He dropped a stack of papers back onto his desk.

"How's she doing?"

The doc grimaced. "Her ribs are bruised but luckily not broken. Her face is black and blue and will be tender for a few days. Don't react if you can. It'll keep her from worrying. Rest and plenty of cool rags against her face will help with the swelling."

James sighed. Her body would heal, but he wasn't sure about her spirit. Maybe between the two of them, they could come up with a plan. But deep inside his soul, he knew he'd likely turn himself in. He couldn't let Elizabeth marry a man who was twice her age and who had no qualms with beating her.

"Can I take her home?" James asked.

"Yes, but she'll need looking after. She's certainly welcome to stay here where Janie can watch over her."

"I appreciate that. I'll ask what she wants."

The doc nodded. "It's chilly this morning." He grabbed a dark blue sweater from his chair and pulled it on. "Follow me and we can see what she wants to do."

When the doc pushed open the door to Elizabeth's room, James had to contain his anguish. While he knew he hadn't caused the pain she was enduring, he wished he could have stopped Mr. Wells. James had to find a way to protect her even if it meant he went to jail. Sitting behind bars was better than her living a life with a man who had no qualms about beating a woman in the streets.

An hour later, James helped her out to the wagon. She hadn't wanted his assistance, but she was wobbly on her feet and needed a hand to steady her.

"Elizabeth..."

She held up her hand to silence him. "I'm fine."

"You are far from fine," he murmured. "He hurt you bad."

She avoided looking at him.

James lifted her into the wagon, trying his best to not squeeze her mid-section. She thought she'd be safer at home. He hadn't had the heart to tell her she had everything to fear. Although her pa wasn't at the ranch, he knew where they lived and would return within the week.

He placed a wool blanket across her legs. Although he wasn't cold, she shivered. He tucked it securely around her.

She placed her hand on his arm and squeezed. "Let's go home."

James slowed the wagon to a stop, every bump in the road causing her ribs to ache. The last few weeks had been rough. If she could lie in bed and forget everything, she would.

James said nothing on the trip home. She didn't know if her pa had found him, but if he hadn't, he was bound to show up soon. He was a snake in the grass, just waiting for a moment to strike. She didn't want to marry Mr. Wells, but she was afraid of what her pa would do if she didn't follow his wishes.

James helped her from the wagon. She took a couple of steps before her legs collapsed, but her brother was at her side and didn't let her fall. He lifted her into his arms as if she weighed nothing. Laying her head on his chest, Elizabeth felt protected and loved. It brought tears to her eyes. She loved him so much.

James climbed the stairs to the front porch. Her friend Susan waited for them, a loving smile on her face. She had rushed to Elizabeth's side when she'd been attacked in town and had promised to be there for her when James brought her home.

"It's so good to see you. Bring her inside." She clucked around them like a mother hen. Why couldn't James court a woman like Susan, who was sincere in her concern for those around her? She wasn't a classic beauty like Suzette but she was happy, kind, and never had a cross word to say about anyone.

James took her to the settee and placed her on the plush cushions. Exhausted from the trip, she wanted to sleep her life away. Susan bustled around, getting her a thick blanket and a plump pillow to make her more comfortable.

"Can I make you tea?" Susan asked.

"You don't have to fuss over me. I can make it. Just give me a few minutes to catch my breath."

"Nonsense. I'm happy to help. I'm so glad you're alright. Let me help you, please." She looked earnestly at Elizabeth.

Realizing Susan's need to help wasn't strictly for her, she nodded in acquiescence. "I'd love tea. Thank you."

Susan smiled and headed toward the kitchen. Shouting over her shoulder, she said, "I have chicken soup simmering on the stove and a thick loaf of fresh bread. It'll be ready for you when you are up for it."

James leaned against the edge of the fireplace in the front parlor, the sharp edges digging into his side as he tried to find the right words. Susan had left an hour ago, and Elizabeth had woken from her nap and had insisted on sitting on the settee in the parlor instead of in her bed. She tried to smile, but it fell short. He knew she was scared, and he couldn't blame her. He had to tell her what her pa threatened.

Decisions had to be made before her pa arrived. James didn't have the power to protect her anymore, and only one thing could —a husband. Unfortunately, she didn't want to marry. She made it known she wasn't interested.

"Elizabeth."

"James." They spoke at the same time.

"Let me speak first, please," she said, her woolen shawl held tightly across her shoulders. Her fingers gripping the sides.

Nodding, he waited.

"My pa. He's here in town, isn't he?"

He couldn't lie to her. "Yes. I spoke with him yesterday."

"He wants me to marry..." she gulped, "Mr. Wells."

He sighed. "Yes, but you don't have to."

"We both know that's not true. I'm worried he'll figure out your past. I couldn't let him do that to you."

Crinkling the brim of his hat, he shifted and looked at his feet. "He already knows."

"No," she cried. "How could he know? I shouldn't have found you. Now everything is ruined. It's all my fault."

"It's not your fault. Somehow he guessed and I was so shocked, I didn't deny it." He turned his head to look out the window for a long moment before returning his gaze to her, raising his hand to touch her before he dropped it to his side. "I'm glad you found me. Our ma..."

She stopped him. "We'll leave. Right now." She shifted to the edge of the settee and tried to stand but fell back against the seat with a whoosh. Her limbs were weak and she didn't have the strength.

"Elizabeth, it's too late." It was now or never. He had to tell her. "He said... he said if you don't marry that man, he'll let the law know what I've done."

"No, no, no." Her voice broke with torment. "I'm so sorry."

"You have nothing to be sorry for. I can't change my past, but I can help you. There's no time to waste. I have an idea."

"I don't understand. What could possibly save both of us from my pa?"

He took a deep breath. She wouldn't like the idea, but it was the only one that would keep her safe from harm. "You can't marry that man if you're married to someone else."

Startled, Elizabeth shook her head in dismay. "There's no one, and besides, if I marry someone not of his choosing, he'll be so furious he'll still turn you in to the law. I can't take that chance. You've given me so much. I can't ruin your future."

Stepping away from the fireplace, James sat next to her. He took her hands in his. "Don't worry about me. We can get you married to someone safe and then I'll disappear. I've done it before. I can do it again."

"I can't let you give up everything you have. It isn't fair. I'll survive." She let go of his hands and turned away from him. Her body was stiff, unyielding, as though she had resigned herself to a life of hell.

"Being married to Mr. Wells isn't a life," he murmured, hoping she would understand that anyone was better.

"Better for me to marry Mr. Wells than have you thrown in prison. You've been trying to change your life, do better, and I can't let my pa do this to you," she said, her voice cracking under the strain.

"Enough," said James. He put his arm around her shoulders and pulled her close to his side, being careful of her bruises. "I'll come up with something. Your pa won't be here for a couple more days. There's still time for a plan."

Twenty-Four

June 1893

B en rose before the sun peered over the mountains. His conversation with Stanley when he arrived weighed heavy on his mind, but before he could resume his life at home, he had unfinished business in Spring Creek. He couldn't in good conscience leave James without explaining why, and he needed to see for himself how Elizabeth was faring. He hadn't spoken with her after her ordeal and wanted to make sure she had suffered no lasting damage. His saddlebags were packed and ready to go. He hoped to be in Spring Creek in a couple of days.

Stanley wanted to leave, to find Connie, to bring her to justice. Ben felt the same way, but he didn't think Stanley had the physical or emotional strength to go after her just yet. They would find her and make her pay for what she did, of that he was certain, but not today and not until he returned to Thundering Mountain Ranch.

He convinced Stanley to stay until he returned with the promise he'd be home as soon as he could. Running away wouldn't ease Stanley's pain and guilt. He, better than most, knew that leaving family didn't solve your problems. He made that mistake and had paid for it in more ways than just the loss of his parents.

He wasn't close to his siblings any longer, and he wasn't sure they trusted him. His mind whirled with the responsibilities that weighed him down. He never imagined he'd become the head of his family this way, but once he wrapped up his business in Spring Creek, he'd be able to return and start the life of his dreams, one his ma would've been proud of.

Standing on the porch of his family's ranch, he could see Elizabeth sitting at his table, her dark brown hair cascading down her back, her smiling face gazing at him with love as their future children ran around, laughing and playing as they built a life together. Wait. He shook his head and his stomach seized. He had just pictured Elizabeth, not Suzette. Lusting after one after one woman while married to another would not do. He had to make a decision.

Giving his sisters a big hug, he promised he'd be home before they knew it. Wanting to say goodbye to Michael and Luke, he gazed around and wondered where they were when he saw them leading their horses from the barn.

"Where are you headed?" Ben asked.

"With you, of course," Michael said.

"I'll be fine. I don't need you to come with me," Ben said.

"You aren't the only one who left Spring Creek with unfinished business," Luke said.

"Besides, I want to check on Elizabeth, make sure she's alright from her ordeal with the river. We left so fast, I didn't have time to talk to her," Michael said.

He gave his sisters another quick hug. Stanley had stepped outside, his arm still in a sling but his back straighter. Confessing what his wife had done appeared to have lifted a burden from his shoulders. He looked more like the younger brother he had left behind. "Take care of 'em, Stanley. I'll be back soon."

~

They rode into Spring Creek after a long few days of traveling. They had moved as quickly as they dared. Ben was saddle sore, and eager to see and speak with Suzette. He wanted to share everything with her. Michael and Luke didn't have the same urgency, but they followed his lead.

He stopped at the General Store so he could pick out a gift for her, something special. Since he had left with no warning and hadn't told her where he was going or why, he wanted to make it up to her. Bouncing up the steps, he headed inside the wide doors. He saw the storekeeper and smiled. "Mr. Crockitt. It's good to see you."

"Mr. Seymour. Welcome back. I hope all's well?" he said, straightening from behind the long counter.

"It's good now. Thanks for asking," Ben replied, not wanting to give too many details. His family's problems were not something he shared with just anyone. "It seems awfully quiet around town."

"There was some real excitement earlier this week."

"Should I be concerned?" Ben asked.

"No, except..." Mr. Crockitt leaned against the counter and waved Ben closer as though he had a secret he had to be careful of sharing. "I'm not one prone to gossip, mind you, but Doc Wilson's sister-in-law caused quite a ruckus and Miss Eliza—"

"Oh?" Ben said, interrupting. "What happened with Suzette?"

Mr. Crockitt's eyes widened with glee, and he practically salivated at the telling. "Her parents came to town. They were planning on taking her back East to marry her off, so she took matters into her own hands. She ran off with that Mr. Breckenridge."

"Wait, what did you say?" Ben's voice cracked as he swallowed the bile that rose in the back of his throat.

"Are you alright?" Mr. Crockitt asked, looking at him as though he had lost his marbles in a game of chance.

"Yes, yes, I'm fine," he said, his voice curt. "Suzette wouldn't have done that. Are you sure you have that right?"

"As sure as I am of standing here," Mr. Crockitt said, stepping away from the counter and wiping some dust off the countertop. "She and that dandy left on the train and haven't been seen since. Her parents were mortified and left in a huff."

Ben thanked Mr. Crockitt and turned to leave. He brushed past Michael, pushing him to the side in his haste to leave the store.

"Ben, what's wrong?" Michael said, but Ben ignored him as he strode across the dirt road. He reached the doc's door and pounded on it. A few moments later, Doc Wilson opened it and his eyes widened.

"You heard?" he said.

"Yes," Ben said, frustration and anger curling inside him like a fiery flame. "What happened?"

"Come inside. I'll explain."

Ben sat in disbelief as Doc Wilson and Janie explained how Suzette's parents had come to town, bringing a suitor with them. The man had bailed Suzette's parents out of the poorhouse with the promise of Suzette's hand. However, Suzette had her own mind and instead ran off with Mr. Breckenridge. She left a note saying she had fallen in love and they'd marry at the next stop.

Ben's heart shattered at the realization he'd never hold Suzette in his arms. The dreams he had were gone. It should've been a good day, a day of celebration. Instead, it was far from that. All his plans of having the ladylike Suzette as his wife had gone up in smoke.

As the doc finished, he mentioned that the confusion over the attack on Elizabeth was what allowed Suzette to slip out unnoticed.

"I'm not sure I understand what happened while I was gone."

"You haven't heard? I assumed James told you."

"I haven't made it to the ranch yet. We stopped at the General Store first. I wanted to get something for..." He shook his head in dismay. "When I talked to Mr. Crockitt, he mentioned Suzette disappeared, and I came straight here. What happened to Elizabeth?"

"The poor girl was attacked and beaten up quite badly," Janie said as she reached for her husband's hand and squeezed.

"By who? Is she alright?"

Sharing a glance with the doc, she said, "Yes, she'll recover, but she's hurting and has a number of bruised ribs. Unfortunately, her father believes that the man, a Mr. Wells, is a good fit for his daughter. He's been telling everyone in town how Mr. Wells is going to be her husband, that it was a misunderstanding, that she attacked Mr. Wells, and he was only defending himself." Janie's voice brokered the disgust she felt.

"Why would he want a man like that for his daughter?" Ben asked.

"No one knows, and speculation is rampant. We're hoping Elizabeth can convince her father otherwise, but it's not looking promising," Janie said.

"I don't know what to say."

"Nothing anyone can do, I'm afraid. She's of age, but we think she'll end up marrying him. The wedding's set for a week from today," Doc Wilson said.

"Maybe James can talk to their pa—" Ben said.

"Oh, it doesn't appear they have the same pa. From what her pa was saying, he doesn't think highly of James. Said James isn't what everyone thinks he is," Doc Wilson said.

"I wonder what he means by that," Ben said.

"No one knows and the gossip, as you can imagine, has been flying," Janie said. "I... Well, Ben, I'm sorry about my sister. I know you had feelings for her and as much as I love her, I'm not sure you could've made her happy."

"I'm not sure I understand," Ben said as he stiffened with unease.

"Can I be perfectly blunt with you?" Doc Wilson said.

Ben nodded.

"Suzette wanted the world and was very much focused on money. My in-laws spoiled her and gave her everything she wished for until she pushed them too far and they sent her here." Doc Wilson paused and shared a look with Janie before continuing. "Not to put too fine of a point on it, but she wouldn't have settled for a life with a ranch hand. Not that being a ranch hand ain't a fittin' occupation, but she wanted money and lots of it."

Ben stiffened. He was sure they just misunderstood her. Family rarely understood the true meaning behind one's actions. His own pa hadn't understood his need to leave home and see the world. Perhaps it was the same thing with Suzette. "Doc, that's the funny thing. I inherited my pa's ranch. It's a long story, but I could have given her that life."

"You might've been able to, but I'm not sure she would've made you happy," Doc Wilson said. "I admire you, Ben, but Suzette went through men like pieces of candy. She used 'em, played with their feelings. She was sent here with the hopes we could get her to appreciate the simple things. Unfortunately, we failed."

Ben was shocked, but if she married another, she no longer had a place in his life as much as it pained him. "I'm not sure what to say."

"Take comfort you weren't caught more in her web," Doc Wilson said, his eyes full of pity.

$$Twenty\text{-}Five$$

Ben, Michael, and Luke rode up to James's ranch. The wind whirled around them. With the dry conditions, it had kicked up a dust storm. Ben was glad they'd arrived before things worsened. The last thing he wanted was to get caught in a windstorm. Lightning strikes could be dangerous.

The work had grown while they were gone. James had also gained more horses, and a few more heads of cattle roamed in the pasture. He met them at the entrance to the barn, his face covered with a kerchief, and his hat pulled down low.

Ben pulled his horse to a stop and took a second look. Something tickled the back of his mind, but before the thought took hold, James pulled the kerchief from his face. "Boys, it's good to see you. I hope you found everything alright at home?"

"It is now. We have much to tell you," Michael said.

"Bring the horses on back. The wind's been brutal the past few days. I'm sure they need feed and water. Let's get 'em settled first."

Later, Ben explained what had happened over the last month at what was now his ranch.

"It'll be hard to see you go," James said.

"About that. Not too sure I'm leaving," Michael said. "That is, if you're alright with my staying."

James nodded. "I've gotten used to you." He winked. "So I'd be mighty appreciative if you'd stay. I'd understand if you needed to leave, though."

"Since we're being honest," Luke said. "I'm staying as well."

Startled at this announcement, it took Ben a moment for him to realize that neither of his brothers were coming home with him. Things were spiraling out of control. Not only had he lost Suzette, he was losing his brothers as well.

Michael's eyes darted to Ben. "Didn't mean to spring this on you, Ben, but I've been pondering it for some time."

"I don't know what to say. I didn't expect this," Ben said. "But I can't stop you. You're both grown men. Just know that you're always welcome back home."

"I'll be back, don't you worry about that," Luke said. "Thundering Mountain Ranch will always be my home, but for now," he turned back to James, "from the looks of it we came back just in time. You've increased your stock and likely could use the help."

"The cattle arrived while you were gone. I got lucky when rounding up the horses. I caught the stallion, and the rest followed. It's gonna take a minute to get 'em broke before I can sell 'em to the Army."

"As long as you need us, we'll be here to help," Michael said.

Ben swallowed back a lump in his throat. This wasn't the end of the world, just a change he hadn't expected. It was only a few days' ride to see them. It wasn't as though they lived on the other side of the country. They could always write letters, send telegrams. They weren't living in the dark ages.

"Boys, I'm hungry and I've got dinner on the stove." James gestured toward the house. "There should be enough for everyone."

"We'll wash and be up in a bit," Michael said.

James left the three of them and walked up to the house.

"Didn't mean to spring this on you, especially right now," Luke said. "But I—"

"No reason to explain, Luke. I understand. I can't expect you to come home just cause that's what I'd want."

"Thanks, Ben, I appreciate that. I know I was angry when we arrived, but—"

"I understand now why you were." Ben slapped Luke on the back in a gesture of love and friendship. He then stepped into Midnight's stall and picked up a brush.

"What happened with Suzette?" Michael asked. "You said little on the ride." He led his own horse into a stall and followed Ben's lead.

"Not much to say," Ben said. He avoided looking at his brothers. "She ran off with Mr. Breckenridge." With that, he finished brushing Midnight's side and placed the brush on the ledge outside the stall. Closing the doors, he latched it firmly. "Let's wash up. I'm right hungry and could use a bite to eat."

Resting against the back fence, Ben stood staring at the red and orange hues of light as the sun melted behind the mountains. His life had taken unexpected turns over the last few months.

When they had left Thundering Mountain Ranch, he thought he'd return to Spring Creek, marry Suzette, and then they'd head back to his pa's ranch a happily married couple. But he hadn't stated his intentions clearly enough to Suzette and had ignored her after the river incident. He couldn't blame her for going with someone who had comforted her instead of leaving her high and dry while he searched for another woman.

He also should've realized his brothers wanted to live their lives their own way. It had been so long since he'd been with his family, he made assumptions he shouldn't have. Running his hands through his hair, he rested his elbows against the fence, holding his hat in his hands, and shifting to get comfortable. His pillow was calling his name, but he wasn't ready to go there, not yet.

A door slammed and Elizabeth ran from the house. She wasn't looking where she was going and ran straight into him.

"Hey, there. Is everything alright?" he asked, holding her arms to steady her. His eyes widening at the severity of the bruises on her face. "Seems we keep doing this."

"Let go of me," she said, wrenching her arms out of his grasp.

"I didn't mean no disrespect," he murmured, stepping away from her and placing his hat back on his head. "I can't ever seem to say the right thing to you, can I?" His heart softened at the despair in her eyes.

Taking a deep breath, she wiped her eyes with her hands and sighed. "No, I'm sorry. I wasn't watching where I was going. I shouldn't have yelled at you."

"No harm done. Can I help?"

"Not unless you can convince my pa I shouldn't—" Gulping back sobs, Elizabeth covered her face with her hands.

Not thinking twice about it, he took her into his arms, being careful of her ribs. James had told them over the evening meal what had happened, not giving too many details, but enough for him to know things were not alright in their world. Between what both Doc Wilson and James had told him, he had a pretty good idea of what had occurred in town the last few days.

She cried harsh sobs for a few minutes, her face cradled in his chest. He rocked back and forth, whispering words of solace in her ear. It felt right to have her close to him. He had missed her and that surprised him. Eventually, her cries subsided, and she sniffled as the last of the tears fell. She pulled back and his arms fell away. He didn't want to let go.

"I'm so sorry. Didn't mean to do that. I've gotten your shirt all wet." She patted at the wet spots she had made on his chest and his belly tightened from her touch. The blood rushed to his ears, his senses sharpened. He had only meant to comfort her, but instead his body reacted in ways he couldn't fathom.

"It'll dry. I'm more concerned about you." He reached for her hands, needing to feel them, and held them loosely in his before she tugged them away. "Sounds as if things aren't going too well."

"If you mean having my whole life upended because of what my drunk pa wants, then yes." She brushed at the long, dark strands of hair on her face.

"Care to walk a bit? Maybe that'll help." The words came from his lips before he could stop them. For reasons that were beyond his grasp, he wanted to be there for her more than he wanted to be somewhere else. It wouldn't hurt to walk, or so he hoped.

"That'd be nice, thank you." A small smile lifted her plump, pink lips.

He had a sudden urge to kiss them.

She turned, and the moment disappeared. They walked along the fence line, not talking, just being together. She took a few deep breaths and wiped the remaining tears from her face.

"Thank you. I needed this." Her arms wrapped around her waist, and she frowned. "I'm sorry you had to see me this way."

"No need to apologize." He looked down at the grimace on her face. "Are you hurting?"

"Oh," she said. "Just sore from... Well, from the other day."

He nodded. If she didn't want to talk about what had happened, he had no cause to push her. It wasn't any of his concern and he'd be leaving soon, anyway. Best to not interfere.

"Going for a walk helps. I do appreciate it."

They continued to amble next to the newly constructed fence. Ben and his brothers had put new posts and rails up weeks before, and they still stood strong. He'd miss James's ranch, but Thundering Mountain was his future. He had ideas and plans to make it his own while being there for his family. What more could a man ask for?

The sun disappeared behind the mountains and darkness

settled across the valley, but the moon was bright, high, and full that night. It cast a glow on them as they continued to stroll along the path. The quiet was disturbed only by the sound of the dry grass brushing across their legs with each step they took.

Breaking the silence, Ben asked, "Are you healing? I don't want to interfere or butt in where I don't belong, but I was told a friend of your pa's hurt you."

"How do you know?" she faltered, surprised.

"Secrets are hard to keep in a small town," he said. "On our way back to town, I stopped at the doc's house. I wanted to, well... That doesn't matter. He mentioned you'd been hurt again."

"My body'll heal," she whispered.

"What can I do?"

"Why would you ca—" She stopped and turned to look at him, her eyes probing, searching his as if trying to determine if he was sincere or if this was another reason for him to hurt her. He couldn't blame her for thinking that. He hadn't been kind to her.

"I do care," he whispered. He raised his hand to his hat and lifted the brim. His hands shook, and he dropped them behind his back. He had said more than he should have. This woman was not someone he could spend the rest of his life with. She was everything he didn't want, and just because he had lost Suzette didn't mean he had to compromise his convictions.

Her shoulders dropped and her hands twisted in her skirt. "No, I don't believe you. Every time you look at me, you seethe with disgust. You don't think highly of me, and I can't say that I blame you. I'm nothing like the women in town and I'll never be."

She turned to walk away, but he reached out and stopped her, and gently turned her around. He smoothed back a lock of her hair, pushing it back behind her ear. Her head lifted, her lips opening slightly as though she wanted to say something. He stopped her before she could by placing a finger against them. She inhaled and stared at him.

He swallowed the lump in his throat. "I've been nothing but

unkind to you, and I'm sorry for that. You never deserved it. There are things in my past that, well, don't matter now. I'm sorry I hurt you. But I'd like to help, if you'd let me." His finger dropped away, and he stepped back. He had gotten too close and needed to put some distance between them.

She nodded, accepting his apology. "I appreciate the sentiment, but there's nothing you can do, unless you can convince my pa to let me marry anyone besides—" Her voice caught. Taking a deep breath, she said, "I'm sorry. I didn't mean to ask that. It isn't any of your concern."

"It sounds as if you've every reason to be upset."

"I'll live with it." Tension laced her every word.

"Is your brother alright with this?"

"No, but he doesn't have much of a choice."

Confused, he held out his hand and went to touch her forearm, but stopped. He had touched her too much already this night. "He hasn't been able to convince your pa?"

"He can't. My pa has information that could... could ruin his life."

"I don't understand. A brother should protect his sister. Seems only prudent."

"Don't judge him." Her eyes flashed. "I shouldn't have told you that. James would be horrified I mentioned it." She clasped her hands together and squeezed them, the knuckles appearing white under the glow of the moonlight.

"Anything you tell me, I'll keep to myself."

She paused and regarded him, as if weighing the truth to his words. "James has done things I can't, I won't let..." She took a deep breath and then continued. "He's trying to change his life. He's made strides by coming here and building a future. My pa... He knows things. I'm afraid of what he'll do if I don't do as he says. I can't do that to James. He took me in and cared for me. He didn't have to, but he did. Now everything he's built will be thrown away if I don't agree."

"I'm sure it's not as bad as you think."

"I wish it wasn't, but it is." She blinked back tears, her lashes dark against her pink cheeks.

"There isn't another way?"

"No. Mr. Wells offered my pa a large sum of money. My pa doesn't have much, and he's a drunk. He has me as a bargaining chip now... Now that he knows things. He's selling me to the highest bidder."

"What if someone else offered to marry you? Would your pa agree?"

"There isn't anyone else. James and I considered that, but we don't know anyone with that kind of money, and I couldn't ask anyone to do that. It's bad enough I'm having to marry someone like him. I couldn't do that willingly to anyone else." Her smile sad, she gazed at the sky. "It's a beautiful night, isn't it?"

The conversation was over. "Yes, it certainly is."

"Thank you for trying to help. I hope you have a better night than me. Good night." She smiled at him, though her eyes didn't share the same brightness.

"Good night, Elizabeth."

Ben stared at her as she walked away. His heart was heavy. He was saddened by what her future held, and it seemed unfortunate the situation couldn't be rectified. A few moments later, James stepped outside and walked toward Ben.

"Didn't expect to see you out here. Figured you'd be in bed by now, what with the long trip," said James.

"I couldn't sleep. Too much on my mind."

"That I can understand." James chuckled, although it wasn't a happy one. "It's gonna be quiet around here without you."

"I hope I'm not leaving you in a bad way."

"No, I understand, and since your brothers are staying on, we'll make it work. When you headin' back home?"

"Depends. Up to you, I suppose. I'll stay as long as you need."

"I can always use your help, but I understand responsibilities. I have plenty of those." An unreadable expression lined James's face.

Ben wondered if he should say anything about what Elizabeth had told him. He didn't want to break her confidence, but it seemed mighty strange James wasn't doing everything in his power to stop what was happening to his baby sister. He'd never do that to his own sisters. "It sounds as though it's been a mite stressful."

"Yep, something like that."

Wondering how much he should ask, Ben stayed silent for a moment before saying, "Elizabeth mentioned she's to be married against her wishes."

James scratched his chin and leaned up against the fence post. "Her pa's pushing the issue. I want to help, but I can't."

"Why not?"

A long silence followed Ben's question, and he wondered if he had gone too far.

Just as he opened his mouth to apologize, James said, "If I try to stop the wedding, then... Doesn't matter now. I want to help, but she won't let me."

"That makes little sense," Ben said but immediately backed away when James pushed at the fence and looked at him, a deep red fury lining his face. "I shouldn't have said that. It ain't none of my concern." He held his hands out to show he was of no threat.

James sighed and shook his head. "I can't blame you for wondering. It makes little sense. I should do more to protect her. Too many years between us and too many things have happened. It's all a waste. I'm sorry for it, more than you'll ever know."

"Is there anyone that could help?"

He laughed, low. It was hollow and filled with pain. "Not unless you know someone with money and lots of it. I don't have enough. My money's tied up in the horses and cattle. Even selling 'em won't be enough. I want to help her, I do, but I just don't have what he wants," he said, a crack in his voice showing the first bit of emotion Ben had ever heard from him.

"How much does her pa want?"

"More than I have or anyone else I know."

Ben thought over what James said and surprised himself by asking, "Can I speak with him?"

James looked at him in astonishment. "Why? He ain't nothing to you."

"Maybe I can convince him to change his mind."

"I doubt that. The man's a mean drunk and is using Elizabeth to his advantage."

"Perhaps, but I'd like to try."

"You don't have a stake in this."

"I know, and I don't know if I can help, but I saw the look in Elizabeth's eyes. She doesn't deserve this." Ben surprised himself with his words. He hadn't expected to feel this way, but what else did he have to lose? Suzette was gone and his brothers were living their own lives.

James held his hands up in surrender. "I guess it wouldn't hurt. Don't think it'll help, but you're more than welcome to try."

"Is he in town?"

"No, he's here, as a matter of fact. He just arrived to let Elizabeth know of his good news."

Ben grimaced. There was nothing good about making your only daughter marry a man who'd beat her in the streets all so he could line his pockets and fill his belly with more liquor.

"He's in the parlor with a bottle of whiskey if you still want to talk with him, but watch your step. He's a mean drunk and doesn't take kindly to anyone's suggestions."

"I'm not too worried about that. I've been around rotten people in my life. A drunk old man don't worry me none."

James shook his head, a rueful smile on his face. "Maybe you'll have better luck with him than I did."

Twenty-Six

Ben headed inside to find Elizabeth's pa. He didn't know what to say to the man, but he had to try. No woman should be married to a man who'd have every intention of hurting her. An older, scruffy man sat on a chair in the parlor with his booted feet on a stool. He looked like he had been run over and spit on ten times over. His face was lined with wrinkles, and his jowls were hanging prominently from the bottom of his chin. Elizabeth must've gotten her beauty from her ma as he didn't see a lick of her pa in her features. She didn't have a cruel bone in her either—unlike her pa, who was a drunk old man determined to ruin his daughter's life. A bottle of whiskey in one hand and a cigar in the other, he dropped his feet on the floor when he saw Ben. "Who are you?"

"Name's Ben Seymour. I work for your son."

"He ain't my son, just my worthless wife's. What do you want?" His words slurred as he lifted the bottle to his lips.

"I'd like to speak with you. If I may?"

Slurping back a drink, he waved his hands as though he cared little for what Ben did, the liquid sloshing over his fingers.

"Is there any more of that whiskey?" Ben asked.

"There's some over there. Help yourself." He put his feet back on the stool.

Ben went to the sideboard, grabbed a glass, and poured himself a whiskey. He then took a seat. "Thank you, sir."

"Don't thank me. Ain't my whiskey you drinkin'."

"Just the same, I appreciate you letting me sit here."

"Why you here?"

"Your daughter." Ben kept the words brief and to the point.

"What's she done now?" He squinted at Ben.

"Nothing, sir. Just concerned about her future, that's all."

"Nothing you need to be troubled with. I'm her pa. I decide what's best."

"I understand. You're looking out for her. A pa's duty and all that."

"Exactly," he said, lifting his cigar and taking a whiff before blowing out a thick cloud of grey smoke. "Glad someone 'round here understands."

"I just worry about men who beat their womenfolk."

"Doesn't hurt a woman to be smacked around a little. Gives 'em character," the old man said, chuckling to himself.

Smothering his disgust, Ben's stomach clenched at the thought of ever laying a hand on any woman. "Maybe a pat on her bottom, but beating a woman unconscious seems a little extreme."

"What a man does to his lawfully wedded wife is up to him," the old man said.

"Can't argue with that?" Ben said.

The old man grinned, his yellow teeth showing in the dim light. He took another swig of the whiskey straight from the bottle. "What's your name again?"

"Ben Seymour, sir. Yours?"

"George Winslow."

"It's a pleasure, sir. May I call you, George?"

"No skin off my back what you call me. Don't know you, so don't care."

"Well, George, the way I see it, Elizabeth needs a strong young man to take care of her, don't you agree?"

"Nope, she needs a man with lots of money to help pay off my debts. To care for me in my old age."

"It's a matter of money, then?" Ben had known the man wanted money, but it horrified him to realize how little the man cared for his daughter.

"Always a matter of money. He offered enough. I accepted."

"If someone else offered more, would you let her marry him instead?"

George cocked an eyebrow, looking at Ben carefully before responding, "I guess it depends. You willing to throw your hat in the pasture?"

"I could consider it," Ben said. No need to give the man a reason to believe he was too willing. If he didn't play this man's game, Elizabeth would suffer. At least as his wife, she wouldn't want for anything and he'd treat her with respect.

"Oh, she's worth it, I can assure you." George cackled.

"Never planned on paying for my wife."

"Never planned on my wife dying on me, either, so I might as well sell her to get my due. I always wished I had a son, to help me out and all. Instead I was stuck with *her*."

It was all Ben could do not to glower at the man. "Well, let's get down to brass knuckles then. What's she worth to you?"

Ben and George continued to talk long into the wee hours of the night. Her pa was a cagey old man who surmised Ben must be a man of substance and wrangled as much as he could out of him.

By the time Ben headed to bed, he was engaged to a woman he didn't love. He did care for her safety and well-being, that was more than most marriages were founded on. Elizabeth was going to be furious when she discovered what he had done. He wasn't looking forward to that conversation. He consoled himself with the fact that he saved her from a lifetime of agony and even protected James's secret, whatever it might be.

The next morning, Elizabeth woke to her pa hollering, "Get out here, girl. I ain't waiting all day."

Slipping her wrapper on, she found her slippers and stumbled into the parlor. She stopped and wrapped her arms tight around her waist as she saw James and Ben standing in front of the fireplace. Her pa was sitting like a king on his throne. She should have dressed, but she hadn't expected company.

"Yes, Pa."

"There's been a change in plans."

She waited to hear what he had to say.

"You won't marry Mr. Wells."

A rush of relief poured through her. "Oh, Pa, thank you! Can I stay here then?"

"No," her pa said.

"But—"

"No buts. You're going to marry that there Ben Seymour instead." His long, pointy finger aimed straight at Ben.

"What?" Her head swiveled to Ben, but he avoided her eyes, instead looking at her pa with an unreadable expression.

"He's agreed to marry you. We came to an arrangement."

Elizabeth was shocked. Ben would never agree to marry her. He was in love with Suzette. It made no sense.

"Ben's offering you a better future than the one you could've had," James said.

"But he's been courting Suzette."

"Don't worry none about that," Ben said. "I'm happy with my choice."

"But I'm not."

James moved from the fireplace, took her hands, and whispered harshly in her ear. "Do you want to marry Mr. Wells?"

"No, but I can't ruin Ben's life just to save mine," she hissed. Not to mention she didn't want to be with a man who couldn't stand her and constantly compared her to Suzette, as though she were some perfect standard every woman should live up to.

James sighed. "He's offered for you and he's the best chance you've got. If you don't agree, your pa will marry you to Mr. Wells and he'll... well, never mind that."

"But—"

"But nothing, Elizabeth." James's gaze was direct, saying more than his words.

Shoulders slumping, she turned to Ben. "You don't have to do this."

"I know, but I agreed," Ben said.

"I don't—"

"Enough. I've decided. You're to marry Mr. Seymour," her pa interrupted. "If you don't, you know what'll happen."

Once again, a man had decided her future. The bright side was she wouldn't have to marry Mr. Wells. The downside was she was marrying a man who wanted someone else.

Twenty-Seven

On the day of her wedding, Elizabeth had a heart full of conflicting emotions. This was not how she had imagined her future. Ben didn't think she was a lady. He was only marrying her out of obligation to her brother. Ben wouldn't hurt her, but he didn't love her.

She needed to stop brooding over her future. It didn't matter. Her pa was only keeping James's secret if she married Ben. She would protect it, no matter what.

In a few brief hours, she would be Mrs. Ben Seymour. Lying in bed, she stared at the ceiling and wondered what that would be like. A loud rap on the door startled her. She sat, pulling the blankets to her chest.

"Come in," she said, her voice uncertain.

The door opened, and Susan peeked around the corner. "I hope I didn't wake you," she said. "May I come in?"

"I was awake. Come in." Elizabeth smiled.

Susan opened the door wide. Her arms were full of frilly, frothy dresses in a variety of colors. "Isn't this exciting? You're getting married today." Susan's cheeks were rosy, and her lips lifted wide from her grin. "I know we had little time to plan your wedding, but I've collected a few dresses for you to pick from. I'm hoping you'll love one of them. You're going to look lovely."

Elizabeth wanted to scowl, but Susan didn't know this wasn't Elizabeth's choice. She couldn't explain what was behind the quick wedding to a man who had paid her no mind. "Thank you. I appreciate your thoughtfulness."

Susan dropped the dresses on Elizabeth's bed and clapped her hands together. "Now, let's get started. There are seven of them."

"That's a lot." Elizabeth wrinkled her nose. Every girl wanted to look beautiful on their wedding day, but that was about six dresses too many to try on. Digging deep to garner enthusiasm, Elizabeth tried to look delighted.

Susan held up a dark burgundy dress with white lace around the collar. "What do you think of this one?"

It was a stunning gown and she reached to touch the fabric, her fingers lingered on the silk. "It's lovely. Nicer than any dress I've ever owned."

"Let's see what you think."

An hour later, Elizabeth had tried on the dresses. They decided the first one, the burgundy dress, was what she'd wear as she walked down the aisle. It was the only one that truly made her feel beautiful. It was loose in the waist and snug across her chest, but with a few minor adjustments, Susan was confident it would be stunning. Susan pinned it and took it from her.

"I'm going to return to town and have my mother alter it. We'll see you at the church in a few hours. I'll have it waiting for you."

Giving Susan a hug, Elizabeth tried to hold back the tears and swallowed back the lump in her throat. "Thank you so much for doing this."

"I'm so happy for you. Ben's a good man and well respected. You're going to have a wonderful life."

"I hope so."

Susan squeezed Elizabeth's hand. "Now, let me skedaddle, so I can get this altered. I'll see you at the church." She gathered the dresses and left.

Elizabeth sat on the bed, exhausted from trying to appear happy, when another knock sounded on her door.

"Elizabeth?" It was James.

"Yes."

"Can I come in?" he asked.

"Of course."

He opened the door and stood in the doorway, hesitating. "Susan just left."

"I know."

"She was excited this morning." He shoved his hands into the back pockets of his trousers, his eyes skittish looking everywhere but at her.

"Yes, she was."

"Did you like any of the dresses?" He removed his hands from his pockets and then rested against the door, his arms folded at his chest. He appeared uncomfortable and likely as miserable as she.

Wanting to make this as easy on him as she could, she forced a smile. "Yes. We decided on one of them. She's taking it to her mother to alter it so it'll fit better."

"That's good. Are you ready for today?"

"As ready as someone heading to a loveless future." The words flew past her lips before she could stop them. She cringed at how ungrateful she sounded.

Before she could apologize, he said, "Ben's a good man. He'll take good care of you."

"I don't need a man to take care of me." She's raised her chin and pursed her lips.

"I know you think that, but I'm positive you'll be happy."

"I wish I was as confident as you."

"Maybe you should look at this differently. I know this isn't what you wanted, but it could be worse. Ben's providing you a home, a safer and happier home than what you would've had if he hadn't stepped in."

"But why did he do that? I still don't understand."

"It surprised me too, but he's willing to protect you. I believe that says a lot about him."

James's future was on the line, and she couldn't ruin it for him. If she had never found him, he wouldn't be in this predicament. "I hope so, but everything's happened so fast." She wanted to believe that her future was brighter but it was hard when she hadn't been given a choice.

"I wish you could have everything you've ever wanted, but Ben's heart is in the right place. He'll give you a good home and will treat you right."

A few hours later, Elizabeth stepped outside and found a tall, black carriage led by two magnificent black geldings, their tails swishing. The carriage's brass fittings gleamed under the bright sun, and Michael stood next to it with a beaming smile. She was still sore from her bruised ribs, but he was gentle as he held her hand and helped her into her seat. Her hands shook and she tried to hide them in the folds of her skirt.

As the carriage rumbled down the dirt road toward town, she turned and looked around at what she was leaving behind—the ranch house she and James had repaired together, the fence posts and railings she had helped to secure, the bunkhouse where they had slept those first few weeks. She might not have had much time with her brother, but the time they had would be held securely in her heart.

Before she knew it, they'd arrived at the church. Wagons and horses filled the meadow, and Elizabeth wondered if another event was happening. She wanted to get this over with and quick and didn't want to have to wait for another ceremony to end.

Michael led her to the pastor's inner sanctuary, where he left her in Susan's capable hands. Susan helped her into the dress, which fit her curves as though Susan's mother had sewn it for her. With magical fingers, Susan took her straight hair and created an elaborate updo, even getting a few strands to curl around her face. She placed a delicate veil on her head. Finally, Susan held up a mirror.

Elizabeth was in awe at the vision in front of her. *Is this really me?* She hadn't ever looked as pretty as she did in that moment. Her heart raced and she began to sweat, droplets forming on her forehead. She had to leave. This wasn't right. She turned to run, but Susan stopped her with one question. "Are you ready?"

She stood, quiet. What was she doing? She couldn't leave. She had to protect James. She took a deep breath and let it out slowly. "As ready as I'll ever be. Thank you for... for everything."

"Of course, it was my pleasure." Susan beamed, took her hand and led her through the hallway to the vestibule in front.

"Where are we going? I thought we were saying our vows in the pastor's office."

"No, not today." Susan smiled, a twinkle to her eye. "We are going to the chapel."

Elizabeth glanced through the open doors and was surprised and dismayed that so many people were sitting in the pews. Turning to Susan, Elizabeth whispered, "Why are all these people here?"

"They're here for you."

"But why?"

"Everyone's happy for you." Taking her veil, Susan lifted it up and over her head so it covered her face. "James told me what's been happening and what your pa's been doing. I'm so sorry."

Elizabeth's eyes filled with tears and she blinked furiously to get them at bay.

Susan smoothed back any wrinkles from the veil and placed her hands on Elizabeth's arms, squeezing lightly. "But you need to smile. Most everyone thinks Ben just swept you off your feet. There are a few who have questions, but not everyone saw what happened with Mr. Wells. Your Ben has been attempting to convince everyone you're in love."

"He isn't *my Ben*, and we aren't in love."

"That's where you're wrong, my friend. He is now and forever after *your* Ben." Smiling, she gave Elizabeth a quick hug. "Here is Milly, I'll leave you in her capable hands." Susan left them and walked inside the chapel.

Milly handed her a fragrant bouquet of wildflowers. "Elizabeth, we're so happy for you. I hope you like the flowers?"

"They're lovely, thank you." Elizabeth hugged her.

"When you're ready, just let me know, and I'll have the organist start the music."

James walked in, looking handsome in his black suit with crisp white shirt. His dark brown hair had been slicked back, and he had a string tie around his neck. He looked nervous, but his eyes twinkled when he looked at her. Elizabeth hadn't even known he owned such a nice suit. He was so handsome and she was lucky to have had him in her life even if it had only been for a few months.

"You look stunning," he said.

She blushed, her cheeks hot. "Thank you. You look just as wonderful. I almost didn't recognize you."

"Ready to do this?"

She nodded, her chest tight, her breath shallow.

The music began and James took Elizabeth's arm. "I truly believe this is for the best." He looked straight out to the congregation, his stance stiff, his voice cracking. "Ben will make you a good husband and your pa won't be able to hurt you again."

"I pray you're right." She took a deep breath, trying to ease the butterflies in her stomach and walked with James down the aisle.

Twenty-Eight

The wedding ceremony had been blessedly short. As soon as James handed her to Ben and Pastor Williams began the ceremony, her heart had pounded so hard she'd been afraid all those watching had heard it. She had mumbled, "I do," her voice cracking but clear. When it came time for Ben to kiss the bride, he leaned in and brushed his lips against hers. It was nothing dramatic, but goosebumps ran all the way to her toes. Their eyes met and a sensation that she had made the right decision pierced through her. Before she could comprehend what that meant, they were pronounced husband and wife, and the congregation broke out in applause. Elizabeth was now Mrs. Ben Seymour.

After the ceremony, their friends and family celebrated their union in the church's community hall with food and drink. It had surprised Elizabeth. She never expected the congratulations. It was difficult to pretend that their marriage was a love match, but Ben was making the effort and she didn't want to disappoint him.

As the evening wore on, Elizabeth's unease grew about what was going to happen that night. She knew the basics of what happened between a man and a woman, she'd been raised on a

ranch after all. She just didn't know what Ben would expect
from her.

He hadn't left her side all evening, being attentive to her. His
hand rested on the small of her back, his thumb moving back and
forth, sending small waves of awareness through to her skin. He
acted as a loving husband should. He smiled and engaged in
conversations with their friends, yet he was as much a stranger to
her as she was to him. Perhaps they could find their way to a
normal life, one filled with friendship and mutual respect.

As the evening came to a close, their friends gathered their
belongings and left, expressing their well wishes. Ben left her side
to retrieve her cloak and his coat, but was back within moments.

She thanked Doc Wilson and Janie for coming before turning
her gaze to Ben.

"I think it's time for us to say our goodbyes." He placed her
cloak across her shoulders, and she startled at his touch. His hands
lingered for a long moment before dropping away far sooner than
she would have liked. His hands had been soothing and gave her a
small measure of comfort that perhaps the night would end well.

"I need to say goodnight to Susan and thank her before we
leave."

He smiled. "I'll wait. Go find her and say your goodbyes. We're
staying at the hotel, and we'll walk over when you're ready." He
shrugged into his coat.

Elizabeth walked toward her friend. "Susan?" she asked, interrupting her conversation with a handsome young man who
blushed and scurried away.

Susan's blue eyes trailed after him for a long moment before
she looked at Elizabeth and smoothed back a strand of brown hair.
"I'm so glad you didn't leave without saying goodbye." Susan
grabbed Elizabeth's hands and squeezed them. "I hope you've had
a wonderful day."

"It's been very nice. I can't thank you enough for arranging
this."

"I was glad to help. I hope it was everything you could've asked for in your wedding."

"It was. Thank you." Giving her a hug, Elizabeth pulled back. "All of this was wonderful."

With tears shining in her eyes, Susan grinned at her. "It was my pleasure, now get. I think your groom's eager to leave." She pointed to the other side of the room, where Ben waited in his crisp black suit. His burgundy vest that matched her dress caught her eyes. She imagined it was all Susan's doing in trying to make their wedding a day to be remembered. He hadn't shaved and his thick beard was growing on her. The rakish look was absolutely mesmerizing. He was talking with his brothers and didn't appear to be in any rush. She still had time.

Giving Susan another hug, she left to find her brother.

"James. We're leaving. I just wanted..." She gulped back the lump in her throat. "Thank you for everything. I love you."

He pulled her into his arms and whispered in her ear, "I love you as well. Give him a chance."

She nodded, even though she wasn't as sure as he was, and drifted to her husband. As she stepped next to Ben, he reached out and pulled her gently to his side, his hand resting against her waist, holding her securely against him.

Michael smiled. "Welcome to the family, Elizabeth. Our ma would've loved having you as a daughter."

She blushed with pleasure at the thought that their mother would have wanted her in their family. "Thank you. I hope I can be a proper sister to you all."

"I have no doubt you will be," Michael said, grinning impishly.

"Have you said your goodbyes?" Ben asked.

"Yes."

"Good night," Michael and Luke echoed as they turned and left the church.

∽

Ben said little as he led Elizabeth down the dirt road. He was unsure of what to say, as he still couldn't believe he had married her. He didn't want Elizabeth to believe she was his second choice, but ultimately, she was.

They reached the hotel, and Ben held the heavy oak door open for her. He signed in with the clerk and received the key to their room. He had brought their bags over earlier and had requested the hotel have dinner ready for them. Holding her arm in his, he led her up the flight of stairs and through the hallway. Opening the door for room number twelve, he followed her inside.

Candles flickered, and the flames cast a soft glow across the room. Their dinner rested on a small table, and the aroma of roasted chicken and garlic potatoes filled the room. His stomach rumbled. He hadn't eaten and was pleased the hotel had granted his wishes. He wanted to give her a pleasant night to remember.

As he took in the room, the rose petals sprinkled on the large four-poster bed caught his attention. That surprised him. He hadn't expected that and was apprehensive of what it suggested. It was their wedding night after all, but he hadn't wanted it shown quite so plainly.

He cleared his throat. "Can I take your cloak?"

Her eyes were wide with fear, but she shrugged out of it and handed it to him. He couldn't help but notice the delicate, creamy skin above the neckline of her dress. The light from the fire sparkled across her skin and his heart raced. He should have expected it, considering his lustful thoughts of her since they met. Still he was unprepared for the feelings she invoked in him. His gaze followed Elizabeth as she wandered around the room. Her hair had been pulled up into a loose bun and tendrils fell around her long neck.

"Is something wrong?"

Realizing he had been staring, he said, "No, I was just thinking about—" His voice trailed off as she saw the bed. He knew at once what she was thinking, because he was thinking the same thing. They were now husband and wife. They would share that bed tonight. He just hoped it wouldn't be a disaster.

Elizabeth was nervous. Not wanting to stare at the massive bed with the white coverlet strewn with red rose petals, she instead walked to the window to peer outside.

"Are you hungry?" she asked.

"Yes," he replied. "I ate little. Did you have anything?"

Gathering her courage, she looked back at him. "No. Too many people wanted to wish us good luck, so I didn't have a chance. Did you do this?" She waved toward the table.

He nodded. "Would you like to eat?"

"Yes, that'd be nice."

Ben pulled out the chair for her. She sat. He pushed in the chair, his fingers brushing against her shoulders because he sat across from her. Avoiding his gaze, she looked at her plate. She didn't want to know what he was thinking for fear it would be regret and disappointment. Neither of them uttered a word.

Finally, Ben broke the silence. "Our food is going to grow cold if we sit here much longer. Let's eat."

She tried to laugh but it came out as a squeak but he didn't seem to notice.

Elizabeth dug into the food as it gave her a chance to ignore what loomed ahead of them. When they finished, it would be time for bed, a marriage bed that lay just a few feet away.

After some hesitation, Ben said, "We've never really talked so perhaps we should get to know one another before—"

A piece of potato caught in her throat, but she forced it down. "Yes, that is a welcome idea. What would you like to know?"

"How did you become such a good horsewoman?"

She smiled. "Pa thought I should learn. He was quick to get me on the back of the horse when I was young. I loved to ride and would watch others when given the chance. Before long, I became almost a natural at it."

Their conversation relaxed her as they shared moments from their childhoods. They'd seldom had moments alone to talk peaceably, other than the nights they were stranded in the cabin, so they took advantage of their unspoken truce.

As the evening wore on, the excitement and trepidation caught up with her. She yawned and tried to hide it, but Ben saw it. "Getting tired?" he asked.

"I'm sorry. It's been a long day."

"Yes, it has, and it's late. I suppose we should get some sleep. The next few days will be hard and long as we travel back to my ranch... I mean our ranch."

"Oh," she said. "Um, well, I should—" She was at a loss for words. She needed to remove her gown, but there wasn't anywhere to do that in private.

Seeming to sense her discomfort, Ben said, "I need to head outside for a moment."

She sighed with relief. She could remove it without his watchful eyes and be in her nightgown before he returned.

Pushing his chair back, Ben stood. "Is there anything you need while I'm out?"

"No, thank you."

"If you need me, I'll be right outside."

Smiling with relief, Elizabeth nodded but then stopped him. She realized she did need his help. "Ben."

"Yes." He turned back to look at her, questions in his eyes.

"I do... I need your help."

He tilted his head slightly, waiting for her to continue.

"I can't reach the buttons on the back of my dress. Can you?" She swallowed.

His face grew red, but he rubbed his hands on his legs and

came to her, not saying a word. She turned her back to him and he brushed away the tendrils of hair that had fallen across her neck. His fingers were cool against her hot skin. He quickly undid the row of buttons until he reached the last one at her waist, where he rested his hands for a long moment. Her skin tingled and grew hotter with every second. A part of her wished he would say something.

"There you go," he said and then stepped away. A moment later the door opened and closed with a soft click.

Breathing a sigh of relief, Elizabeth stood holding the front of her dress as though it were a shield of armor. She hadn't turned for fear of what she'd see. She knew he was going to see her in a way no man had ever seen her before, but she wasn't in an all-fire hurry to speed it along. She also wasn't naïve enough to believe their marriage would be in name only.

She loosened the ties of her petticoats, and shoved both the dress and petticoats down over her hips before stepping out of them. Standing only in her corset, shift, and drawers, she shivered as the cool air hit her bare skin.

Not wanting to lollygag and take the chance he'd return before she was in her nightgown and buried underneath the thick blankets, she looked for her bag. It sat waiting for her at the foot of the bed.

She rifled through the contents but couldn't find her cotton nightgown. In fact, most of the items were not familiar and looked new. Frustrated, she dumped everything onto the bed and found what appeared to be a nightgown, but it certainly wasn't hers.

It was elegant, the fabric soft and silky, but not something she would've chosen for herself. Her throat closed and she tried to hold back the panic that was threatening to overwhelm her. She looked through the items again, hoping her old cotton nightgown would be among the clothes, but it wasn't. Instead, she found a white envelope with her name on the front. She ripped it open and found a letter from Susan inside.

. . .

Elizabeth,

You have by now noticed the items enclosed are not what you had packed. I wanted your wedding night to be special and to start your new life out right. Please don't be alarmed and take this gift with the love that was intended. I have grown to love you as a sister. You mean the world to me. Ben Seymour is a good man and will protect you. You may not realize it now, but over time, you will see that he will be the best husband you could ever ask for.

With all of my love,

Susan

Holding the letter to her chest, she was overcome with love for her friend. Her heart exploded at all she had found in Spring Creek. It was sweet of her to give her this gift. All the items in the bag were of the finest quality. The dress was made of a dark velvet green with hints of gold threading woven throughout, and the undergarments were created with the finest silk. There were two new skirts and shirtwaists, some new boots, and a pretty set of slippers that matched the dress.

But the nightgown. The nightgown, if that was what she'd call it, was indecent. It was made of a sheer, thin material that left little to the imagination. She might as well be naked for all it covered. Small straps held the top of the bodice, and the silk pleated where her breasts would sit. A thin, pink ribbon was woven along the top with tiny pink and yellow rosettes scattered throughout. The skirt was long, essentially translucent, and flowed delicately to the floor.

She didn't want Ben to think she was a woman of loose morals for who else would wear something so indecent? Groaning, she shivered but was resolved. She had to wear it; she wasn't going to bed without at least something on. Stuffing the rest of the items back into the bag, she removed the rest of her clothing and threw on the nightgown.

By the time Ben returned, only a few candles remained burning, and she was buried under the blankets. She trembled with fear, anticipation, dread, and excitement. The jumble of emotions made her want to hide, but there was nowhere to go.

Twenty-Nine

Elizabeth stretched her arms above her head. She'd slept little, but it had been worth every missed minute of sleep. She didn't have the words to describe what had occurred between her and Ben. He generated emotions in her she didn't even know she possessed, Nothing had prepared her for what had happened the night before. He had been so sweet, so gentle, yet passionate and exciting. Closing her eyes, she wanted to relive those feelings again and again.

The mattress shifted underneath her as Ben climbed onto the bed and kissed her on the lips. "Good morning, love," he said.

Opening her eyes, she looked at him. She wanted to reach and pull him to her but hesitated. Even though they had an amazing evening, she wasn't sure his emotions would be the same in the light of day.

"Good morning," she whispered.

She blushed and glanced at the blanket.

He lifted her chin with his finger. "You don't need to be shy with me. I want to make sure you're alright."

"I'm alright."

"Would you like a bath?"

"Yes."

He scooted off the bed and came around to her side. Reaching for the blankets, he dragged them off her. Startled, Elizabeth tried to grasp them back, but it was of no use. He had removed them before she could stop him. She wasn't wearing a stitch of clothing and didn't want him to see her.

He chuckled. "You don't have to be afraid."

"I'm not afraid, I just... I—"

Before she could stop him, he put his arms under her legs and around her back and pulled her up into his arms.

"What are you doing?" she screeched, hitting him on the chest.

Surprised, he dropped her back onto the bed. "I'm sorry. I have a bath ready for you in the other room. I thought you'd enjoy it." His voice trailed away as his eyes raked over her.

The heat built in his eyes. Bending, he brought his head close and kissed her deeply. She could feel the fire he evoked all the way to her belly. She wrapped her arms tight around his neck.

Sometime later, Elizabeth lay curled next to Ben, her head on his chest. Her body floated. She didn't even know how to explain how she was feeling.

His fingers trailed across her shoulder and back, soothing motions that caused her eyelids to droop with fatigue. "It appears we got a little distracted."

Smiling into his chest, she nodded.

"We better get you into that bath. You're going to need it now more than ever." He lifted his head and gave her another sweet kiss. "I didn't hurt you, did I?"

"No." Red heat filled her chest and face from his questions.

Climbing out of the bed once again, Ben dressed. Elizabeth watched. She couldn't help herself. He was a handsome man, all solid muscle, and he was hers. Realizing she had stared too long and had dawdled long enough, she scooted to the edge, the sheet held across her body. He once again swept her up into his arms. This time, she didn't fight him, wrapping her arms around his neck and resting her head against his shoulder. She could smell him and nuzzled her nose into his neck.

"I can walk to the bath," she muttered.

"I know, but I want to make sure you get there safely," he said, a cheeky grin on his face. "Besides, it gives me an excuse to hold you in my arms."

Sighing with pleasure, she pulled his head to hers, her fingers tangled in his thick, soft hair, and kissed him. With deep reluctance, he pulled away.

"We can't keep doing that," he said. "At this rate, you'll never make it to your bath."

"And is there something wrong with that?" she asked, taunting him.

His arms tightened around her and his breathing grew heavy, but he shook it away. She grinned. Knowing she could evoke such a response out of him with just one look thrilled her to her toes.

"No, but we've much to do today, and you need to heal. You were an innocent, sweetheart, and I did hurt you, even if you don't want to admit it."

"Then," she murmured, "take me to my bath, my lord."

Thirty

Ben and Elizabeth left the hotel and returned to James's ranch. They were tempted to linger longer, but Ben needed to return to Thundering Mountain. He also wanted to get Elizabeth away from Spring Creek and her pa, who had cheered with unrestrained glee when they were pronounced man and wife. The money made him happy, but there was no love for his daughter. Ben didn't believe Elizabeth knew the finer details of the arrangement between him and her pa, and he preferred to keep it that way.

He'd considered going on the train, but Elizabeth told him she didn't mind riding a horse or sleeping on the trail. Traveling by horse allowed them more time together before reaching their new home. He didn't like putting Midnight on a train, so he was thrilled she had suggested it. Her bruised ribs were worrisome, but she insisted she'd be fine. The doc agreed she'd be alright if they took it slow. James would send her possessions by train.

When they reached the ranch, everyone was waiting to say goodbye. Elizabeth headed straight for her brother and hugged him tight.

"You look happy," he said, stepping back and holding her at

arm's length. His eyes looked her over as though reassuring himself
no harm had come to her.

"I am. Thank you for... for everything. I'm going to miss you."

"I'll miss you too, but it'll give me peace of mind knowing
you'll be safe from your pa." He wrapped her arm around his.
"Come, we have stew simmering on the stove. I thought we'd have
one last meal together before you leave... if you have time, that is."
He looked at Ben for approval.

Ben nodded. Elizabeth needed to have these last few moments
with her brother. It could be months before they'd see each other
again.

Slapping Michael and Luke on the back, the three of them
headed toward the bunkhouse to gather Ben's belongings. With
both of them staying in Spring Creek and Stanley leaving the
ranch, things were changing. He knew it had to be this way for
now, but at least his sisters weren't leaving. He prayed they'd be
fond of Elizabeth. Her unladylike behavior concerned him,
though. He'd have to school her on appropriate behavior and to
avoid cussing and wearing those awful trousers. No wife of his
would wear them. It wasn't proper and just wasn't done in polite
society. He believed Elizabeth could be a genuine lady if she tried
hard enough. The last thing he wanted was for any other man to
get a good enough look at her in those trousers. They made his
blood boil, and he'd not let any man glimpse what was now his.

Michael handed him letters to take home to their sisters and a
knapsack of food for their trip.

"I put fresh fruit and sweets in there. Thought Elizabeth might
enjoy them," Michael said.

"Thank you. I'm sure she'll appreciate that."

"Take care of her," Luke said. "She's something special and
you're lucky to have her." Ben eyed Luke thoughtfully. Was there a
hidden meaning in Luke's words? He wished he had the time to
analyze them, but they needed to be leaving soon.

Picking up his saddlebags, he placed them on Midnight and

tightened the straps on the horse James had given them as a wedding present. His tent and his bedroll were in place. He secured any loose fittings.

Turning to his brothers, he held out his hand.

Michael grinned and pulled him into a bear hug. "I love you and wish you the best."

Stepping back, he put his hand on Michael's shoulder and looked into his younger brother's eyes. "Take care of yourself. Don't be a stranger. You're always welcome at home. When you're ready, we'll build you a cabin on a parcel of the property that'll be yours. Pa would've wanted that."

Turning to Luke, Ben said, "The same goes for you."

"Thanks. We won't be strangers," Luke said.

"I'm counting on that." Ben held out his hand, and they shook. Luke wasn't as affectionate as Michael.

He tugged at the lapels of his coat. "I think it's time for us to leave. Let me go find my bride."

As he reached the stairs of the main house, the door opened and Elizabeth stepped outside. Ben sighed with relief. She wasn't wearing trousers. Maybe he could avoid having to school her on proper behavior. She was in a brown woolen dress, her hair pulled back into a simple braid, and an old brown hat sat on her head. Sturdy boots covered her feet, and she carried a couple of leather bags. Ben took them from her hands. James followed with her bedroll, which he attached to the back of her saddle.

Turning back to her brother, she gave him a tight hug. James held her for a long moment before letting go. She stepped back and kissed him on the cheek. Ben knew what it meant to leave your family, especially when it wasn't of your own doing. He'd be sure to let Elizabeth visit her brother often.

"I love you. Please visit when you can," she said.

"I love you, too," James said.

Helping his wife into her saddle, Ben turned back to James and shook his hand.

"Don't make me regret putting her in your hands, Ben. I'm depending on you. Make sure she's well taken care of. She deserves it."

Ben nodded. "I will. She'll never want for anything, I promise."

James waved goodbye. The ranch faded in the distance as they headed away and toward their future.

They traveled far that night before making camp in a thick grove of trees. Ben removed the tent and bedrolls, and led the horses a few feet away from where they'd sleep. As he tended to them, Elizabeth put up the tent and started a fire. When Ben returned, he was pleased at what she'd accomplished.

"Can I help?" he asked as she poked her head out of the tent.

"No." Her smile was wide, her eyes twinkling. "I've got it. I'll make us something to eat in a minute."

"I can do that since you've done so much already." He rifled through their food bag and pulled out slices of smoked ham, a loaf of bread, and a couple of crisp apples.

"Do you know if we have any coffee?" he asked as she crawled out of their tent. He handed her the food.

"Yes, there should be a small bag of it somewhere." She pushed a stray hair away from her cheek. "Do you want me to look for it?"

"No, I'll find it."

She sat on a log and tore the loaf of bread in half. He found the coffee pot and filled it with water before putting it over the fire. She gave him a piece of the bread and a slice of ham. As they waited for the coffee to brew, they ate.

They talked and shared stories as the sun dropped, casting a soft yellow glow across the valley. It was a crisp, clear night. Before long, the temperature dropped enough that Elizabeth headed to the tent to get warm. Ben put another log on the flames, cleared the dirt around the fire pit of brush so it'd be hard for any embers to catch, and joined her. They were both too tired and sore from riding to do more than curl up in each other's arms.

The next morning, they had a breakfast of biscuits and cold ham and broke camp. Elizabeth didn't complain or argue and followed Ben earnestly. She was as eager to see her new home as he was to get there. They traveled fast while taking care not to overtax the horses or further injure her ribs.

A few days later, they rode through the gates to the Thundering Mountain Ranch. Tall, stately pine trees graced the entrance and lined the edge of the lane for as far as they could see, with enormous green and blue mountain peaks framing it from behind. It was an impressive sight, and her mouth opened in awe. He was plumb pleased she enjoyed what she saw.

They headed down the lane to Elizabeth's new family. Waiting for them were Katy, Anne, and Stanley. Ben had regaled her with stories about his brothers and sisters while on the trip and hoped they'd be pleased she was his wife. She also appeared to be getting more comfortable around him.

"Suzette, welcome. We've heard so much about you," Katy said before Ben could stop her.

Elizabeth's face turned red with embarrassment as Ben frantically tried to wave his siblings quiet.

"No, Katy. This is Elizabeth. She's my wife."

"What? Elizabeth? I thought you were marrying Suzette," Katy said, confusion masking her youthful face as she misread their unspoken words.

"Hush, Katy," Anne said, elbowing her.

"What? I just thought—" Katy's eyes were wide with confusion.

Ben would have to do some explaining later, but not in front of Elizabeth.

"Elizabeth," Anne said. "Welcome to the family." Anne reached for Elizabeth's hands and squeezed them with affection.

"Thank you," Elizabeth said.

"I'm Anne and that blathering young lady over there is my sister, Katy."

Giggling, Elizabeth said, "Hello, it's nice to meet you."

"And over here is our brother, Stanley."

"Welcome," Stanley said.

"Come inside," Anne said. "You must be tired and exhausted from your trip."

"Not as much as you'd expect," Elizabeth said. "I enjoy riding and sleeping under the stars, so it was nice to be out for a few days. I could stand a good wash, though."

"I can definitely arrange that. We have a room made specially for baths. Pa built it for Ma. You'll love it."

"That'd be mighty welcome," Elizabeth said.

Anne took Elizabeth by the arm and guided her inside the main house. Ben was pleased that Anne was taking her under her wing. Maybe this wouldn't be a calamity after all. Despite the awkward introduction and Katy's confusion over mentioning Suzette, he was a mite surprised he didn't have a twinge of regret in his heart for marrying Elizabeth. It was a welcome realization to know that perhaps Elizabeth could replace Suzette in his affections.

Elizabeth woke a few hours later and studied the room she had been given. It was nicer than anything she'd ever been in before. The brass fittings on the door, the armoire, the tables, and chairs shimmered from the sun. The rug under her feet was thick and plush. Her toes sank into it. The window coverings were made of a pale blue velvet and gathered on the floor like a puddle of water, rippling and calm all at the same time. They matched the blue coverlet on the bed. The chairs in front of the fireplace were encased in a soft white fabric she was afraid to touch. Her room at

James's had been comfortable, but the room here was practically palatial. She was afraid to touch anything for fear she'd break a table or one of the delicate figurines that lined the fireplace mantle.

Leaving her room, she wandered through the hall. She wanted to find her husband. Her husband. She tingled at the knowledge that she was married to him. She hadn't expected to like him, but with every minute they spent together, her opinion of him was changing, growing into something she didn't want to lose.

All the doors were closed on the second floor, and she didn't want to intrude. She found the primary set of stairs and headed toward the sound of voices. The door was cracked, and as she went to push it open, she heard her name followed by Suzette's. Her hand hesitated as she listened.

"Elizabeth and Suzette are different as night and day," Ben said, his deep voice carrying through the crack of the door.

"When you left, you said you were planning on proposing to Suzette. What happened? Why didn't you marry her?" Stanley asked.

"It's a long story and started with Suzette running off with another man."

"Oh, sorry to hear that. But I still don't understand how you ended up marrying Elizabeth. You never mentioned her when you were here."

"In the end, it was the right thing to do."

"How so?"

There was silence for a long moment. Elizabeth knew she shouldn't be listening in on this private conversation, but she wanted to know why Ben married her. She knew he'd been courting Suzette, but everything had happened so fast she hadn't had the time to study his actual reasons, nor was she left with the choice when her pa demanded her compliance. She hadn't even asked why he wanted to marry her when her pa told her the plan.

She reached for the handle to reveal herself when Ben said, "It was her father. He threatened to marry her to a cruel man, one who hurt her in town while I was here."

"What?" Stanley asked, his voice incredulous. "How could a father let that happen?"

"He was interested merely in money and was selling her to the highest bidder."

"How'd you get involved? I'd always believed you'd marry for love, like Ma and Pa. Never expected you to rescue a woman, especially one you've never mentioned. I understand your concern for a woman whose pa has no care for her well-being, but seems unfortunate that you'd saddle yourself to someone even if it was honorable."

"It surely ain't a love match and not sure it'll ever be, but her brother hired me on and treated me well. I felt I owed him for that. Her pa was threatening to reveal a secret of his. I didn't want to see his future ruined because of a cantankerous old drunk with a vindictive streak. As to how I convinced him to let me marry his daughter... well, that was just a matter of how much I was willing to pay," he chuckled, sardonically.

"You didn't?"

"I did. It wasn't easy coming to an agreeable amount, but I basically paid for my wife."

Shock, fury, and dismay swept through her. Her fist flew to her mouth to cover her cries of despair, shame, and humiliation. She should've known he hadn't wanted her, nor her heart. He wanted as much as any man wants from a woman, and in her estimation that made him as lowly as Mr. Wells, only instead of a kick to her ribs, it was a punch to her heart. It took everything she had not to lose her vittles right there on the floor as the bile rose in her throat.

Ben continued, "I cleared out a good sum of our cash reserves to quiet him and..."

Elizabeth couldn't hear any more. She ran down the hall as quietly as she could. Furious and filled with pain, she didn't want anyone to see her crying. She was a brood mare going to the highest bidder. If it hadn't been Ben, it would've been Mr. Wells. A part of her had hoped Ben had offered for her because he cared about her, not because he wanted to protect James's secret. Instead, it was only out of obligation to her brother's kindness and to be a God-fearing Christian who takes pity on the helpless.

She wanted to guard her heart and never let him know her real feelings, but it was too late. She had fallen for him and fallen for him hard, but he didn't love her and never would.

Thirty-One

After a rousing dinner of laughter with Ben's family, where they'd recounted embarrassing and heartwarming stories, Elizabeth excused herself, claiming to be tired from the trip. As much as she had enjoyed listening to Ben's brothers and sisters, she could only contain her despair for so long. They told stories about Anne and Katy's escapades in the kitchen when their ma was trying to teach them to cook, then one about Stanley trying to kill his first deer. Instead, he had hit a rabbit and claimed he meant to hit the rabbit the whole time. The stories were told with laughter and a sincere affection for one another.

Her cheeks hurt from trying to smile. Once she reached their room, she wasted no time undressing and blew out the candles. She wasn't tired, but she wanted to be asleep when Ben came upstairs. She needed time to adjust to what his true feelings were after hearing why he had really married her.

She tossed and turned, trying to fall asleep. She was wide awake when he entered, but she closed her eyes and pretended to be in dreamland.

When he whispered, "Elizabeth," she didn't respond.

Not stirring, she slowed her breathing as he whispered her

name again. He sighed, and the bed shifted as he climbed in next to her. He pulled her to him, but she still didn't stir. Within a few moments, his breathing slowed and he was asleep, the smell of whiskey on his breath.

When she was certain he wouldn't wake, she lifted his arm and scooted out of the bed, away from him. She couldn't bear to be near him. It was too hard. Wrapping herself in a blanket, she curled up in the chair next to the window and held the blanket to muffle her sobs.

She needed to stop crying. This wasn't like her. She had been through worse, and this didn't even compare. She had a new home, and new sisters and brothers. It was time to appreciate what she did have. There was no time to be miserable or ungrateful. Staring out the window into the dark sky, she looked at the twinkling stars and before long, her eyes drifted close.

Something woke Ben. Reaching for Elizabeth, he found nothing but empty, cold sheets. He was alone. Sitting up, he rubbed his eyes and gazed around the dark room. The rounded shape of Elizabeth was nestled in the chair next to the window, her white nightgown like a lighthouse on a stormy night. A blanket she had held lay crumbled on the floor. Her small hands tucked under her cheeks and her braided hair laying across her shoulder.

His heart seized with feelings he couldn't identify. When he reached for her and couldn't find her, his mind raced with where she had gone and fear had furled in his chest until he saw her curled in the chair. His feelings were changing. She made him laugh and smile with her determination and grit.

Elizabeth didn't let him take care of her. Instead, she believed she could take care of herself. She hadn't complained about anything on their trip to his ranch, and in fact, had been downright thrilled to be on the dirty trail. The dirt and dust didn't stop her. She would halt her horse to admire the views and would jump from her saddle to look at a new plant or pick a wildflower to tuck behind her ear.

She didn't startle easily, even when they crossed the path of a bear. She pulled her horse to a stop, keeping as still as possible as the bear ambled along the riverbed, focused only on the fish for his afternoon meal. When it was safe to cross, she had led her horse carefully across the riverbed so as to not cause it to stumble or to startle the bear. No fear lined her features, and no sudden movements came from her. She was as different as night and day to any woman he had ever known.

Shaking his head in puzzlement, he shivered. The room was chilly, as the fire had burned low. She was bound to be frozen sitting there next to the drafty window. He went to her side, put his arms under her legs and around her waist, and lifted her to him. She was warm, and the depth of emotion he was having for her made him awkward and uncomfortable. He thought he had fallen in love with Suzette, but his feelings for Elizabeth were deeper than he first thought, like a hidden crevice on the side of a hill only discovered when the snow melted from the mountains.

She shifted in his arms and settled into his chest, but didn't wake. She must've been bone tired. Striding back to the bed, he laid her on the white sheets. Her long brown hair draped across the pillows. Grabbing the thick, blue blankets, he pulled them to her chin. Brushing the stray hair off her cheek, he smiled.

She wasn't a classic beauty, but when she smiled, her cheeks brightened and her eyes twinkled sending hot, flames across his skin. She needed work to become the lady of the house, and with patience and understanding, she'd become someone his ma would've been proud to call her daughter. Still a part of him wondered if he was expecting too much of her. Would he snuff out the joy in her if he took away the things that made her most happy? Or would his expectations only make her bloom like a rose reaching for the sun?

As he gazed at her, the sun peeked up over the horizon and streaks of yellow light crossed the room. The time had passed far too quickly. As much as he wanted to crawl back into the warm bed, cuddling with his new wife could wait. They had their whole lives together.

Thirty-Two

July 1893

As the days and weeks progressed, Elizabeth tried to settle into her new life. She wanted to be useful, but no one needed or wanted her help. Their housekeeper did the cleaning and cooking. Ranch hands groomed the horses, fixed the corrals, and managed the cattle. She couldn't even help with the garden, as the housekeeper's husband did that, and he didn't appreciate her opinion.

Instead, she spent her days sitting in the parlor looking out the windows or trying to read books, but they couldn't keep her attention. She was going crazy with boredom, and her frustration grew. She needed something to do or she'd scream.

After weeks of doing nothing but twiddling her thumbs and suppressing yawns, she'd had enough. She decided to go for a ride and explore the ranch, and she was going to wear her trousers.

Ben's opinion of her trousers was clear, and she knew if he caught her in them, he'd have a few words to say about it, but she was tired of being bored. She didn't want to anger him, so she'd wait until she was alone and slip out unnoticed. If he didn't see her, he wouldn't have a reason to complain.

Later that morning, Ben left her alone in the parlor, telling her he'd return in time for their evening meal. He was checking the fences on the north end of the property, and he'd be gone most of the day.

When the door closed behind him, she dropped the book she had been pretending to read and ran upstairs to her room. Slipping on her trousers, she tightened the belt around her waist. She dug in the armoire and found her old hat. She slapped it on and headed outside to the barn.

As she opened the barn doors, the fresh smell of hay hit her, and she breathed in the scent. She had missed this and smiled in gleeful anticipation. She found her saddle tucked in the tack room. As she finished tightening the cinch, the barn door creaked open. Peering around the stall door, she breathed a sigh of relief. It was only Anne and Katy.

"Elizabeth, are you in here?" Anne asked.

"Yes, I'm back here." She waved her arms.

She tugged on the horse's reins and led him out of his stall.

Anne's eyes flew open when she got a good look at her. "What are you wearing?"

Elizabeth glanced at her trouser clad legs and blushed. "Um, well, nothing special."

"You're in trousers. That is scandalous," whispered Katy, beaming, "but something I wish I had the gumption to do."

"Katy," Anne replied, shocked. "No lady should ever go..." Anne looked at Elizabeth and backtracked, "not that you aren't a lady, Elizabeth. It's just, well—"

Elizabeth grinned and burst out laughing. "It's alright. You're right. A lady shouldn't wear these in polite society, but I'm not in polite society. I'm going to explore the ranch, and I don't want to wear a skirt. These are much more comfortable." Rubbing her horse's nose, she pulled a sugar cube out of her pocket and gave it to him, his whiskers tickling her fingers. "I'm in need of a bit of fun."

"Can I go with you?" Katy asked.

"I'd love it if you came, Katy, but you might get bored when I go exploring."

"No, I won't cause I'm going to put on trousers, too. I'll grab a pair out of Michael's room. I'll be right back." Turning, Katy ran out of the barn, the door swinging in her wake.

"Katy, you can't do that!" Anne yelled. She glared at Elizabeth. "You can't let her wear trousers. It's... it's unseemly."

"Anne, I'm the last person to decide what she should wear. If she wants to put on trousers and come with me, she's more than welcome. And so are you."

"I... well..." Anne hesitated.

Elizabeth could tell Anne was struggling with what to do. She thought Anne was going to scold her, but to her surprise, she shrugged and said, "Why not? I'll be right back."

Ten minutes later, both Anne and Katy returned to the barn, laughing. They were both wearing a pair of Michael's old trousers. They'd rolled up the legs and found belts to secure them on their thin waists. They didn't waste any time saddling their horses before all three headed out to explore.

Elizabeth had missed the freedom of riding as though she didn't have a care in the world. Before her pa realized what she could do for him, he had let her ride unchecked and untethered whenever her heart desired. She had missed the movement of the horse's flanks under her thighs as she leaned over his neck and let him travel where he desired. The horse, too, needed the freedom that came from not having a man on his back telling him where to go and what to do. Her hair had come undone from its tight braid and flowed behind her, a tangled mess that needed the release as much as her soul had.

Elizabeth had shown Katy and Anne different plants and flowers, and even pointed out a rabbit she saw scurrying away from them. She recognized the foliage and could tell which plants were edible and which ones weren't. She even recognized a few poisonous ones and explained what the fresh animal tracks were. They dismounted from their horses, picked flowers, made flower crowns, and even laid in the grass and watched the clouds amble by.

When they headed back, Katy and Anne encouraged their horses to gallop just as fast, if not faster than Elizabeth, as they too experienced the joy and independence of doing what they wanted with no societal rules holding them back.

Neither Anne nor Katy had ever been allowed to explore as their father had worried. They wanted to see more, but as the sun dipped behind the mountains, they reluctantly returned. They had been gone longer than planned, and Elizabeth didn't want Ben or any of the ranch hands to worry.

They returned to the big, red barn, giggling as though they had known each other for years. Covered in dust and dirt, they each had wide grins and twinkles in their eyes. The three dismounted from their horses, and Katy and Anne had already entered the barn when the door to the house flew open. It banged against the outside wall with such force, it was a wonder it didn't fall off the hinges.

"Elizabeth." Ben hollered. "Where have you been?"

Uh, oh, she was in for it now. She could sense his anger burning from where she stood. Throwing her shoulders back, she stood her ground as he marched across the dirt. The dust billowed around him like a sudden and ferocious storm cloud.

"What are you wearing?" he asked, his face beet red with anger. His eyes raked over her from head to toe, and not with lust, but with a pulsating fury that should have shaken her to her core. In the back of her mind, she thought she should worry but she'd had too much fun today to worry about what Ben thought.

"I've been out exploring, and it's undeniable what I'm wearing," she said, her tone obstinate and challenging.

Sputtering, he said, "Did my sisters go with you?"

"Yes, as a matter of fact, they did."

"And they saw you in, in... those?" he said, gesturing toward her legs.

"Well, it's not as if I hid them."

"I can't believe you exposed them to this... this unladylike behavior."

"I guess you'll be angry when you see that not only did they see me in these trousers, they put a pair on too," she said. She didn't want him to yell, but she wouldn't bend to his will. He may be her husband, but she wouldn't be bullied. Never again.

"You didn't?"

"I did nothing. They wanted to wear them, and I didn't tell them they couldn't. I'm not their mother, and they're grown women. If they want to wear trousers, I won't stop them."

"I can't believe you paraded my sisters around the ranch where anyone could've seen them. Are you determined to ruin their reputations and their ability to make a good match?"

Anne and Katy chose that moment to step out of the barn. Their movements were hesitant as though they were afraid to confront their brother. They had surely heard his roar as he stomped toward her.

"Anne, Katy, get inside now and remove those... those things."

"Trousers," Katy said, her eyes belligerent as she stared down her nose at her brother. "They're called trousers. You should know what they're called 'cause you put them on every day."

He glared and pointed to the house. "Go inside and change at once. Ma would've been appalled if she'd seen you in those."

Alarmed by the fury in his voice, Anne and Katy ran past him and into the house.

"How dare you talk to your sisters that way? They only wanted to come along. They didn't know how you'd react."

"But you did." His hands were balled into fists at his sides. "It's not proper. No wife or sisters of mine will ever be seen in those."

"You have no right to tell me what to do."

"I have every right. You're my wife, and your behavior shall reflect as such."

Frustrated at his controlling attitude, Elizabeth brushed past him. He grabbed her by the arm and pulled her to a stop. She ripped her arm out of his hand, his fingernails scraping her delicate skin. "Don't touch me."

"Get back here. We're not finished," he yelled.

"Yes, we are. I'm done. When you want to act civilized, come find me. Otherwise, go muck out a stall or stick your head in cow dung, but don't come near me!"

She headed inside and up to her room, slamming the door behind her. "What an arrogant, overbearing oaf," she muttered. Throwing her hat on the bed, she sat on the bench, untied her boots, and yanked them off. The door to their room crashed open. Ben stood in the doorway, shaking with anger.

"Don't you ever walk away from me."

"I'll do what I want," she hollered.

He started toward her. She stood and threw her boot at him. He ducked as it sailed out into the hallway, hitting the wall with a loud thump. That stopped him for a moment, and then his anger intensified. He continued toward her, and she looked around for something else to throw, but nothing was handy. He backed her up against the wall. She had nowhere to go.

"Don't touch me!" she screeched.

"How are you going to stop me?" he said as he placed his arms on either side of her, trapping her. "I said, never walk away from me."

"Let me go!" She tried breaking the circle of his arms, but he wouldn't move.

"No, not until you learn you're my wife and will do as you're told."

"Not if I don't agree with it," she sputtered.

"Why can't you act like..."

He was always thinking of *her.* "Like who? Suzette? Maybe you should've married her."

"Maybe I should have. She was a lady."

"Of course, Miss Perfect Suzette." Her chest heaved with anger and pain. "You don't think she could do anything wrong, do you?"

"She never did."

"That's what you think?" She pushed at him, but he was a solid wall of masculinity that didn't move and as her anger grew, so did her desire, and she hated herself for it.

"And what's that supposed to mean?" he roared back.

"She isn't as innocent as you'd like to believe." Why did he believe Suzette was such an example of ladylike behavior? "She ran off with another man, for heaven's sake."

His face contorted with rage. "Enough. She has nothing to do with this." He stepped back away from her as though he could no longer bear to touch her. She shouldn't be surprised. All he thought about was his precious Suzette.

"Of course she does. You're comparing me to her. You think she can do no wrong?" She was furious and continued to rail at him. He couldn't continue to think Suzette was perfect. It was too much to bear.

"She did nothing to you," he said, his voice lowering in volume.

"Didn't she?"

"What do you mean?" He looked at her, confused.

"It doesn't matter. Please, just leave me alone." Her anger subsided, slowly being replaced with sorrow.

"This is ridiculous." He ran his fingers through his hair. "This has nothing to do with her. It's about you and what you should do as my wife. Don't bring her into this."

"You mean the wife you felt obligated to buy, is that it?" she sneered.

Shocked, his eyes opened wide. "What are you talking about?"

"You know. I heard you."

"You must've misunderstood me."

"I didn't. You paid for your wife." She placed her hands on her hips before waving them in front of her. "So, I guess you think you own me. But you got a raw deal if you believe that. Might need to ask for some of the money back from my pa." Hot tears burned her eyes. She kept blinking them back. She would not give him the satisfaction.

"Elizabeth," he whispered. He once again came close, trying to break through her defenses, but she wouldn't let him. He slumped against her and placed his forehead against hers. "You weren't supposed to hear that."

"Doesn't matter if I was supposed to or not, I did," she mumbled. "Now get away from me. You might have bought and paid for me, but you'll never own me. Please leave my room. I want to be left alone. And don't worry, I won't wear the trousers again."

"Sweetheart, let's talk this through."

"Don't call me that. I don't want to talk to you. Please leave."

"I'll leave, but this isn't over. We'll discuss this later."

He kissed her on the forehead, his touch gentle before he left her standing rigid against the wall. As soon as the door closed, she slid to the floor and burst into tears. What had been a fun afternoon had turned into a nightmare.

She knew he was against the trousers but didn't think he would've had such an awful reaction. And she got so angry. *He isn't worth it*, she told herself as she swiped at the tears, but they didn't stop. They rolled down her cheeks unchecked, soaking the top of her shirt. She cried herself to sleep right there on the floor.

∾

A knock on the door startled Elizabeth awake.

"Elizabeth," Katy said, her words muffled through the thick door. "Are you alright?"

Elizabeth pushed herself up and stretched, groaning with the movements. Her body ached from the tears and pain from her fight with Ben. She was filthy, exhausted, and her neck hurt from sleeping on the floor.

"I'm fine, Katy."

"Can I come inside?" she asked.

"Um, can you give me a minute?"

Elizabeth headed to the washstand, picked up a clean cloth, and submerged it in the lukewarm water. Wringing it out, she wiped her face, hands, and arms. She looked a fright, and her face was puffy, but it'd have to do. Running a brush through her hair, she pulled it back into a tight bun at the base of her neck. She tugged at her shirt before she opened the door.

Katy looked her over, concern apparent. "You haven't changed. He didn't hurt you, did he?"

"No, your brother would never touch me like that. I fell asleep before changing." Elizabeth smiled to reassure her.

Katy didn't appear to be comforted, however. "I don't want to overstep, but we heard Ben. Me and Anne wanted to make sure you were alright. He was harsh." Her eyes were filled with regret.

"I'm fine. We argued, but it'll blow over. I should wash." Trying to change the subject, she said, "I haven't missed dinner, have I?"

"No, that's why I came up here. It should be ready soon. Come downstairs when you're ready."

"I'll be down as soon as I change."

Katy turned. "I'm sure he didn't mean to get so angry, but he has these"--she waved her arms--"these notions based on what our ma taught him, taught us. She had this belief that all women controlled their fate, but the slightest misstep could ruin your future. Something happened in her past that she never talked about, but she was mighty particular about what a proper woman was and what she wore as though a skirt would protect our virtue. I'm sure she had her reasons, but they were unreasonable, especially in today's modern world. I mean, it's almost 1900. Things are changing." Her voice was hoarse and thick with emotion. "I'd never tell Ben this, but there are plenty of women on some of the nearby ranches who wear trousers while working with their husbands, and no one seems to mind. I can't understand why he is so against it, but I think it has to do with our ma."

Elizabeth tried to smile, but it was difficult. Her ma had never taught her much since she had died when Elizabeth was far too young to remember.

"I think he just wants to protect you," Katy said.

"I understand, Katy." But she didn't understand because in her world, the trousers had kept her safe. She never would have been able to escape her pa that last time if she had been wearing a skirt. The ability to run saved her when he came roaring out of the house, his bottle of whiskey in one hand as he tried to grab her. She had sprinted across the field to her horse and catapulted herself into the saddle. He had already beaten her once and if he had caught her, he would've hurt her permanently if not outright killed her. If she had been wearing a skirt, she never would have been able to run as fast. She never would have been able to sit in that saddle to get away.

Whatever Ben's ma had taught him was what he believed, and she would never change his mind on that. She'd have to resign herself to a life full of boredom as she sat in a frilly skirt, watching her life fade away all so Ben could have a proper wife.

Thirty-Three

Frustrated, Ben was at a loss. Elizabeth had said little to him over the past few days and had given him the cold shoulder every night since their fight. He had overreacted but didn't know how to apologize. If he were honest, his anger over her wearing trousers was due mostly to jealousy and his inability to control his anger. He didn't like that they showed every inch of her, but he also understood the practicality of them. Skirts could get caught on fences, trees, and shrubbery but she was his, and he wanted to keep it that way.

Between his jealousy and her overhearing his conversation with Stanley, their home felt like a freight train running down the tracks without an engineer. He also wanted to explain what she overheard, but she didn't respond when he tried talking to her. Sure, she was polite and nodded her head when he spoke, but she refused to look him in the eye and didn't start or continue any conversation.

He may have married her to save her from Mr. Wells and the secret James was trying to hide, but his feelings had changed, and he wanted to share that with her. He just wasn't sure how he could if she wasn't willing to speak with him.

He had a reprieve, though. Luke was coming for a visit. Luke had sent a telegram as he had something important to discuss with him. Perhaps the tension would ease with Luke at home. If nothing else, it would be a welcome distraction.

Luke arrived one night later that week, and after a nice evening meal and some catching up, the men headed into the study to have a drink. Luke had news to share but wanted to do it behind closed doors. Ben, Stanley, and Luke settled with tumblers of whiskey and talked of ranch business before Ben asked Luke why he had come home.

Luke sighed. "I'm afraid it isn't good news." He took a large swallow of whiskey, wiped his mouth, and braced it against the arm of the chair, his fingers fiddling with the glass. "They've thrown James into jail."

"What?" Ben said, the glass in his hands slipping onto the arm of the chair before falling to the rug underneath him. He sat forward, his hands braced against his knees. "What happened?"

"Elizabeth's pa went to the Marshal. He's claiming James robbed a stagecoach last summer and took a large cache of money and gold."

"Wait. The stagecoach robbery. I was there. I didn't see him but..." He sat back and thought for a long moment. There was one day when he had returned to the ranch and James's face had been covered. It had reminded him of something, but at the time, he couldn't place it. Now it made sense. "I couldn't see their faces before I was hit over the head," Ben said. "This must've been what they were trying to hide."

"You knew about this?" Luke asked.

"No." He sat back and ran a hand through his hair. "I knew there was something James had done but he never said what. My arrangement with her pa was supposed to keep James safe *if* I paid him the agreed-upon amount."

"Have you paid him?" Luke asked.

"I paid him half, but the other half was going to be late. I sent him a telegram two weeks past, letting him know it'd be soon. He must not've believed me, and now that I know what they were trying to hide, I'm not sure I'm too inclined to pay her pa a penny more. I can't believe I was party to this."

"What are you going to tell Elizabeth?"

"I don't know. She won't take the news well, and I wonder how much she knew. It might be better if I say nothing for now and wait 'til I discover more."

"Is that a good idea?" Stanley asked.

"Probably not. Things have been tense. This is only going to make it worse. For now, I'll tell her I must go back to Spring Creek to take care of unfinished business."

"Whatever you think is best. I just hope you don't regret it," Luke said.

The next morning, Ben knocked on Elizabeth's door—their door —before opening it. He didn't want to walk in unannounced, but he needed to talk to her without interruption. He'd been sleeping in a guest room the last few nights trying to give her the space she wanted. She had made it abundantly clear she wanted nothing to do with him.

She slept soundly and didn't stir when he walked to the edge of the bed. He stared at her. She looked so peaceful, and he hated to wake her, for when he did, the peacefulness would disappear and instead anger and frustration would reappear. She shifted on the bed, and the covers fell from her shoulders. She was wearing the sheer nightgown he liked so much.

He wanted to spend one last moment with her before he left. He sank onto the mattress and pulled her into his arms. Her eyes flew open and she pushed at his chest.

"Please, let me hold you," he pleaded.

She stopped fighting and stilled in his arms. Taking a breath, he inhaled her sweet scent. He wanted to remember that she smelled of roses with a hint of sugar and lemons. He knew he needed to talk to her, but he didn't want this moment ruined. It was an occasion to treasure.

Knowing it was getting late and he needed to leave if he wanted to catch the train, he sat and let go of her, his arms itching to hold her again. As she swung her legs to get out of bed, he touched her arm and said, "I need to tell you something."

She turned toward him, holding the sheet to cover herself. He wished her inhibitions were less around him, but one step at a time.

"I'm leaving for a few days. I'll be back as soon as I can." He shifted out of the bed.

"Is something wrong?" She snatched her wrapper, tied it close, and shimmied out of bed. She strode to the window and stood in front of it, her brown hair tousled from sleep.

"No, I just need to return to Spring Creek."

"I'll pack my bags and be ready to go." She made her way to their armoire.

"No need to pack a bag. You're staying here."

She whipped around like a goddess on a mount. "That's ridiculous. Of course I'm coming with you. Besides, it'll give me a chance to see James."

"You're not coming with me." He hadn't wanted to make things difficult, but she never cooperated or listened. "There are things I need to attend to, and it's better to have you here."

"What? No. Something's wrong. What is it?" she cried, her face growing red with anger.

"Nothing you need to be concerned with." He sat and pulled on his boots.

"If it isn't something I need to worry my little head about, why won't you tell me what it is?"

"Because I'm not going to."

"What are you trying to hide from me?"

He blew out his breath in exasperation. "I'm not trying to hide anything from you." He hated lying to her, but until he knew what was going on, it was best to keep her in the dark.

"Then tell me what it is," she said, her voice once again rising in volume.

Ben ran his hands through his hair in frustration. He didn't know how she did it, but she pushed his buttons like no one had before. "I need to do this. You'll stay here with Anne and Katy. When I get back, I'll explain everything."

"Why can't you explain it now?" She stomped her bare feet on the floor. If it had been any other time, he might have laughed at the picture she made.

"I don't need to explain every decision I make. You're my wife and you'll do as you are told."

"So, we're back to that again."

"What do you mean?" he asked, exasperated with her.

"Telling me what to do, like I'm a piece of property you've bought and paid for. Oh, that's right, you have bought and paid for me, so I must sit here like a good little girl and do as her master demands."

Elizabeth's face was red hot with anger. She was furious with him, but there was something so enticing about her, even when she was incensed with anger. Tamping back his urges, he tried not to smile, as he knew it would set her off again.

"I'm not going to argue with you, especially right now. I need to leave. I just wanted to say goodbye before I left."

She stalked to the window, her back to him. "You can leave, Ben. I'll stay here as your good little wife and wait for your return."

Annoyed, Ben wanted to shake her until she quit acting like a spoiled brat, but he knew that wouldn't solve a thing. He hesitated, wanting to say more, but he was afraid any words he said now would go through one ear and out the other. She wasn't willing to listen.

"I'll be back in a couple of days. We'll see if we can't resolve this as the grown adults we are."

She continued to stare out the window, not turning to look at him. He gazed at her back for a few moments, willing her to say something, but she didn't. Every time he tried to talk to her, he said the wrong thing and he wished he could fix that, but right now, he had to get to Spring Creek.

If he couldn't help her brother James, she would have more reasons to hate him.

Climbing down the metal train steps, Ben and Luke headed straight for the jail. Ben wasn't sure he could help, but he had to at least make sure James was alright for Elizabeth's sake. He was still stunned to discover that James had been involved in the stagecoach robbery. On the one hand, he might be responsible for James's current plight since he hadn't paid Elizabeth's pa as planned. On the other, he was angry because he never expected James's secret to be of this magnitude. He didn't want to be party to any criminal activity, and it couldn't appear he was involved. He had to clear his name with the Marshal first, before he could help James.

Opening the door to the jailhouse, Ben and Luke walked inside.

"Marshal," Ben said.

"Mr. Seymour." The Marshal stood and glared at him. His hands hovered above his guns, ready to pull them if need be. "I'm astonished you're here. Didn't think you'd show your face. I should arrest you."

Ben wasn't surprised at the Marshal's words, but he wouldn't admit it. "Why would you say that?"

"Sounds as if you knew who robbed the stagecoach. I should've trusted my instincts all those months ago when you claimed you were hurt. What happened? Did you slow them down?"

"I swear I didn't know who robbed the stagecoach, and I certainly wasn't involved. I could see why you'd have questions, but I'm as surprised as you are. I knew James had a secret, but I was not aware he was a criminal."

"I think you better sit and explain everything to me because I'm not inclined to believe you."

He had just stepped into a hornet's nest. Ben held his hands out to show he wasn't a threat and sat. The Marshal sank into his own chair and waved Luke to a seat across the room.

Ben explained what he knew and when he knew it, not leaving out any detail. He wouldn't go to jail for something he didn't do. He'd cooperate and answer any questions the Marshal might have.

Thirty-Four

The next morning, Ben and Luke headed back to town to see James. After an hour of questioning the night before, the Marshal reluctantly agreed Ben likely had nothing to do with the stagecoach robbery. But the Marshal refused to let Ben see James that evening and was told to return the next morning.

Ben returned, not because of any sympathy for James, but for Elizabeth's sake. He didn't remember her ever hinting that she knew what James's secret was, and he prayed James had never told her. However, deep inside, he wondered if he was deluding himself. She knew James had a secret, and she'd been willing to protect it. It was just a question of what she knew.

With all the politeness he could muster, Ben asked the Marshal if he could talk to James. Pulling out his keys, the Marshal nodded. They went through a thick wooden door to the cells. Luke stayed out front. Opening the jail cell, the Marshal waved Ben into the cell and locked it behind him. The slamming of the metal door was jarring, and he hoped never to find himself stuck behind them.

"Let me know when you're done and I'll let you out," he growled, giving James the evil eye.

When the Marshal left, James stood from the worn cot and glared at Ben. "You shouldn't have come. Is Elizabeth with you?"

"I had to come. This appears to be my doing and no, Elizabeth's not with me. I thought it best to keep her in the dark until I figured out what happened."

"Wasn't your fault. My past caught up with me, that's all." James sat heavily on the cot and avoided looking Ben in the eye. "Her pa stumbled into a saloon with one of my men, one who I didn't particularly get along with. The two of them got to talking and well, as they say, the rest is history."

"I still feel somewhat responsible. Elizabeth's pa might not have done this"-- Ben waved his hands around the cell--"if I'd gotten him his money sooner. Although, I'm a mite annoyed to find out it was you who robbed the stagecoach. I don't want to be party to any criminal schemes."

"Sorry 'bout that. I should've known getting him the money wouldn't have mattered. From the way he was acting, he would've held the information over our heads for years until he sucked you dry." James ran his hands up and down his pant legs. "Probably better this way. Now you don't have to pay, and he can't get to Elizabeth."

"Perhaps, but now you're in jail. This is going to devastate her."

He shrugged, his shoulders dropping with unmasked sorrow. "I can't change what's happened. I'll survive and so will she."

Ben stalked back and forth in front of James, trying to decide if he wanted to ask the next question. He wasn't sure he wanted to know the answer.

"Just ask, Ben."

He stopped pacing. "Was she aware of this?"

There was silence, and Ben looked over his shoulder.

"What I did to survive?" James sighed and said, "Yeah, she did."

Ben cursed under his breath. "Did you involve her in any of your robberies?"

"Not intentionally, no." James's head hung in shame.

"What does that mean?"

"I'm not sure you want to know." His voice was low.

"Why wouldn't I?" He shouldn't be pushing James, but he had to know. If there were additional secrets, it was time to lay them on the table.

"You watched me rob the stagecoach, didn't you?"

"Well, I didn't know it was you, but yes, I watched."

"What happened? Why didn't you stop it?" James asked.

"I couldn't. Someone hit me over the head. Knocked me out."

James said nothing. It took Ben a moment to realize what he was implying.

"Wait, are you... no... that can't be. She did that?"

Nodding, James said, "Yeah. She followed when I refused to let her take part. I guess she was hiding when you came up over the hill."

Ben laughed hysterically. He couldn't believe it. His wife, *his wife*, was party to a stagecoach robbery.

"I can't have a wife who's a criminal."

James stood, no longer contrite, and glared at him. "I don't know what you're thinking or what you're planning on saying next, but I'd suggest you think carefully first."

"Don't threaten me." Ben said.

"I'm not threatening you." James stepped forward until they were nose to nose. "She's innocent in this, no matter what you believe. She was only trying to protect me and didn't know what I'd been up to when she first found me." His breath was hot and stale. "I tried to keep her out of it. A criminal is the last thing she is, and don't you ever accuse her of such."

Not backing away, Ben said, "It certainly doesn't look that way. I'm married to a woman who was involved in a stagecoach robbery. What am I supposed to do with that?"

"You're supposed to forget it and never bring it up again. She's had a hard life and the last thing she needs is to have her husband accuse her of being a criminal."

"I can't just forget."

"You better," James said. "I'm taking the fall for everything and will swear left, right, up, and down she had nothing to do with it. Don't you dare say otherwise!"

Ben took a step back and looked at James hard. He wanted to hit the man. "You better not be lying to me. She better not have been involved in anything else."

"She hasn't been and wasn't involved in this either. You remember that."

"I'll respect your wishes, but don't think I'll ever forget it."

"I don't expect you will," James said.

Breathing hard, they each stood with fists clinched at their sides, but sanity prevailed because neither took a swing. Ben wanted to lay James out, wanted to punch him and beat him until he paid for this. His fears regarding her behavior were further confirmed from her own brother's lips. No matter what James said, nothing could change that.

Ben ran his hand through his hair, thinking hard, before he said, "What am I to tell Elizabeth?"

"Nothing for now. Not sure how long I'll be here, or if I'll hang or be sent to prison. It's better if we just don't mention it. Once we've a better idea of my future, then you can tell her."

"I'm not sure that's a good idea." She would be furious and the longer he kept this from her, the worse it would get. If she discovered he was keeping secrets of this size, she'd never forgive him.

"Likely ain't, but she'll fret and blame herself."

"This isn't a good idea." Ben pushed back.

"You didn't tell her before you came here, so you can keep it to yourself a mite longer."

"I don't know."

"Please," James implored. "I'm asking a lot, and I know I have no right, but she's truly innocent in this. I'm begging you, let's keep this to ourselves for now."

"Alright, I'll stay quiet."

"It won't be for long, just 'til we have a better idea of what's next. You best leave. I think we've said all we need to."

Ben couldn't believe what he had just learned. Elizabeth had been the one to hit him during the robbery. She could've been hurt or killed if it had been someone intent on misdeeds. She was lucky it had been him, although he was still mighty embarrassed a woman had caught him unawares. He wouldn't reveal this information to anyone. The last thing he needed was to have his wife painted as a criminal. It could ruin his family's reputation, not to mention his own. He'd be the laughingstock of Montana.

Leaving jail, Ben and Luke went to send a telegram. He had to let Elizabeth know they'd made it to Spring Creek. Once he did that, he'd find Elizabeth's pa. They had an agreement. He had intended on keeping his end of the bargain, but now he didn't feel obligated to do so. He'd be happy to let the old man know that.

After Ben sent the telegram, he told Mr. Crockitt he'd return for any messages while Luke headed back to James's ranch. Without James, chores were piling up, and Michael needed the help.

After a couple of hours of searching, Ben wanted to scream with frustration. Elizabeth's pa was nowhere to be found. No one had seen him since James's arrest, and no one knew if he had left town, either. As he headed back to the hotel, Suzette pranced out of the doc's office and waved him to a stop.

Dismounting from his horse, he nodded to her. She was the last person he expected to see. He thought she was long gone.

"Good afternoon, Mrs.—" He couldn't even spit out her married name. He had no wish to talk to her, but he wouldn't be rude.

"Ben, it's great to see you," she said, her smile bright.

"What can I do for you?" he asked, his voice hollow and terse.

Startled at his tone, Suzette's face fell. "Are you not happy to see me?"

"Why would I be happy to see you? You left town with another man," he said with clenched teeth.

Her eyes wide with sorrow, she said, "I'm so sorry. He made these promises and then..." she murmured. "Then things took a turn for the worse. I can explain everything, if you'd give me half a chance." Her eyes were wide with unshed tears.

His heart tugged. He hated to see her cry. Even though she'd left him for another man, a part of him wanted to know why. "Alright. I'm willing to listen."

A sparkling smile illuminated her face. She was the most charming woman he had ever known. He couldn't help but wonder what might have been if she had only trusted him.

"Thank you. Will you meet me tomorrow at the new cafe around two? I'll explain everything."

Nodding, he said, "I'll see you then."

Smiling, she turned and sauntered away, her hips swaying under her blue skirts. He knew he shouldn't meet her, but hearing her out was the neighborly thing do to.

Thirty-Five

When the telegram arrived, Elizabeth was the first to see it. Not waiting for anyone else, she tore it open. The envelope fluttered to the floor, forgotten.

ARRIVED IN SPRING CREEK STOP

WILL BE HERE LONGER THAN EXPECTED STOP

WILL SEND WORD WHEN HEADED HOME STOP

BEN

Dread clenched her heart. Something was wrong. She just knew it. Ben didn't mention her brother, and now he'd be gone longer than planned. It drove her to distraction, not knowing what was happening. Ben wouldn't have gone to Spring Creek just to help at the ranch. It didn't feel right.

She'd pack a bag and catch the next train. She didn't care if he had told her to stay. He might be her husband, but she was her own woman. She made her own decisions, not him.

She threw clothes into a bag and flung a cloak over her arm. Within minutes, she entered the barn looking for Sam, the ranch foreman. She needed his help to take her to town. Instead of Sam, she found Anne and Katy.

"Elizabeth, where are you going?" Anne asked, her eyes wandering to Elizabeth's bag.

"I'm headed to town to catch the train to Spring Creek."

"Ben wanted you to stay here," Anne protested.

"I know he did, but something's wrong."

"Why do you believe that?"

"We received a telegram and—"

"Oh, no. Did something happen?" Katy asked, interrupting.

"I don't know. He said he'd be staying longer than expected. He didn't mention my brother, but I know something's wrong, so I'm going to go find out what it is."

"Don't you think you're overreacting?" Anne asked.

"Maybe I am, but I won't sit and wait. I'm leaving."

"If you're going, then I'm going with you," Anne said.

"No." Katy said. "Ben'll be mad if we ignore his wishes. Don't you remember what happened when he caught us in those trousers?"

"We can't let her go by herself, so I'll go with her."

"If you're going, then so am I," Katy said.

"That's ridiculous. Only one of us should go." Anne folded her arms across her chest.

"I'm going too, so you might as well accept it. Elizabeth, can you find Sam to get the wagon? Anne and I will grab our bags and be right back."

Katy led Anne to the house. Within the hour, the three of them were headed to town. Sam protested but since he was fighting a losing battle, he took them to the train station. He also informed them he was going. No way was he letting the three of them go without protection, he said. Not wanting to fight with him, Elizabeth reluctantly agreed.

Hours later, they stepped off the train. Sam had their bags and headed to the livery for a wagon and horses. Thirsty and hungry, the girls walked to the cafe for a bite to eat. As they approached, Elizabeth stopped, having noticed the couple sitting in the front window. It was Ben and Suzette. Ben held her hand and gazed at her with adoration. Suzette reached for his cheek, running her fingers to his chin.

Why was Ben with Suzette? Ben looked out the window and saw Elizabeth. Dropping Suzette's hand, he stood and glared. Fury rippled across his features. He threw down his napkin and said something to Suzette before storming out the door.

Turning, Elizabeth brushed past Anne and Katy but was stopped by the anger in Ben's voice.

"What the hell are you doing here, Elizabeth?" he roared. Elizabeth stood with her back to him, not wanting him to see the hurt she felt at being placed aside for that woman. *Was that why he had returned to Spring Creek?* Suzette must've sent Luke to retrieve him, which was why he left her at the ranch.

Well, she had followed and now she knew. Her husband had always wanted another woman and wasn't afraid to leave her to be with Suzette. She was humiliated and now her new sisters had also seen what he tried to hide.

"We, uh, well—" Katy took a few steps back, seeing the anger in her brother's eyes.

Elizabeth could hear both Katy and Anne trying to placate their brother, but his barely concealed rage tore through her like a knife. She couldn't let his sisters take the brunt of his anger. She turned and glared at him. Anger was better than sorrow, and she'd let him see that.

"I guess I now know why you had to return to Spring Creek without me?"

"You shouldn't have come here. I told you I had unfinished business."

"And that unfinished business just happens to be Suzette?"

"What?" he asked, confused at her question.

"I thought something was wrong, seriously wrong, but now I

know it was *her* the whole time. You just can't stay away from her, can you?"

His anger drained as he digested her words. He almost looked contrite, but she didn't care anymore. He held his hand out, then dropped it.

"Nothing to say," she snarled, her disgust with him palpable. "I guess I shouldn't be surprised. Go back to her, stay with her. Rot in hell with her for all I care, but stay away from me."

With that, she turned and left.

"Elizabeth, get back here," he yelled, but she didn't stop.

"Ben, no," Anne said. "Let her go."

"And why should I do that?"

"I think you know why," Anne said, the last words Elizabeth heard as she ran away.

Elizabeth was beholden to Anne for her interference. Turning the corner out of Ben's view, she started running. She tried to contain her tears but couldn't. They streamed unchecked.

She had never expected to find Ben with Suzette, but she should have known better. Why else had he rushed back to Spring Creek without her? There was no other explanation. He had been in love with Suzette when he married her. Now that Suzette was back, it seemed he would throw Elizabeth away for Suzette. *What do I do now?* The thoughts tumbled over and over in her head, smashing into one another like waves against a rocky cliff.

She reached the pond at the rear of the church and leaned against a tree. Sliding to the ground, the roughness scraped at her back and snagged her cloak, but she didn't care. The physical discomfort didn't compare to the grief ripping her in half. She pulled her knees to her chest and wrapped her arms around them, crying for everything that could've been. Everything he had done and said had been an act when all he wanted was

Suzette. Just thinking of that woman's name made her skin crawl.

The morning he had left for Spring Creek, she had wanted to stay mad at him and tried so hard to do so, but as soon as he'd touched her, she'd forgotten everything but him, his body, the way he smelled, the feelings he evoked inside of her. She couldn't control the love that was unfurling in her. *Love.* No, it couldn't be love. She liked him. She'd enjoyed the moments they'd had when they weren't fighting, but she didn't love him. Did she?

The days they had spent camping after they had been wed had blissful. There had been no anger or displeasure, only the joy of getting to know someone truly for the first time.

She did love him, loved him with everything in her. The realization rippled through her like a tornado through a field, fast and furious.

What she felt for Ben did not compare to the love she thought she had for Timmy. Timmy had been her first love, and she'd always treasure those memories, but what she felt for Ben far surpassed that. Ben made her laugh, made her smile, made her squeal with excitement and anticipation. She wanted more of that. She wanted a future with him, but it was becoming clear that what he wanted was Suzette.

What little happiness she thought she possessed was gone. He returned to Spring Creek to see *Suzette,* to plan a future with *her,* to get rid of his wife so he could spend the rest of his life with *her.* Did he run his hands across her body, making her body sing with pleasure? Her heart broke at the thought of Ben treasuring Suzette's body as much, if not more, than hers.

What a fool she had been. Once again, she gave her whole heart, only to have it shredded. She never learned. The pain tore through her. It was a wonder she could breathe.

After some time, her tears dried and the hiccups faded. The emptiness inside of her grew with each breath she took. She stared at the pond and the ripple of the water as the wind flowed around her. A leaf fell from a nearby tree and blew across the water. She watched it flutter before dropping to the surface. It floated, the edges bouncing and twirling as the wind continued to push it.

Why couldn't life be as simple as nature? She knew she needed to go back and find Anne and Katy. They didn't deserve her disappearing on them, but she'd needed to gather her thoughts first.

The sun burned bright, and although she'd rather stay here and drown her sorrows, it was time to head back. She pushed to a standing position, wiped away the remnants of her tears, and brushed the dirt off her skirt.

As she walked around the corner, she ran straight into Ben. He clasped her by the arm, then stared at her. His apologetic look disappeared into something she couldn't quite identify.

"Where have you been? Why are you here?" he asked.

"I don't need to explain myself to you." She wrenched herself from his grasp.

His hands fell to his sides. "Oh, yes, you do. You're my wife. I told you to stay at the ranch. You willingly disobeyed me, and you brought my sisters with you."

"I don't need to obey you. I'm my own person." She avoided his gaze. She didn't want to see his lies. "I need to find your sisters. Then I'm going to my brother's ranch. You can spend the evening elsewhere."

Brushing past him, she marched by with her back straight and her head held high. She would not give him the satisfaction of knowing how much he'd hurt her. He'd been caught doing something he shouldn't have been doing. He was in the wrong, not her.

Conflicted, Ben watched Elizabeth storm away. It had alarmed him to see her standing outside the cafe window. Her cloak blowing in the wind, her body rigid as she had seen him sitting at a table with another woman. He was even more humiliated to realize what she was thinking wasn't that far from the truth. He'd been living in a moment of fantasy, imagining what could have been with Suzette, when he saw *his wife* stricken with agony across her beautiful face.

For a few hours, he had pushed the real reason he was in Spring Creek to the back of his mind and enjoyed his time with Suzette. She had been everything he thought he'd wanted, thought he'd needed, until he saw Elizabeth standing outside that window. He saw the hurt, the pain in her eyes, and he regretted it.

He had been out with another woman while hiding why he had come to Spring Creek. Her reaction, her assumption he had come for Suzette, was unfounded, but it didn't appear that way to her.

Suzette and Elizabeth were as different as night and day. Suzette exuded propriety and was every inch the lady. She'd made a slight miscalculation in judgment when she ran off with Mr. Breckenridge, but that wasn't her fault. Mr. Breckenridge had tricked her into believing he would marry her. He'd been after one thing, but she escaped before he took her innocence. It took courage for Suzette to tell him that.

When he reached across the table and held her hands, he was trying to comfort her, to let her know she was safe, and that she'd have a future. After a time, she regained her composure, and that was the moment he saw Elizabeth.

She stood there looking at him, confusion in her enormous eyes replaced with a suffering that haunted him. He then saw his sisters, and a rage he hadn't felt before rushed through him. He knew he was being unreasonable, but he hadn't wanted his time with Suzette to be interrupted. In that moment, he didn't want to explain himself and didn't feel as though he should, but he'd been wrong and was ashamed to admit it.

Thirty-Six

Elizabeth returned to the cafe. Anne and Katy sat eating at a small table covered in a red checkered tablecloth with Sam. Plates of juicy steaks, beans, and fresh bread lined the table.

Anne saw Elizabeth first. She dropped her napkin and gave Elizabeth's hands a squeeze. "We were worried. Are you alright?"

Elizabeth nodded. "I'm so sorry for disappearing. I hope I didn't cause too much trouble."

"No trouble at all." Anne gestured to the empty chair. "I'm just glad you weren't hurt. We ordered for you. I hope that's alright?"

"Of course it is," Elizabeth said. "I don't know what I'd do without you."

Elizabeth had no appetite, but she didn't want them to worry. The problems between her and Ben needed to stay there. She wouldn't drag his sisters further into their mess. She picked at her meal while the others finished. Once done, they headed to her brother's ranch where Michael greeted them, although he was surprised at their arrival.

"What are you doing here?" he asked, helping Anne and Katy

out of the wagon. Elizabeth ignored his question and headed into the house. Darkness greeted her.

"James, I'm home. Where are you?"

She lit a candle, the silence broken by her striking the match. The house was too quiet and empty.

"James," she said, her voice loud and uneasy. She hollered his name once again, but he still didn't answer.

Coming back outside, she asked Michael, "Where's James?"

"You don't know?" He cocked his head to the side, his hands holding their bags.

"Don't know what?" she asked. "Where is he?"

"He, well, uh—" he stuttered, unsettled by her questions.

"What's going on? Where's my brother? Has something happened? Is he hurt?" Fear jolted through her. James should be here.

"He's fine, but he's... well, I'm not too sure how to say this."

He dropped their bags on the porch and ran his hands through his hair. His eyes skirted in every direction but hers.

"What's going on?" Her voice sounded shrill, even to her.

Michael sighed. "He's behind bars."

"What? Why?"

"They arrested him for the stagecoach robbery that happened last summer. Your pa made the allegations."

"Oh, no," she cried. "I've got to return to town."

"It's late. There's nothing we can do tonight," Michael said.

"But I need to see him. Make sure he's alright."

"He's fine. You can see him in the morning. That's why Luke returned to Thundering Mountain. Didn't he tell you?"

"Wait, what? Ben knew?"

"Uh, yes?" Michael bent the brim of his hat between his hands and avoided looking at her.

"He didn't tell me. How could he do this to me?" Furious, she yelled at him.

"Elizabeth, please, you're getting upset." Anne gently touched her elbow to lead her away. "Let's go inside and sit. I'll make coffee. We can discuss this," Anne said.

Elizabeth was losing control. She took a deep breath and nodded. Walking to the kitchen, she stumbled to a chair and sat, her body shaking with fright. The others talked quietly, trying to calm her, but she didn't hear their words. She was too upset.

This was her fault. If she hadn't found James, he wouldn't be in jail now. He'd be safe. Her pa wouldn't have threatened him. James's future would've been secure. Everything had gone wrong. It was because of her that nothing would be the same again.

She didn't sleep. Nightmares of losing James and Ben divorcing her for Suzette plagued her through the night. Her eyes and body were sluggish and heavy with fatigue the next morning.

She needed to face her brother and ask him for forgiveness, beg him if needed. He could have lived on his ranch and had a happy life, perhaps with a wife and a passel of little ones, but her pa had ruined it all. Although she hadn't been the one to report him to the law, her pa had, and she was an extension of the man who had hurt James when they were little. James was sure to hate her, and she couldn't blame him. If she had never arrived, he would've had the life he'd always wanted.

Bacon and eggs were simmering in the kitchen, and it turned her stomach. She wasn't hungry, but she walked down the hall anyway. Anne stood above the hot skillet, her skin glistening with sweat from the heat of the wood-burning stove. Tendrils of her dark blonde hair clung to the nape of her neck, but she smiled when she saw Elizabeth.

"Good morning," Elizabeth said.

"You're awake. How did you sleep?" Anne picked up the skillet and dumped the warm eggs onto a platter on the table.

"Good," Elizabeth said, but her tone gave her away.

"I wonder if you aren't just telling me that so I won't worry." She squeezed Elizabeth's shoulder before returning to the stove. "The coffee's hot and ready. Everyone'll be here soon."

Elizabeth poured herself a cup. She blew on it before bringing the hot liquid to her lips.

"Thank you. I didn't realize you could cook," Elizabeth said, trying to force normality into abnormal conditions.

Anne laughed. "I can. I just don't do it very often. Ma made sure we knew how, even though we have a cook. She said there was no guarantee we'd have one once we married. She said our husbands would expect us to know how." Anne smiled at the memory. "I enjoy cooking and try to whenever I can. I just don't get a chance very often."

"Your ma sounded like a very smart woman. I wish I could've met her."

"She would've liked you." Anne wiped her hands on her apron, picked up a mug, and took a sip.

"Thank you for saying that, but I can't see how. Your brother doesn't approve of me. I'm not a lady like Suzette."

Anne sighed and pulled out a chair to sit. "Elizabeth, my ma would've loved you. She didn't have it easy before she met Pa and even then, they had their trials. Ma had an independent spirit, and it took Pa years to convince her to trust him and marry him. They had a lot of misunderstandings and could have solved many of 'em if they'd discussed them instead of assuming the worst about each other."

"Still doesn't explain why Ben has such disdain for me. He returned to Spring Creek to—"

Anne interrupted. "He returned to discover what happened with your brother. From what Michael and Luke have said, Suzette is not the woman Ben thinks she is. I think he's just having a hard time reconciling what he thinks he wants with what his heart wants."

"I don't know. Seeing him yesterday with her just made my skin crawl, and I got so angry."

"And with good reason, Elizabeth, but I think there's more to what you saw than meets the eye. I've seen the way Ben looks at you when he thinks no one is looking."

"But—"

Anne rested her hand on Elizabeth's. "Going on about six years ago, right before Ben left home to make his own way, he'd been infatuated with a neighbor's daughter. She was a flighty thing and ended up with a child out of wedlock. Thank heavens it wasn't Ben's, as Ma would've tanned his hide if it had been. When Ma caught wind of Ben sniffing around her, she took him aside and told him he needed a woman to be proud of, one with morals, one that could make her proud." Anne took another sip of her coffee and shook her head, lost in her thoughts. "I think he took her words to heart and placed Ma on this pedestal that he's measured every woman against. What he's forgotten is that Ma was far from lady-like, truth be told. She was independent, stubborn, and the disagreements Ma and Pa would have would be legendary. She wouldn't let Pa run roughshod over her and gave him hell." Anne laughed. Her eyes sparkled at the memories. "But she let no one outside the family see any other side of her, and I think that's what Ben's afraid of."

"Your ma sounds like a wonderful woman. I don't think I could've lived up to her expectations, or to Ben's for that matter."

"Oh, she was wonderful, but so are you."

"I don't know."

"Give him a chance, please. He's a good man who's been misguided. He'll come around once he realizes what he might lose. Besides, I think he came here to help your brother and Suzette just got in the way."

Anne set the cup down, went to the back door, and hollered. "Food's ready."

Katy, Luke, and Michael entered a few moments later and took their seats at the large, round table. The back door opened once again, and Ben entered.

Elizabeth stilled as she saw her husband. She figured he'd stayed in town so he could be near Suzette. She hadn't expected to see him this morning, and she wasn't sure what to do. She couldn't reconcile what Anne said about her brother with the man she thought she knew. Was he just as confused as she and having a hard time admitting it?

His eyes found hers, and he hesitated. It was as if he wanted to say something but didn't. He sat across from her instead. "Thank you for cooking, Anne."

"It was my pleasure. Everyone dig in before the food gets cold." She gestured to the table.

They passed the food around. Eventually, the murmur of voices filled the awkward silence. Elizabeth said nothing and tried to eat, but the food stuck in her throat. She pushed the food around until she couldn't stand it any longer. She dropped her fork and looked at Michael.

"Michael, can you hitch up the wagon? I want to head to town."

"Sure—"

"I'll take you to town," Ben interrupted.

"No, thank you." She didn't know if she could sit next to him and pretend. She needed time away from him to determine how she felt and if what Anne told her was true.

"Nonsense. I'll take you. I need to speak with the Marshal." His tone suggested Elizabeth not argue, but she so wanted to tell him how she really felt.

"Fine," she muttered. "I want to leave as soon as possible."

"Are you finished?"

"Yes," she said, placing her napkin on the table.

"It doesn't appear you ate," he said.

"Don't you worry whether or not I ate. It isn't any of your concern."

"Elizabeth, are we going to do this right now?" He pushed to stand, his hand dropping his own napkin.

"I told you I was done. I'm ready to go. Are you ready or not?" she said, her tone belligerent.

Everyone had quieted—no sounds of eating, no forks hitting plates, and no slurping of coffee. No one moved or said a word. She hadn't wanted to make the others uncomfortable, but once again, she had. Ben would use this as another example of her unladylike behavior. It would give him a good reason to divorce her and be with the woman of his dreams. Divorces were common in Montana, and it appeared anyone could get one. She would be another pitiful woman whose husband threw her over for someone else.

He shook his head in frustration. "Go get your cloak. I'll get the wagon ready."

She watched him walk out the door.

Seething with anger, Elizabeth thanked Anne for the meal. She didn't want to spend any time with him, but she had no choice if she wanted to see her brother. She would pretend he was just one of the ranch hands. Even if it killed her, she could pretend.

Elizabeth jumped to the ground as soon as Ben set the brake. She ran up the stairs and went inside the jail before he could stop her. She politely asked the Marshal if she could see her brother.

Nodding his head in the affirmative, the Marshal snatched a set of keys from his drawer and stood. He motioned for her to follow and led her to his cell.

"You have a visitor," he said, stopping in front of a dark, dank cell.

"Who is it?"

"It's me," she said, stepping out from behind the Marshal.

"What are you doing here? This is no place for you." Whiskers covered his face, and he looked awful. His tall, broad frame looked as though it had shrunken inside itself. She held back the tears at what her pa had done to him.

The Marshal opened the cell.

"You can go on in and see him, Mrs. Seymour, but only for a few minutes."

"Thank you, Marshal," she said. He closed the door behind them and left them alone. "James," she said as she rushed to him and wrapped her arms around his waist, burying her face in his chest. "I'm so sorry you're in here. It's all my fault."

He squeezed her tight before pulling away.

"I wish you hadn't of come," he said, "and it isn't your fault. It was just a matter of time before I got caught."

"But it was my pa who did this."

"He might've been the one, but I knew I was taking a risk. If it hadn't been him, it would've been someone else."

"I should've just stayed with him and married Mr. Wells. You never would've been involved."

"Stop that." His eyebrows furrowed in frustration. "I'm glad you found me. Our ma would've been overjoyed to know we were together. You didn't deserve to marry that man, no matter what you think. Ben is the far better man. I'm happy for you and if this is the price I must pay, then so be it."

Little did James know that her future was as bleak now as it would have been being married to Mr. Wells. Forcing a smile on her face, she said nothing. Better for James to believe she was happy and safe. He didn't need her mess of a life weighing on his conscience.

"What can I do to help?" she asked, her hands fisted in the folds of her skirt.

"Not much you can do." He walked to the bars on the window and placed his hand around one of them. "They have me dead to rights. One of my men was caught and with help from your pa, he's testifying against me. No point in denying it. The traveling judge'll be here soon. I'll either hang or be imprisoned."

Her fingers stilled, and uneasiness crept up her spine. "There must be something we can do. What if you paid the money back?"

He laughed mirthlessly as he turned back around. "There isn't any left. My portion of the last haul paid for the ranch and the horses."

"Sell the ranch, then. Give them the money."

"It won't do no good. I've done things I'm not proud of. It's time for me to pay for my crimes."

"Please. We've got to try. I can't lose you." She raised her hands to her lips, trying to stop herself from crying, but it was no use.

"No. It's over. I've accepted it and the consequences."

Tears streamed down her face. She was desperate to fix this mess. His eyes filled with pain. "Don't cry. Go home with your husband. Remember me with fond memories and try to get on with your life. You deserve happiness."

"I don't know if I can do that," she cried. "You mean the world to me. I don't want to leave you. I don't want you to go to jail or be hang—" She couldn't say the words. They were too painful.

"You don't have a choice. Now go. Don't come back."

He gave her a tight hug and then yelled for the Marshal. As the Marshal opened the cell door, James shooed her away. She stood waiting, the pain agonizing as the Marshal turned the lock with a loud click.

"I'll leave for now," she said, "but this isn't over. I'll find a way to help you whether you like it or not."

She followed the Marshal out to the front where Ben stood waiting for her. "Is everything alright?"

"No, nothing is alright." She eyed the Marshal. "Are there any lawyers in town?"

"Yes, one. His name's George Black."

"Can you point me to him?" She was on a mission, and nothing was going to stop her.

"He has a room next to the General Store. Can't miss it."

"Thank you."

As she grabbed the door handle, the Marshal hollered, "Tell George the judge'll be here next Tuesday unless something stops him. He can get the details from me."

She nodded and left, Ben following behind her. The blazing sun beat down on her almost as hot as the hole Ben's eyes were burning in her back as she headed to the lawyer. She'd convince him to help James. It was the only way.

"Elizabeth, wait," Ben said, grabbing her arm.

"What? I don't have time for this. I need to find the lawyer. See if he can help."

"He confessed."

"That may be, but he's a good person. The judge needs to know. He's changed his life and is trying to do better."

"He doesn't want help. I've talked to him. He's determined to accept the consequences."

"Well, I'm not. He's taken care of me. Now, it's my turn to take care of him."

Thirty-Seven

Exasperated, Ben stared at Elizabeth. Why couldn't she do as she was told? James said he didn't want her help, but did she listen to her brother? No, not any more than she listened to him. He didn't know what to do with her. She had a mind of her own. Nothing he said or did made a lick of difference.

She found the lawyer's office and yanked it open. He wanted to follow her, to help her, but he hesitated.

"Ben, oh, Ben," a sweet voice called.

It was Suzette. His smile grew when he saw her. She, at least, was pleased to see him.

"Suzette."

"I'm so glad I caught you," she said, her angelic smile warming his heart. "I was worried when you left so abruptly." Her smile dropped just a bit to show he'd hurt her feelings.

"It wasn't my intention. Please accept my apology."

"No need." Her fingers brushed against his arm. "I wanted to make sure nothing was amiss and ask if there was anything I could do for you."

"Do for me?" he asked.

"Why yes. I've been concerned there was something I could help you with, what with you leaving so sudden. I felt perhaps I could offer advice or just be available for you to talk with. If you wanted to, that is."

Her fingertips trailed down his hand, leaving him breathless. His focus shifted at her soft touch, and he gazed into her pretty eyes, the color of the bright blue sky.

"I appreciate that. You're too kind, especially with how I treated you yesterday afternoon."

"Oh, now don't you worry," she said as her other hand reached up and caressed his cheek. "I understand." Her hand dropped to his chest and patted him, her hand light and delicate, a true reflection of who she was. "Would you care to join me for a cup of coffee?"

"I'd be honored, but I've something I need to attend to. How about tomorrow afternoon? Would you be available?"

"That would be most welcome, Ben."

His name across her lips was like a breath of fresh air on a warm spring day.

"I'll meet you tomorrow at noon?"

She nodded, pushed open her parasol, and sashayed away. He watched her go, once again wishing Elizabeth could act like Suzette: so sweet, so endearing, so everything he had ever wanted in a wife.

After making an appointment to see Mr. Black later that afternoon, Elizabeth's fears that Ben had returned to Spring Creek to reunite with Suzette were further confirmed when she saw Ben canoodling with that woman on the public street. There was no end to his constant reminders to act as a lady, yet he was not behaving as a gentleman should. He let a woman who wasn't his wife have her hands all over him. She stared in horror at the expression on Ben's face. It was filled a look she had never seen directed at her before. It further broke her heart.

She had received brief moments of affection when they had traveled to his ranch, but after their argument, he'd only looked at her with frustration and anger.

Very much in love with Suzette, he'd never love her the same way. Knowing he could leave her, Elizabeth decided she wouldn't let him break her. She'd be strong and focus on helping her brother. Once he was free, she'd then concentrate on her future. She was intelligent and capable. The two of them could find work in Helena or maybe head east. They had options. With her head held high, she made her way to the church to talk with Pastor Williams. Perhaps he could offer her some wisdom.

The church doors were locked, and no one answered. Sighing, she headed to the grove of trees at the rear of the church. She might as well wait there until her appointment with the lawyer.

Sitting with her back against the tree, she gazed over at the pond, her thoughts scattered about her future.

"Elizabeth."

She scowled. Once again, Ben had found her.

"What do you want?" She could see the tips of his boots, but refused to raise her head.

"I want you, of course."

"Humph. Not so sure about that."

"I'm not sure what you mean." He bent his knees. His hand reached out and lifted her chin.

"It doesn't matter. Leave me alone." She jerked her chin out of his hand, staring at him, defiance oozing out of her in spades.

"Why do you have to be so difficult?" He rocked back on his heels, but continued to be closer to her than she liked.

"I didn't realize I was being difficult. I'm sitting here enjoying the *stunning* weather." Her voice was sarcastic and filled with loathing. "How is *that* being difficult?"

"Did you talk to the lawyer?" he said, choosing to ignore her comment.

"No, he wasn't in. I'll see him this afternoon."

"Good. I'll go with you."

"There's no need. I can get my brother a lawyer without you."

"Your brother's my friend. I want to help."

"I would really rather you didn't."

"I would really rather I did. I won't discuss this any further. You'll learn to accept what I say," he said, glaring at her.

"No, I won't." She glared right back. She wasn't a woman to be pushed around, and she wouldn't give in.

"Why do you have to be like this?" he said, clearly vexed.

"I'm not. If you wanted an obedient and dutiful wife, then you shouldn't have married me."

"Maybe I shouldn't have," he muttered, his tone scathing. "But you're my wife, whether I like it or not."

"Why don't you go be with Suzette if you don't want to be married to me? You want to spend more time with her than with me, anyway."

He stood and paced in front of her. "That's not true."

"I saw you last night with her and then today. It seems to me you'd sooner be with her since you frequently seek her out and enjoy her attention."

"At least she doesn't argue with me every time I turn around, doesn't run around in men's trousers, doesn't cuss, and acts as a lady should."

"You knew who I was when you married me. Besides, does Suzette act like a lady, or is that just the way you see things?"

"Of course she's a lady."

"She wasn't a lady on the church trip, nor a lady when she ran off with that man."

He whipped around and frowned at her. "You know nothing about what happened with Suzette and Mr. Breckenridge. And I can't believe how selfish you're being. She could've been killed that day. When you pushed her out of the way, she barely saved herself from falling after you."

"That isn't true."

Ben paced back and forth. "I know what happened. She tried to calm you and instead you pushed her. She fell because of you. You're lucky she wasn't hurt as well."

"I—" Elizabeth couldn't believe what she was hearing. He thought she caused Suzette to fall. "I don't want to do this anymore. Leave me alone. I'll meet you at the lawyer's office." Dismissing him, she turned her gaze to the pond, trying to hold back her despair.

Thirty-Eight

B en and Elizabeth met with the lawyer and then returned to James's ranch. Mr. Black didn't hold out much hope for James's release. He had spoken with both the Marshal and James and had nothing positive to say. Not only had James confessed, the evidence against him was solid. The lawyer said six years in prison since he confessed, and he likely wouldn't hang.

Ben tried to remind her that James could be out in six years, but she only saw that he was going to jail. No matter what he said to her, she was inconsolable.

After several attempts at engaging her in conversation, he gave up, and the silence was broken only by the sounds of hooves and the crack of the reins. When they reached the ranch, Elizabeth ran inside, the door banging behind her.

Leading the horses and wagon to the barn, Luke and Michael stepped outside and met him at the entrance.

"It isn't looking good." He told his brothers what the lawyer had said.

Michael shook his head. "How's Elizabeth taking the news?"

"Not well. She said little on the way home. She believes it was her doing."

"You told her it wasn't, didn't you?" Michael asked. He unhitched the horses.

"She isn't listening to me. To make matters worse, she's pretty upset I had dinner with Suzette. I don't think she'll be thrilled when I tell her we're going to meet her for coffee tomorrow."

"Why would you make Elizabeth go see Suzette?" Luke asked, disgusted.

"It's the neighborly thing to do. Suzette's had a difficult time of late. She invited me and since I was rude in leaving her alone at the cafe yesterday, I feel it's only right to make it up to her."

"I can't believe you'd want to spend any time with her after what she did to Elizabeth," Luke said.

"She hasn't harmed Elizabeth in the slightest. If anything, Suzette should hold a grudge."

"Are you so taken in by that woman that you can't see the truth?" Luke said, his words coming out in a snarl.

"Suzette could've been seriously injured on the church trip. If it hadn't been for Elizabeth panicking—"

"She didn't cause that fall. Suzette did."

"No, that isn't true. Suzette told me what happened. Elizabeth pushed her off the trail."

"Is that what you truly believe? Elizabeth, who rides horses like a man, isn't afraid to get her hands dirty, works harder than any woman I know, and knows how to shoot a rifle better than most men. She survived a fall into a raging river, found her way out of it, survived over night with a nasty bump and gash to her head, and you think it was her that caused the ruckus on that trip?"

"I..." Ben gulped. Did he have the facts wrong? No, Suzette had explained. She wouldn't have lie to him. "That's what happened," he insisted.

"Perhaps you should ask someone who witnessed it instead of believing every word that comes out of that lying, conniving woman's mouth," Luke muttered.

Ben's mouth opened in shock. "Don't say that about her. That's cruel and unnecessary."

"I'll say anything I'd like about someone who ran off with a man while stringing multiple men along and treats the other women in town with disdain."

"I don't understand. She's not like that and would have no reason to lie to me."

"Are you so blinded by lust for that woman that you can't see what's staring you in the face?"

Ben stared at Luke in shock.

"I can tell you the truth if you're willing to listen," Luke said, rocking back on his heels.

"Luke, whatever you need to tell me, why don't you just spit it out?"

"Fine, but I hope you're prepared to hear it." Luke leaned against a stall wall. He bent his knee as he rested his foot on a bale of hay. Michael, who had been working in the stall, leaned over the wall, watching them with fascination. "Elizabeth didn't push Suzette. Elizabeth waited for you and the pastor to deal with the mountain lion when Suzette became hysterical. She was crying and screeching like a wet hen." Luke grinned at the image he described.

"This isn't funny, Luke," Ben said.

"I didn't say it was. Anyhow, Elizabeth was calm, but Suzette wouldn't hear of it. She pushed Elizabeth so hard that Elizabeth lost her balance. Even as Elizabeth fell, she prevented Suzette from falling into the river. Elizabeth could've saved herself. Instead, she saved a woman who has scorned and ridiculed her since she moved to town."

Ben was stunned. "Are you sure?"

"Of course I'm sure. It happened so quick there wasn't a thing I could do," Luke said, pushing away from the stall wall. "When we got back from the trip, Suzette was telling lies. I should've said something then, but it wouldn't have made a difference. You believe Suzette above everyone else."

He stalked back and forth in front of the horse's stall. "I wish you would've told me."

"Would you have listened? You believe Suzette is a lady, but she isn't. I mean, she left town with a married man."

"She didn't know what Mr. Breckenridge was up to. He lied and told her he was going to marry her."

"And yet she had you courting her, too, along with a few other men in town, including James. You were a pleasant diversion to her, but that's it. Her parents sent her to Spring Creek to protect her from the scandal she created back East. Then she comes here and creates more of the same."

"She didn't know he was married."

"Maybe she did, maybe she didn't, but for whatever reason she's trying to claw her way back into your good graces, especially now. Don't forget, you're the proud new owner of a major cattle ranch."

"I'm married to Elizabeth."

"All of us can tell there's tension. You're more enamored with Suzette than you are with your own wife. I suppose if you wanted to, you could divorce Elizabeth. I wouldn't be surprised if that's what Suzette's angling for."

"I'd never divorce my wife." His gut pinched at the thought. He cared for Elizabeth. He wouldn't intentionally hurt her.

"You had dinner with Suzette yesterday and are planning to spend more time with her. Every time you look at Suzette, there's adoration in your eyes. You don't even look at your own wife that way. Don't you think Elizabeth's noticed? She isn't a naïve young lady, your wife. She's been through a lot."

"I don't know what to say. I—"

"Your wife deserves more and doesn't appear to have your support." Luke poked a finger in his chest and Ben stumbled back. "If I was married to a woman like her, I'd never treat her the way you have."

"But you're not," Ben said. "She's my wife."

"Yes, she is," Luke replied, looking at him warily. "Do you care for her at all?"

"Of course I do," he muttered, ashamed at the fact that Luke even had to even ask him that question.

"Do you?" Luke folded his arms across his chest and spread his legs. In that moment, he looked just like their pa scolding him for wrongs he had done.

Ben pondered Luke's words. They had a ring of truth to them. He had believed everything Suzette told him without question. He thought back over their relationship and saw the things he ignored because of his infatuation with her and his dream of having the perfect wife. He ignored the inconsistencies of Suzette's character and her disdain for him when it didn't suit her. There were plenty of times where she hadn't wanted to be in his company, but the moment he was with another woman, especially Elizabeth, she had come back and diverted his attention. His ma would have been horrified if he had brought Suzette home, as she wouldn't have survived a harsh winter on a cattle ranch. He just hadn't wanted to believe it and was appalled that he hadn't recognized it earlier. Even her brother-in-law, Doc Wilson, had warned him, and but he'd ignored it because she seemed to be the epitome of perfection. Her beauty had swayed him, not her character.

He remembered how he had treated Elizabeth at the barn dance, how he'd left her standing on the dance floor when Suzette had called his name. He remembered how Elizabeth had listened to him when they got caught in the snowstorm, not judging him but instead showing compassion. Suzette always talked about herself and never asked him questions. It was always about her.

He was horrified that he hadn't been as kind to Elizabeth as he should have, constantly comparing her to Suzette and finding her lacking when, in reality, she was the superior woman. She had tried hard to be a good wife to him and he was angry over her wearing her trousers. He had been jealous, not wanting any other man to see what he believed was his. From the moment he had realized she really was a woman, that day when he had first arrived on James's ranch, he had been smitten, but he hadn't recognized it because she was so different from any other woman he had ever met. Contrary, stubborn but enticingly beautiful. He hadn't wanted to believe that she could be the perfect woman for him because of trousers.

Elizabeth deserved better. He needed to think long and hard about what he had done and how he could make it up to her. His belly clenched. "You're right, Luke. I've much to consider. Thanks for being honest."

Slapping him on the back, Luke gave him a goofy grin. The tension in the barn eased.

"Hey, that's what younger brothers are for. You know, to point out the inadequacies of our older brothers."

"Inadequacies," Ben muttered. "Let me tell you—"

"Ah, come on, you two," Michael said, closing the stall door with a loud click. "I'm hungry. We can compare who is the better brother later, especially since the two of you will never measure up to me." Michael grinned and laughed hysterically at the shocked look on his brother's faces before sauntering off, cocky as ever.

Ben rose early the next day. He couldn't predict the future, but he felt it was his duty to help James in any way he could. Making things right with Elizabeth was also on his agenda, but before he could convince Elizabeth he was determined to make their relationship work, he needed to end whatever remained between him and Suzette.

Finishing up their chores, the three men left the women and headed to town. Michael and Luke were going to order supplies while Ben went to find Suzette.

Knocking on Doc Wilson's door, Ben removed his hat and smoothed back his hair. He prayed the sweat running down his back wasn't noticeable. He was not looking forward to this conversation.

Suzette opened the door and smiled. It was calculating and

took him aback. Asking her if she'd like to go for a walk, she nodded and followed him down the steps. After a few minutes of her simpering about the latest gossip, he finally led her to a grove of trees where they'd be sheltered from prying eyes.

Taking off his hat, he turned away to calm his nerves before taking a deep breath and looking back at her.

"Suzette, I—"

"Oh, Ben. I knew you had feelings for me." She tilted her head back and gazed up at him, her eyes cunning and deceitful. He had never seen her look at him that way before and if he had, he'd completely misread it. "Now that you've returned, we can have the future I'd always dreamed."

"Future?" he said, shocked. No, no, no—this was not how this conversation was supposed to go.

"I asked the lawyer, and he said getting a divorce from *Elizabeth* is simple enough." She waved her hand in the air like she was swatting away a nasty rodent.

Ben had to swallow his disgust. The way Suzette said Elizabeth's name, made his skin crawl. "Divorce?"

"Yes," she said and twirled around. "You'll get divorced from that uncouth, slip of a girl, and then we'll get married in a beautiful church in Helena. You can build me a big, stunning house, and we'll be the cream of society. No one'll dare dismiss us." She reached for his hands and tried to pull him close, but he wrenched away, putting distance between them.

"No, Suzette. You don't understand."

She tilted her head, her eyes narrowing. "What don't I understand, Ben Seymour? You made promises to me, asked to court me, and now that I'm free of that wastrel you can keep your promise."

"I made no such promises to you," he said, his collar growing tight around his neck. "Yes, I asked to court you but you made it clear that you had many suitors and I was just one of them. I'm not divorcing Eliza—"

"Yes, you are," she said, her foot stomping on the ground.

"No, I'm not," he said.

Her face turned a blotchy red, her mouth opening wide as though she was sucking on air. She stalked toward him and lifted a hand to slap him, but he stopped her and gripped her wrist.

He glowered at her. "You don't want to make a scene, Suzette," he hissed, his voice low. "Let's end this amicably, and we can both go on our ways. I love Elizabeth and I'll never *ever* divorce her for someone like you."

Her eyes grew wide and steam billowed out her ears. She wrenched her arm away from his. "You'll regret this, Ben Seymour. One day, you'll wish you had never met me." She twirled around and stomped away, her skirts fluttering in the wind.

Sighing, he shook his shoulders of the weight he hadn't realized he'd been carrying and met with his brothers. As they rode their horses toward James's ranch, a galloping mare raced toward them, with a young woman on its back. It was Anne. Yanking on the reins, she pulled the horse to a stop. She looked a fright. Her hair was a tangled mess, her dress ripped at the sleeves, and tear marks streaked her cheeks. She couldn't get the words past her lips, breathing hard with exertion and fear.

"Anne, what's wrong?" Ben asked, grabbing the reins of her horse to settle him.

"It's, it's Elizabeth," Anne said, gulping in air. "She... She's been taken."

"Taken? I don't understand."

She took a deep breath. "We were eating when a man burst through the door. He held a gun and pushed me out of the way before he grabbed Elizabeth." Her voice hitched, but she continued. "When Sam tried to stop him, he hit Sam across the head and knocked him across the room. He pulled her out of the house, yelling and screaming. He said if we followed, he'd kill her."

"Holy hell," Ben said, his fingers gripping the reins so hard, his horse pulled its head in protest. "Who was it?"

"I don't know, but Elizabeth seemed to know who he was. She

didn't fight back when he threatened her. She seemed resigned. Told us not to worry and that she'd be alright. But I don't think she will be. He was deranged. He kept yelling at her, saying she was his, that she was always supposed to be his, and she had to go with him."

"Which way did they go?"

"I don't know." She shook her head. "He made us stay inside the house. He said if he saw us open the door, he'd kill us. We were so scared, we didn't know what to do. Sam was out cold. We stayed inside until I was sure they were gone before I saddled a horse to come find you. I'm sorry." She trembled from the fear and exertion.

"Michael, take Anne. Head back to town and get the Marshal. Stop at Doc Wilson's and send him out to the ranch. Luke and I'll see if we can find any signs of where they went."

Nudging their horses into a gallop, Ben and Luke raced back to the ranch. Ben had to find her before it was too late. He couldn't lose her, not like this.

"Katy," he yelled as he ran inside, the door slamming open from his hurried movements.

"Back here."

They raced down the hall. She sat on the kitchen floor with a blood-soaked cloth pressed against Sam's head. He had just woken and pushed Katy's hand away.

"Sam, you alright?" Ben crouched next to him.

"Yeah, boss. I should've stopped him."

"I'm sure you did all you could."

"Not enough. Give me a minute and I'll be ready to go."

Sam tried to stand, but he stumbled. Ben grabbed him before he fell and led him to a chair.

"I don't think so. You're in no shape to sit on a horse. Stay here. The doc'll be here soon."

Ben strode to the parlor and pulled two rifles from the gun case and tossed one at Luke. He had left his Winchester at Thundering

Mountain, not realizing he'd need one while visiting Spring Creek. Pulling out a set of six shooters, he stuffed one in his pants and handed the other to Luke. They both grabbed handfuls of bullets and stuffed their pockets full. He wanted to be prepared.

He ran out the front door and mounted his horse. Luke close behind him. They pointed their horses away from town. Ben sensed they had little time. If that man was as deranged as Anne had led them to believe, it wouldn't be long before he hurt Elizabeth more than he already had.

Thirty-Nine

E lizabeth sat on the hard edge of the saddle, terrified. Mr. Wells held her in front of him, his meaty hands and arms holding the reins, preventing her from moving. When she had returned to Spring Creek, she had never thought he would still be in town. He must've seen her and planned his attack when the men had left the ranch that morning.

He was livid and shouted obscenities in her ear. She said little, and that infuriated him more. He repeatedly said she was his, that she belonged to him, and why had she made him come find her?

She sat quietly, not fighting him when all she wanted to do was scratch, kick, and fight to get away from him. She had to tread carefully and plot her escape when the opportunity presented itself. Then, she would run. She would've fought back earlier if Anne and Katy weren't there. She hadn't been willing to put them in danger, so she'd let him drag her away.

Just as the sun set, they arrived at a dilapidated old cabin high in the mountains. He had eventually quit yelling and instead mumbled incoherently, the words making no sense to her ears.

Dismounting from the horse, he yanked her from the saddle

and gripped her forearm, his fingers digging into her soft skin. She yelped slightly. With a powerful thrust, he hit her with his fist. Her head whipped back, and she tumbled to the ground.

"What was that?" he yelled, spittle from his mouth spraying her.

She said nothing, her face ringing from the pain. She tried to sit, her hand holding the side of her face, the throbbing more than she could bear.

"Don't think you can get away, girl," he shouted. "You've always belonged to me. Your pa promised, and I aim to get what is mine."

Jerking her from the ground, she stumbled, tried to keep up with him, and fell hard onto her knees. Trying to stop her fall, she put her palm out, but her arm buckled from the odd angle and her wrist snapped. Sharp, intense agony radiated up her arm. She was sure her wrist had broken.

Even more angry now, he kicked her in the side for good measure. As she lay on the ground, he snorted with disgust, then yanked her up by her hair. Her scalp stung.

He wrenched open the door and threw her inside. She fell to the ground, hitting her broken wrist on the hard floor. Yelping with pain, tears flooded her eyes, and blackness threatened to overwhelm her. He shut the door and locked it with a click.

Elizabeth shivered, the pain all-consuming. The room spun around her. She closed her eyes, trying to swallow the nausea that was bubbling inside her. She lay on the floor for a long while before she found the strength to move.

The room was small, dark, and filthy. A window perched high at one end let in little light, but it was enough to see the large cobwebs in the corners of the room. Was she alone? She didn't know, but she prayed she was.

Holding her broken wrist with her good hand, she stood and winced in agony. Her side ached. Her head pounded. Her wrist pulsated. Every part of her was wounded in some way.

She squinted, her eyes adjusting to the darkness, and saw an old straw mattress in one corner, and a table and chairs in the other. Walking to the chairs, she tested one for stability. It held her weight. She sat protecting her injured wrist and shaking, not from cold but from fear. The nausea worsened, and she tried to swallow back the acid in her throat.

Her life was a giant mess, and now she had been taken by a disturbed, angry man. She took quick breaths, trying to endure the misery. She didn't know how much more she could take. Before he had yanked her from the horse, she'd believed she could get away, but now she wasn't sure—not with a broken wrist and maybe broken ribs. She wasn't even sure her ribs had healed from the last beating she had taken from him.

She steadied herself. Finding an inner strength she wasn't sure existed, she knew she focused on taking care of her wrist as best she could. She pulled it to her chest. With her other hand, she reached for her petticoat. Putting a piece of the bottom ruffle in her mouth, she used her good hand to rip it. It took her a few tries before she removed two ruffles: one for a sling and one to stabilize her wrist.

Sweat beaded her brow, and her ribs were like hot daggers piercing her from the inside. Taking one ruffle, she wrapped it around her wrist, wincing with every single movement. Every twinge sent arrows of fierce, sharp pain from her wrist into her arm and shoulder. Tucking the ends in, she took the other piece of cloth. She used her teeth to help tie the ends together, creating a makeshift sling. Dropping it around her neck, she put her wrist through the hole. The pain lessened once she had it supported. There wasn't too much she could do about her ribs.

She didn't have any idea how long she would be here, but she knew she wasn't going anywhere soon. Ben didn't care enough to bother looking for her. He had nothing to gain in finding her and everything to gain if she never came back. Perhaps he'd presume her dead and would be free to marry again. Her heart was broken and she didn't know if it would ever be repaired again.

Ben and Luke searched for hours. The Marshal and the men he gathered from town caught up with them, and they divided up the search party. It would be dark soon, and there was no sign of Elizabeth or her captor.

He had failed as a husband in so many ways. Not only had he misjudged her, he'd thought she had caused the accident up in the mountains. What an unbelievable horse's ass he'd been to blame her for the incident when she was the one who'd been hurt.

He couldn't believe he'd thought Suzette was the woman for him when it was just an infatuation, one that may have cost him the best thing that had ever happened to him. He should have talked to Elizabeth the night before and let her know how he felt, but he had wanted to end whatever it was with Suzette first. Because he had waited, it might be too late. He didn't know how much danger she was in. She was resourceful, but she was still a woman who had been beaten once already by this man. He was afraid of what more Mr. Wells would do to her.

The man who took her was unhinged—a danger to her, to everyone. She was no match for him in his crazed state. As the sun fell behind the mountains, Luke reined his horse to a stop beside him.

"We need to stop for the night," Luke said.

"No, she's out there. The longer we wait, the further away he'll get. We may never find her." Ben didn't want to consider what atrocities Mr. Wells had planned for Elizabeth at any hour of the day, but especially not at night. She was at his mercy, and based on his past actions, it wouldn't take much to push him over the edge.

"Be reasonable, Ben. We won't be able to search in the dark. We aren't any good to her if we can't see what we're doing. Let's head back to the ranch, get a good night's sleep, and start first thing in the morning. We'll have a better chance of trying to track 'em then."

Ben knew Luke was right, but it was hard to admit. Slumping with fatigue, failure, and worry, he agreed. He prayed she'd survive the night.

Forty

I t had been two days since Mr. Wells had thrown her in the one-room cabin. As the dim light faded in the small cabin on the first night, she'd crawled onto the old straw mattress and tried to sleep. Unfortunately, it'd been useless. Every time she moved, she'd bumped her wrist and pain shot up her arm, waking her. The next morning, she'd attempted to find her way out, but it had been in vain. She didn't have the strength to climb out the small window, and there was nothing to help her pry the door open.

Locked in tight, there was no escape and he'd left her with no food or water. Her strength had continued to wane, and her spirits had dwindled. Her wrist had swelled under her makeshift wrap, was painful to the touch. Hungry and thirsty, she'd wanted to leave this horrible place.

Now, on the second morning, she knew if someone didn't find her soon, she'd be in real trouble. She rested on the straw mattress with her back against the wall and tried to muster all her energy. She must've missed something. Her eyes wandered around the room, trying to concentrate on what she saw when the door flew open and Mr. Wells stormed inside.

He glared at her with such a look of lust and contempt, it

petrified her to her core. She cradled her broken wrist to her chest and prayed to the heaven's above that he wouldn't kill her or something far worse.

"Get up, girl. Get over here. Time to leave."

She tried to stand, but dizziness swirled around her, and she wobbled on her feet. She took a few steps forward but teetered and stumbled. She fell to her knees, and caught herself before falling and hurting her wrist further.

"What's your problem, girl?" he said, sneering.

"I don't feel too good. I haven't eaten. Can I... Do you have water?" she pleaded.

Disgusted, he stalked out and returned with a canteen. He tossed it at her. Relief washed through her as she fumbled to open it with her good hand. Prying it open, she put it to her mouth and had a long drink. It tasted delicious, and she gulped it, water running along her chin. When she got her fill, she took a deep breath. It didn't satisfy the hunger pains, but at least the dryness in her mouth had disappeared.

He snatched the canteen from her. "You've had enough. Get up. We're leaving."

"Where?"

He smacked her across the mouth and she fell, hitting her head on the floor.

"Don't talk back to me, girl. I'm tired of repeating myself. Get on the horse."

Somehow, she stood. She walked with slow and deliberate care to one of the two horses outside the cabin. At least she wouldn't have to sit in front of him. Her cheek smarted from the slap, and it felt as though a hammer pounded on her head, but she found the strength to climb into the saddle. He took her reins and mounted his horse.

"Don't get no bright ideas about runnin' away. I won't have no problem lockin' you up again. Understand?"

She nodded, staring at the pommel in front of her, her spirits diminishing with each passing second. Her body shook with hunger, and she tried not to fall. With little energy left, resignation weighed her down, and it took everything she had to stay on the horse. The sun blazed, and her eyes smarted at the glare. Her hope was were gone. No one would ever find her.

As the day dragged on, Elizabeth struggled to not fall asleep or to fall off the saddle. Later that afternoon, after going through the forest and deserted roads, he guided the horses into a clearing surrounded by thick pine trees.

"Get down, girl. Sleeping here for the night."

Sliding off the horse, her legs quivered with fatigue, but she wouldn't give him the satisfaction of seeing her fall. Propping herself against a tree, she watched as he removed the saddles and pulled a loaf of bread from his saddlebag. He tore a piece off and threw it at her. She tried to catch it and failed. It fell to the dirt. Her hunger overrode her good sense as she bent, brushed off the dirt, and took a bite. It tasted good, dirt and all.

She finished eating and slid along the tree, the rough bark scratching her back but at the same time giving her a small measure of comfort. It was strong, supportive, and stalwart, all the things she wanted to be. He started a fire, pulled out a blanket, and tossed it at her. It surprised her he offered that much. On the trail, he had continued to mutter incoherent words and then would yell that it was her fault. He'd said that if she'd married him as planned, he wouldn't have had to do this. She didn't argue with him, didn't say a word. There was no point.

She took the blanket and held it tight around her. She curled up on the ground and used her good hand as a makeshift pillow. She needed to find a moment to make her escape, but as the darkness enveloped the mountains and pine trees around them, she sunk into oblivion, exhausted.

In the middle of the night, a disturbance woke her. Opening her eyes, she peered into the blackness but only saw the dying embers glowing orange. Mr. Wells was curled next to the fire, his pistol clenched in his hand. He snorted and shifted. She held still, praying he'd stay asleep. She needed to relieve herself, but she didn't think she could even crawl to do it. Her arms and legs were limp. She tried to move but couldn't and before she could stop it, she felt the burn of her urine as it trickled along her thighs. She had never felt so helpless.

Suddenly, someone grabbed her from behind. Startled, she opened her mouth to scream, but a hand covered her lips and muffled her cries of fright.

"Elizabeth, don't move. It's me." Ben's voice penetrated her hysteria, and she stilled. Relief flowed through her, and she slumped against him. As angry as she'd been, she was happy he had found her. She wanted to tell him how she felt, how much she loved him, but it wouldn't do any good. He didn't love her. He loved Suzette. She wanted to cry, to yell, to fight back, to love him every day for the rest of her life but it would never happen. He had made his choice and it wasn't her.

He removed his hand from her mouth and whispered in her ear, "Can you walk?"

She shook her head.

He looked over her body, at her cradled wrist, scowled in anger, and wrinkled his nose at the obvious smell of urine coating her.

"I'm sorry," she whispered. "I couldn't hold it. I made a mess and…" Tears clogged her throat. She didn't want him to be angry, but once again, she'd disappointed him.

He put his finger to her lips. He stood, taking care not to disturb any leaves, and bent to pick her up when Mr. Wells woke. He aimed his pistol at them, shaking with rage. Ben blocked her from him.

"Stop right there. What do ya think you're doing?" Mr. Wells hollered.

Ben held up his hands, no firearms showing. "Didn't mean to disturb you, sir."

"Don't sir me, you bastard. I know you."

Ben dropped his hands. "Then you'll know I came to get my wife."

"She ain't your wife," he sputtered, spittle dribbling on his chin.

"I assure you she is, and I've got the marriage certificate to prove it."

"She belongs to me. I paid for her. She's mine, now get away from her." He waved the gun, his eyes glazed with anger and obvious confusion.

"I'm afraid I can't do that."

"If you don't, you'll be sorry."

Ben stood true, not giving an inch.

"Don't move or I'll shoot you," Mr. Wells screamed, becoming more and more agitated. He continued to wave the pistol at them. Ben was trying to protect her, but Mr. Wells was not predictable. There was no way Ben could stop the bullets if he started shooting.

"Ben," Elizabeth whispered. "Do as he says."

"Don't fret. I'll be fine. I'll make sure he never touches you again."

As Mr. Wells stumbled forward, Ben took a step to deter him. When he moved, Elizabeth saw Luke in the distance. Putting her good hand to her mouth to stifle her cry of dismay, she tried to keep quiet.

Luke snuck behind Mr. Wells slowly, but when he took his next step, he snapped a twig. The sound reverberated through the forest.

Mr. Wells swung around and saw him, but in that split-second, Ben rushed him. He tackled him to the ground, and they both grappled for control. The men rolled, dirt flying, their feet hitting the logs in the fire, sparks soaring. Their grunts filled the air, and Elizabeth watched in horror. She could barely tell where one body began, and the other ended.

A gunshot roared through the forest clearing. Ben and Mr. Wells both lay still. Neither man moved

Luke rushed toward the jumble of bodies on the ground. Time stood still. Then, one stirred and rolled off the other. It was Ben. He was alive, and she sighed with relief.

He paused, seeming sluggish and dazed.

Elizabeth struggled, trying to scoot over the hard ground. She had no strength left to get to him. Ben sat, blood covering his shirt. Luke held out his hand to help him stand.

Seeing Elizabeth trying to reach him with no success, Ben shook off Luke's arm and strode to her, kneeling at her side. He pulled her into his strong, capable arms.

"I'm not hurt," he whispered.

"The blood?" she cried, putting her good hand against his chest.

"It isn't mine."

Shuddering with relief, she tucked her head under his. He held her in his arms as deep, gulping sobs ripped through her. He hadn't been hurt, and he had come for her after all. After a few moments, her tears subsided. She pulled back an inch and wiped her face with the back of her good hand. "I'm sorry. I didn't mean to do that."

"You don't need to apologize. Are you alright?" he asked, concerned. His fingers pushed her hair behind her ears, and he cupped her cheeks, his thumbs stroking her skin sending awareness through her.

"Yes." Her nerves settled and her defenses returned. As glad as she was to see him, she was still bitter about Suzette and wanted to beat the woman into a bloody pulp.

He stood, then bent to pick her up. "Let's get you home."

He pulled her into his arms and cradled her close, careful of her injured wrist. She so wanted to sink into his arms and let him hold her, but was worried he was only interested in getting her back to sign divorce papers. She hesitated to let him see her break any further. He placed her on his horse, squeezing her leg.

"I need to help Luke with..." he hesitated, "with the body."

She nodded. Luke had grabbed a blanket from the saddlebag, and with Ben's help, they pulled the body onto it, wrapped it tight, and placed it onto the back of a horse. The horse smelled blood and pawed the ground, but Ben gripped the reins, settling him with a firm hand and a few words.

Putting out the fire, they packed up the makeshift campsite. Elizabeth forced herself to stay awake. She was so tired and wanted to sleep but knew she couldn't yet. Before long, they were ready to leave. Looping the extra horse's reins to the pommel, Ben mounted behind her and pulled her close. She tried to hold herself away from him, but it was too hard. She gave up and relaxed in his arms. He felt so safe, so warm, so inviting. In this moment, she'd enjoy the comfort he offered, for she knew that once they returned to the ranch, it would be gone.

Elizabeth slumped against him as her body gave up the fight. Shocked beyond belief, Ben struggled to recognize her. She had a broken wrist, and bruises lined her cheeks. She had no energy to move, let alone stay upright in the saddle, and she smelled of dirt, sweat, and urine.

It had taken too long to find her. He didn't know what took place over the last few days, and he feared she wouldn't fully recover. He had no way of telling what that man had done to her, and he was afraid to ask. He wasn't sure how he could help her or if she would accept his help after everything he had done and said.

When he lifted her into his arms, she'd winced and moaned with pain, and he couldn't tell what other physical damage she'd suffered at the hands of that maniac. He wanted to hold her close and never let her go, but she didn't trust him, still harboring anger over their fights.

He couldn't blame her. His behavior toward her had been unforgivable. He hadn't been the husband he should've been. She meant everything to him and he couldn't lose her. He just needed time to explain to her how wrong he had been, how Suzette meant nothing to him, and that he wanted to spend the rest of his life with her. If he could convince her he had genuine feelings for her, maybe—just maybe—there would be a future for them. He hoped it wasn't too late.

They reached the ranch late that night, the moonlight being their guide home. Ben considered taking her straight to town, but he wanted to avoid running into Suzette at the doc's office. He didn't want Elizabeth to believe any love still existed between him and Suzette. Explanations were needed, but not now. He sent Luke to town with the body and asked him to send the doc as soon as he informed the Marshal of what happened.

He nudged Elizabeth. "Sweetheart, we're home. Can you keep yourself on the horse long enough for me to dismount?"

Looking around, confused, it took her a moment to nod yes. He dismounted, lifted her off the saddle, and she cried out in pain. He tried setting her on her feet, but her knees buckled.

"I'm sorry," he whispered as he lifted her back into his arms. Carrying her inside, Anne rushed to him, concerned. Her eyes wide with shock at Elizabeth's injuries.

"How hurt is she?"

"I'm not sure, but let's get her to her room and cleaned up before we ask her what happened."

"Oh, yes, of course." Anne picked up her skirts and ran down the hallway to Elizabeth's bedroom. She opened the door and pulled back the blankets on her bed. Ben placed her on it, being careful of her injuries. He reached for her shoes, but she pulled her feet away from him.

"I can do it." She tried to sit but fell back with a grimace.

"You don't have the strength. Please let me help."

"I said I can do it," she said, but as she tried to roll over, she rolled on her wrist and cried out in pain.

He tried picking her foot up again, but she fought him.

"No. Leave me alone."

Anguished, he ran a hand across his eyes wiping away his tears. He backed away as he realized his wife didn't want a thing to do with him.

Anne, seeing him struggle, urged him out of the room. "Let me tend to her, get her clean and out of those filthy clothes. I'm sure she'll want to talk to you later."

"I'm not too sure about that, but I'll leave." His voice was low, hoarse and if he said much more he might crack under the strain.

He stepped out of the room. He wanted to stay with her, to hold her and let her know how much she meant to him, but in this moment he needed to leave her be. He closed the door to her room while hoping he hadn't closed the door on their future.

Forty-One

D oc Wilson looked Elizabeth over while Ben stood outside the room, giving them privacy. He had told Ben, prior to going inside, that he'd have to set her wrist. That would cause immense pain, as it had been a few days since the first break. Ben wanted to protect her, but he knew the doc was doing what was necessary and wasn't trying to hurt her.

As he set her wrist, she cried out in agony. Ben heard her scream. He doubled over knowing he couldn't help her, but he'd honored her wishes by staying out of the room.

The doc opened her door and gestured him inside. "I've wrapped her ribs, but it's going to take time before she's fully healed."

Elizabeth sat in the bed, her body turned away from the door. His heart hurt from the indifference she was showing him, although he couldn't blame her. He wanted to help her but knew she didn't want it.

He stood next to the fireplace waiting while the doc finished gathering his things.

Showing the doc outside to his waiting carriage, he listened to Elizabeth's care instructions. "She needs to rest. Give her plenty of water and nothing heavy for food. Soups would be best for the next couple of days. I'm sure her body will mend, but I don't know how long it will take her mind to recover."

"What can I do to help?"

"Don't ask her too many questions. Let her tell you what happened if she wants to, in her own time."

"Thank you."

"You're mighty welcome. I'll be back tomorrow to check on her."

Ben returned to Elizabeth's room. He knocked on the door, but she didn't respond. He knew he should leave her alone, but he needed to see her, to see for himself that she would be alright.

The door creaked as he pushed it open. She lay asleep on the bed, her body covered in a demure, white nightgown. Her brown hair lay in direct contrast to the white pillowcase, and her broken wrist was swaddled in a stiff, white fabric. She looked so frail and broken. He couldn't imagine his life without her. He needed to convince her of that, and he didn't know how he could.

After everything she'd endured, everything she'd seen, he wasn't positive he could persuade her to give him another chance, but he'd try because he loved her.

She turned in her sleep and caught her arm between her body and the bed. She whimpered, and her eyes flew open. When she locked eyes with him, she sat up to adjust her position.

"What are you doing in here?" she asked, her voice devoid of any emotion.

"I'm sorry. I didn't mean to wake you. How are you feeling?"

"I'm fine. You can leave now."

"Please. Can we talk?"

"I'm tired. Can we do this later?"

"We could, but I'm afraid that the misunderstandings between us will grow if we don't talk everything through."

"I don't want to, Ben." She picked at a thread on the coverlet.

"I do. I'll try and keep it brief so it doesn't further exhaust you."

She pulled the blanket around her waist and leaned against the headboard. She put her broken wrist against her chest and wrapped her good arm around her waist. She stared at him and waited for him to speak, but it wasn't with an open mind. This was going to be an uphill battle, and he wasn't sure he'd make it to the top.

"I—" he swallowed. Now that he had her attention, he was at a loss for words.

Taking a deep breath, he paced in front of the bed. Maybe it would be easier to say what he had to say if he didn't look directly at her. "I've made plenty of mistakes. I've been so wrong in judging you, and I never gave you a fair chance. I..." he paused as the next words were so difficult to say. "I was captivated with someone else, and I... I let those false feelings and my righteous indignation override my good judgment."

He stopped to look at her, to see if anything he said was helping. It wasn't. She sat there, not giving an inch, not saying a word.

Expelling the breath he had been holding, he said, "It terrified me when I found you'd been taken. My heart felt like someone had ripped it from my chest. Every minute that passed when we couldn't find you was agony. I can't imagine my life without you. I hope you can give me a second chance."

She sighed. "Why should I? You'd all but made it clear you'd rather be with Suzette than with me."

"I misunderstood a few things."

"Did you misunderstand or are you feeling guilty?"

"Of course, I feel guilty," he said, "but Luke set me straight on some things that I mistakenly believed were the truth. I didn't realize that you had tried to save Suzette on the church trip, that you were the one trying to keep her calm. I believed her words over what was staring me in the face. I didn't want to accept the fact that you were strong, independent, and would have never hurt her like that. I was stupid, wrong."

"I don't want your guilt or your pity."

"I don't pity you. I... I'm in love with you."

She slumped, her hands relaxing their hold on the blanket. Her mouth agape as her pink tongue darted out and licked her lips.

Maybe she hadn't given up on him completely. He hoped so. With everything on the line, he strode closer to the bed. He had to look her in the eyes. Then maybe she'd see how much he cared for her.

"I'm in love with you and have been for a very long time. I just didn't recognize it. I thought... I thought I knew what I wanted, but I got fooled by a pretty face. I didn't see Suzette for who she was. I wanted to believe she was perfect, but I know now she wasn't, and she isn't... wasn't the woman for me."

"I..." she swallowed, tears glistening in her eyes. "I don't know."

He knelt next to the bed, trying to be contrite so she could see he meant what he'd said. His hands reached for hers. They were cold. He wanted to warm them and with any luck, thaw the coldness in her heart toward him.

"You'll have to trust me. I'm promising you now and forever, Elizabeth, that you're the only woman for me." He looked deep into her eyes, showing her the best way he knew how. Her lovely eyes looked at him, wide with wonder and hope.

"I love you. Please. Please give me a second chance," he whispered.

She hesitated, trying to pull her hands away but he didn't let go. "I love you too, but how do I know you won't change your mind?"

Hope bloomed inside of him like a rose opening to its full glory and he wanted to be the sun on her petals. "I can only promise that I'll try hard every single day to make you proud, to love you the way you deserve, and to protect you to the best of my ability. Will you let me try?"

She considered him for a moment, and pulled one hand away. Her hand cupped his cheek. Her eyes warm as she looked at him. "What about my trousers?"

He smiled. "Wear them every day, anywhere you want. I'll never utter a single word about them if you'll give me a second chance."

She nodded with a shy smile that made his heart burst wide open with love. He loved this woman with his whole heart and soul and he'd never betray her trust again. He stood and pulled her into his arms, being careful of her injuries but desperate to hold her close. She wrapped her good arm around him, holding onto him as tightly as he wanted to hold on to her. Burrowing his face into her hair, he breathed in her clean, womanly scent. She fit, oh so perfectly in his arms. She was made for him.

She pulled back and looked into his eyes, her smile wide, full of hope and love. She may not have been the woman he thought he wanted, but she was perfect for him.

He would never stop loving this magnificent, vivacious woman who meant the world to him. Her cussing, her trousers, and her unladylike behavior would keep him on his toes; but he couldn't be more thankful he had found her. He would do everything in his power to make her happy, to give her everything she had ever wanted for he was the lucky one, and he would never again regret making her his wife.

Epilogue

Christmas Eve 1899

"Papa, papa." A little girl in a green cotton frock ran to Ben as he strode in from working outside all afternoon. Reaching down, he scooped her up into his arms.

"How's my little angel?" he said, gazing into her dark brown eyes, the spitting image of her mother.

"Good! Guess what? Momma said Santa Claus is coming tomorrow."

"And he is, my sweet girl. Where's your momma?"

"She's in the kitchen with Jimmy, feeding him again," she said, disgust in her innocent little voice. "All he ever does is eat, Papa."

"Vicky, babies need to eat."

"And sleep and eat and sleep and eat."

"That's all you ever did when you were his age."

Shaking her head, she pushed to be let down. Ben set his five-year-old daughter on the ground and gazed at her, his heart full of love.

"Let's go find your momma. I've got news for her."

She danced down the hall to the kitchen and her momma.

"Momma," she hollered as she skipped into the kitchen, her dress in her hands as she twirled around. Her stockings had fallen to her ankles.

"Vicky, shh, your brother just fell asleep."

Vicky skidded to a stop. Elizabeth sat in the rocking chair, holding their son.

"Sorry, Momma. Papa's home."

"I heard," Elizabeth said.

Ben bent and kissed his stunning wife softly on the lips. "Looks as though Jimmy's sound asleep. Can I put him in his cradle, sweetheart?"

"Yes." She lifted him into his father's arms. Only two months old, he added another layer of happiness to their family. Taking his son, he made his way to the cradle that sat next to the warm stove and gently placed him inside the cozy cocoon. Jimmy stirred, but with a full belly from his momma's breast, he was content and would sleep for hours.

Turning back around, he watched as Elizabeth listened to their daughter explain what she'd seen earlier. He still couldn't believe his good fortune. Elizabeth had given birth to Vicky almost a year after they were married, and little Jimmy came five years later. He couldn't be more blessed. They were happy, and he hoped to make her happier.

"I've some good news," he said.

She looked up from Vicky and beamed at him. Her smile brightened him every time she bestowed one on him.

"I received a telegram."

"Oh," she said, "Is everything alright?"

"Yes." He laughed. "I said I had good news."

Shaking her head, she said, "You're right; you did. So, pray tell, what is this good news you're bringing me?"

He paused for a moment to drag out the anticipation. "Your brother's been released. He'll be arriving by train tomorrow morning, just in time for Christmas."

Elizabeth stood, excited, and yelped with joy. "Oh, Ben."

Jimmy stirred and started to cry.

"Oh, no." She giggled, laughter bubbling up in her.

Ben put his hand on his son's tummy, and he quickly settled back to sleep. Then he pulled her into his arms and swung her around the room.

"I didn't think he'd be released until the end of January."

"Neither did I, but his telegram says otherwise."

"Momma, who's coming tomorrow?" Vicky pulled on Elizabeth's skirt.

Squatting to look into her daughter's eyes, Elizabeth said, "Your Uncle James, my big brother. Remember? I've told you about him."

"He has the same name as Jimmy, doesn't he?"

"Yes, he does. We named your little brother after my big brother."

"And he'll be here tomorrow?" she asked, her little forehead scrunching.

"Yes, my sweet darling. It looks as though Santa's bringing us all presents this year."

Vicky's smile was broad as she draped her arms around Elizabeth's neck. Standing, Elizabeth pulled her up.

Ben then wrapped his arms around both of his girls. What a wonderful Christmas gift for his kind, loving, giving wife.

A Sneak Peek

My Dear Readers,

If you've loved Ben and Elizabeth's story turn the page for sneak peeks of *Thundering Meadows* (book 3) and *Thundering Ridge* (book 4) the next installments in the *Thundering Mountain Ranch* series where the Seymour family grows with each happily ever after.

Thundering Meadows

A widowed, heavily pregnant mother. A recently released outlaw. What could possibly go wrong?

A fortuitous meeting on a derailed train turns into a promise of protection and a new beginning for a desperate young mother and a reformed outlaw.

Rose McGaven, widowed and heavily pregnant is on the run from a dangerous man who only has one thing on his mind and it isn't protecting his late brother's wife. She'll do anything to escape his clutches including boarding a westbound train during a Christmas Eve blizzard.

James Dodson's life has been full of regrets, but with a chance to start over as a hand on his brother-in-law's ranch, he'll work hard to prove that he can do right for once in his miserable life.

When Rose and James find themselves stranded together on a cold winter evening, James comes to her rescue in more ways than one. As she looks into his dark brown eyes, she places her trust in the handsome stranger's hands.

As they navigate through starting a new life together and the challenges of their pasts, danger lurks in the shadows and threatens to tear them apart.

Thundering Ridge

Justice, love, or both... Can he find the peace he's looking for or will revenge ruin his forever?

Luke Seymour, cowboy turned aspiring reporter, left his family's ranch to find justice for his Pa's murder. After eight long years, he finally catches a glimpse of the woman who started it all. Beginning a search of parlor houses in Helena, Montana, he attends an auction where his heart stops, his palms sweat, and his interest in one young lady makes him forget for just one moment why he is there.

Louisa, desperate and alone, agrees to an auction that threatens to rob her of her innocence. With courage and desperation, she stands in front of the wealthiest men in town, leaving her wants and wishes behind.

In a life-altering moment, Luke offers Louisa a chance at a new beginning, a respectable position as his housekeeper and cook. Not knowing if she can trust him, she looks deep into his green eyes and decides his offer is far better than the alternative. As their lives intertwine in a booming frontier town, their bond strengthens, but Luke's relentless pursuit draws danger close and he stands to lose everything. Can he find a way to bring evil to justice or will his relentless pursuit endanger the one woman who has buried herself deep into his cowboy heart?

Thundering Meadows

Christmas Eve 1899

"All aboard."

James stood, stiffness in his bones from the hard wooden bench. Pinprick tingles ran down his back and across his shoulders from leaning against the jagged edges of the rough brick station house. Smoke from the engine swirled around him, enveloping him in its thick, moist heat.

Waiting for the train to arrive, he had sat mesmerized watching the snowflakes fall until the conductor broke the silence. A clean winter wonderland had replaced the once ugly, mud crusted platform. The snow was picking up in intensity and a peek at the sky made it clear it was going to get worse before it got better. He prayed the train made it to Helena in one piece.

He rolled his shoulders, the strap of his tattered knapsack slapping against his back as he moved toward the passenger car. He handed his ticket to the conductor, who checked it closely before waving him inside. His gloveless fingers reached for the frosty handle, pulling his weary frame up and onto the metal steps, each step more freeing than the last.

Emptiness greeted him as he moved into the cool train car. No body heat warmed the inside and the small stove was cold to the touch. Clearly there was no reason to keep a fire burning if no one sat in the worn red leather seats. He gripped the wooden backs, one hand at a time, as he made his way to the middle of the car, one seat as good as another. Placing his knapsack in one next to a window, he dropped onto the flattened cushion.

He tightened his thin coat around his gaunt frame, pulling up the collar in a useless attempt to keep what remained of his body's heat. Ice crystals formed from the frigid air inside the passenger car, but at least the four walls kept the wind at bay. He scrunched down and attempted to get comfortable for the long ride.

The engine chugged to life, steam billowing behind the frost covered windows. He ran a hand across the glass to remove the ice and saw a young woman and child run toward the train. The conductor held out his hand to help her scramble up and into the passenger car. She handed him two tickets, and he nodded, gesturing for her to take a seat. Breathing hard, her hot breath formed a mist in the frigid air. She rushed down the aisle. Her heavy coat opened revealing her belly, round with child.

The conductor pulled out a pocket watch and snapped it shut a moment later before stepping outside and shutting the door tight behind him. A few minutes later the train pulled away from the station, the lurch jarring but welcome as James was finally on his way home.

He wondered about the woman's man, but of course, it wasn't any of his concern. She had settled a few seats in front and to the left of his, dumping her two carpetbags onto the dirty floor. She had dropped her head in obvious fatigue before hugging her son to her side. He began to fuss, but she distracted him by pointing out the window and whispering in his ear. Within moments, he ceased crying, and she relaxed, closing her eyes.

He couldn't help but notice her reddish blonde hair streaked with bits of gold. It sat piled high, accentuating her pink cheeks, big green eyes, and plump red lips. Other than her protruding belly, she was small and petite in stature.

The train labored along the tracks, picking up speed, lulling him to a comfort he had long forgotten, and anticipation for a warm feather bed filled him. The simple things were what he'd missed. Everything else could be left behind. He closed his eyes and enjoyed his newfound freedom as he slipped into a restless slumber.

Metal against metal and abrupt jerking movements yanked him from his sleep. The train shook and rumbled as the engineer applied the brakes. The train shuddered to a stop, throwing him forward. He braced himself, but the young woman wasn't as fortunate. She'd wrapped her arms tight around her son, but the abrupt stop caused her to slam her forehead into the hard wooden back in front of her.

She slumped, unconscious. Her son screamed and tears poured unchecked down his rosy, red cheeks as he tried to wake her. "Momma," he hollered. "Momma!"

Jumping up, James hurried forward. Kneeling eye level with the young boy, he smiled. "It's all right, little man, let me check on your ma."

The boy popped his thumb in his mouth. His wet, dark green eyes were the spitting image of his mother's.

James checked the woman over to assess her injuries. She had a nasty gash above her eye, but otherwise appeared to be unharmed. Grabbing a handkerchief from his coat pocket, he tried to staunch the blood trickling from her wound.

She opened her eyes and screamed. She swung her arms and shoved him away, fright in her eyes. He sat back on his heels, startled, giving her room until she realized he offered no harm.

"Ma'am, you've been hurt. I'm only tryin' to help."

She quieted as soon as she saw her son. She softened her gaze before she turned to James. Her eyes were full of apprehension, but her tension eased as though taking his measure with one glance. "What happened? Where am I?"

"It appears the train had some trouble. When it stopped, you banged your head. Your son's unharmed, though. You protected him while at the same time allowing yourself quite the injury."

"Oh." She arched her lower back, and gripped her belly with her hands. She strained the muscles in her neck. She groaned in agony.

He cursed under his breath. She had just gone into labor.

James was the only one with her and the only one to help. He didn't want to do this, but he clearly didn't have a choice.

If you'd like to learn more about me and my books, sign up for my newsletter at www.nicoleneiswanger.substack.com.

All my love, Nicole

Thundering Ridge

June 29, 1900

Luke stuffed the latest piece of news securely in his shirt pocket, and he salivated at what it meant. Hot sweat trickled from his forehead and cheeks, and he wiped it with a worn rag as he finished the morning newspaper run in the basement of the three-story building.

As the typesetter and occasional journalist, Luke straightened his back and stretched his long arms above his head, lifting the sweaty hair from the back of his neck. He had returned late from his brother's ranch the night before and his muscles ached from the quick trip, but he'd still headed into work early to get the day's run complete. Glancing at the clock, he grimaced. He hadn't had the opportunity to talk with Walter, the editor and owner of the *Helena Gazette* and time was passing quickly.

Luke's muscles bulged as he pulled the last of the newsprint into a thick pile and tied it with twine. "Frank, that's it. We're done for the morning. I need to find Walter. As soon as I'm finished, I'll come back and help you in cleaning."

Frank nodded and picked up the broom to sweep the floor.

Walter insisted on a clean press room, and it was a daily part of their work to make sure things were in tip-top shape before they left for the day.

Picking up one stack of newspapers, Luke said, "I'll let the newsboys know they can come and get the rest of these on my way up to see the boss."

"Thank ya kindly, Luke," Frank said. "The missus wants to know if you'd like to come for dinner one day next week. She thinks you ain't gettin' enough to eat." Frank laughed, his grey eyes twinkling.

Frank's wife had been determined to find Luke a wife, and she tried to feed Luke every chance she got. No matter his protestations that he wasn't searching for one, she continued to parade eligible young women in front of him with the hopes he'd set his sights on one and settle down. Until he had avenged his pa's death, he couldn't in good conscience put the woman he married into harm's way. He hated to burden Frank and his wife with his problems, so he smiled and indulged her interference knowing full well he wouldn't court any woman until the time was right.

"I'd like that. Tell her to pick a night and I'll be there." Frank's wife was a kind woman with a good heart, not to mention a great cook, and that alone was reason enough to go. His own cooking was abysmal. He would always appreciate a well-cooked meal, no matter the circumstances.

Frank nodded and continued to sweep up the scraps of paper that were scattered across the floor.

Luke jogged up the stairs, through the spotless front office, to the outside porch where the newsboys sat waiting for the go-ahead to gather the newspapers and sell them. Walter had bought the building just after it was built two years before and it contained the latest modern conveniences of gas-lighting and indoor plumbing. Sometimes, he was afraid he'd track dirt inside the office and Walter would have his head.

Handing the newsboys the stack in his arms, he told them the rest were ready for delivery and then walked up the second set of stairs to Walter's office. A second office was further down the hall, unused at the moment. Luke had been hoping for a permanent promotion to journalist. With any luck, that office would become his when he finally proved himself worthy. He rapped on Walter's door with his knuckles and waited for permission to enter.

"Come in."

Luke opened the door. The sunlight poured in through the dirt-streaked windows, nearly blinding him. Stacks of newsprint lined the far edges of the room. Past issues of various newspapers were stuffed into the tall filing cabinet behind Walter and lay scattered across his desk. It was a wonder Walter could get any work done with the number of papers blanketing the surface.

"Got a moment, Walter?"

Walter raised his eyes from the ledger in front of him and gestured for Luke to come in. Picking up his cigar, Walter sat back in his chair, the leather creaking with movement.

Luke settled in one of the plush armchairs Walter had on the ready for paying customers. Luke likely shouldn't be sitting there, but he didn't think he had much ink on him. Walter didn't seem to mind, as he hadn't told him to get up.

"I kind of have an odd question to ask, Walter."

Walter chuckled. "I can't imagine you asking me anything I haven't heard before. Go ahead." His blue eyes twinkled as he took a puff from the thick cigar that sat between his pudgy fingers. Walter wasn't a small man or a big one, either. He was average size, but he had a large presence. Not afraid to state his opinion on most anything, Walter was a relatively decent man who had given Luke a chance.

"Before I ask the question, I best explain some things about my family and what happened in the summer of 1893." Luke had never told Walter anything about the woman who had caused so much pain and havoc, but considering what he'd just discovered, it was about time if he wanted Walter's help.

Walter nodded thoughtfully. "Go on, then. I don't have all day."

"Yes, well... my older brother, Stanley, married a woman by the name of Connie, or leastways that's what we knew her as. Stanley met Connie in the spring of 1892, and after a few months, they were married. At first, she tried to fit right in with the family, but then things seemed to change. She became demanding and tried to make all these plans to change the ranch."

Luke's gut clenched as he remembered her determination to change the way his pa did things, her snide remarks when she didn't get her way, and the way she chastised his ma over the smallest of things. It still made him sick to his stomach to think about what she had done.

"Pa didn't take to her ideas and things became tense between 'em. Then, Ma and Pa got sick – real sick. Ma went first and then Pa. Pa had been recovering and then he was gone sudden-like. I thought it was strange and part of me suspected Connie, but I had no proof." He rubbed his hands together, a chill running up his spine. "Come to find out, she had everything to do with it. She convinced a ranch hand to smother him to death while he rested on his sickbed." He swallowed back the thick lump in his throat, the heartache very much as real today as it was seven years ago. His voice gruff, he continued, "Then, she manipulated Pa's will to make it seem like Stanley had inherited everything, kicked me and my brothers off the ranch, and then tried to have Stanley killed. Thank the heavens above, she didn't succeed. Stanley survived the attempt."

Walter's eyes were wide with shock. "That's quite the tale. I knew your pa died, but I never knew it was murder."

"Yeah, it's not something I tend to share."

"What happened to her?"

"She managed to escape and disappeared for years."

"So why are you sharing this story with me?" Walter's blue eyes were piercing, contemplative. "I'm sympathetic, but I'm not sure what you need from me."

While they had a good relationship, Luke and Walter weren't the best of friends and rarely saw one another outside of work. Luke shifted uncomfortably in his chair. "My oldest brother, Ben, sent out inquiries, and he received a letter from a friend of his in Texas. We think she might be involved or had been involved in a fancy parlor house." Luke reached into his coat pocket and pulled out the worn and creased letter Ben had given him the night before.

Ben,

I made some inquiries. Connie's real name is Bethany Constance Ashland. She grew up in a Houston brothel. In 1890, when she was nigh on 20 years of age, she left the brothel. It's believed she moved to San Antonio.

She married an older, infirm gentleman in late 1891. He passed six months after they tied the knot and his death was quite suspicious. The law had been questioning her about her husband and a couple other men she was suspected of killing when she disappeared. They followed her trail for a while but then lost track of her.

If she's anywhere in Helena, I'd suggest you look in high-end parlor houses. She ain't one to live simply, and seems to crave attention and money.

Hope you find this information helpful. I wish you and your family the best.

Norman Petterfield

Walter finished reading and handed the letter back to Luke, his face unreadable. "Does this have anything to do with the black eye you were sporting a few months ago?"

Luke folded the paper carefully and placed it back in his pocket. "Yes. I thought I'd seen her a few times but wasn't quite sure. We never expected her to return to Helena. Toward the end of April, I saw her again and followed her. I was careless and paid the price with a shiner. Since then, I swear I've seen her but haven't been able to track her. Ben gave me this letter last night."

"So, what can I help you with?"

Luke shifted forward in his chair and braced his hands on his knees before raising his eyes to Walter's. "From the letter, it sounds like I need to get myself into a few of the parlor houses in town. It never crossed our minds she might be a lady of the night, so I'd like to start looking there. I can't see her belonging to anything other than an exclusive one, but I doubt I'm part of the clientele that gets a coveted invitation."

"And you think I am?" Walter chuckled ruefully.

Luke's collar suddenly felt tight. He raised a finger to loosen it. "Not exactly, but you know plenty of people, and I hoped you might be able to wrangle me some invitations or point me to someone who could."

Sitting back fully in his chair, the cigar held in one hand, Walter gazed at Luke for a long moment. "I'll see what I can do. Not making *any* promises, but I'll put out some feelers and see what snaps back. Might cost you, though."

"I understand." Luke let out the breath he hadn't realized he'd been holding. "Thanks, Walter. I appreciate it."

"You're welcome. Now get back to work. I don't pay you to sit here idle."

"Yes, sir," Luke said, scrambling to stand.

With any luck, Walter would come back with good news. He was determined to find information on Connie or Bethany, or whatever her name was. With any luck, they would find her and make sure she paid for what she'd done. That way, she couldn't harm anyone ever again.

Blurbs

The *Thundering Mountain Ranch* Series continues... You can purchase your copies at all your favorite retailers.

Book 1 - *Beneath The Thundering Sky* - Separated by secrets, reunited by fate. Will Frannie and Cole's love survive or will they continue to let misunderstandings keep them apart?

Book 2 - *Thundering Mountain* - Will an independent, trouser wearing, unladylike Elizabeth break past Ben's preconceived notions of what a lady is? Or will their enemies to lovers relationship shatter into a million pieces.

Book 3 - *Thundering Meadows* - Desperate for a chance to find a better home for her and her children, Rose finds herself on a derailed train with James, a handsome stranger who becomes her only chance at survival.

Book 4 - *Thundering Ridge* - Luke rescues Louisa from an illustrious auction while on the hunt for the woman who upended his family's life a mere seven years before. Will Louisa be able to trust the man who makes her heart spin whenever he gazes at her?

Book 5 - *Thundering Snow* - A chance encounter during a bar room brawl lands Charlotte directly in Stanley's lap. They embark on a dangerous journey that could heal old wounds and spark unexpected love

Book 6 - *Thundering Sunset* - A carriage accident and a belligerent suffragist throw a cowboy into the world of women's rights. Marie's determined to change the world and Michael's determined to change her's.

If you'd like to learn more about my books, sign-up for my newsletter at www.nicoleneiswanger.substack.com.

About the Author

Nicole is a Senior Business Analyst by day, a reader during meal time, and a writer while watching historical dramas. She rediscovered her passion for writing during a summer vacation when her husband's truck died. While being stranded for five days with nothing to occupy her time she began writing. She writes American Western Historical Romances set in the heart of Montana and Idaho with swoon-worthy cowboys and feisty, independent women.

Please get in touch
www.nicoleneiswanger.substack.com
nicoleneiswanger@gmail.com

Help other readers find this book by writing a review with your favorite retailer or by sharing on your favorite social media platform.

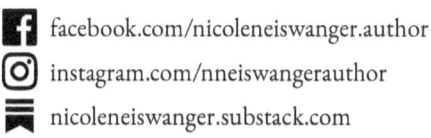

facebook.com/nicoleneiswanger.author
instagram.com/nneiswangerauthor
nicoleneiswanger.substack.com

Also by Nicole Neiswanger

Thundering Mountain Ranch Series

Beneath the Thundering Sky

Thundering Mountain

Thundering Meadows

Thundering Ridge

Thundering Snow

Thundering Sunset - **Available January 15, 2026**